Praise for *Mur*

"Fans of European sleuths with a taste for good food . . . will have fun."
—*Publishers Weekly*

"What really makes Longworth's writing special is her deep knowledge of French history, landscape, cuisine, and even contemporary cafés and restaurants. This is that rare atmospheric mystery that is street-wise and café-canny."
—*Booklist* (starred review)

"Longworth's gentle procedural succeeds on several levels, whether it's for academic and literary allusions, police work, or armchair travel. With deftly shifting points of view, Longworth creates a beguiling read that will appeal to Louise Penny and Donna Leon fans."
—*Library Journal*

"French-set mysteries have never been more popular [and] among the very best is a series set in Provence featuring Monsieur Verlaque, an examining magistrate, and his sometime girlfriend, law professor Marine Bonnet."
—*The Denver Post*

Praise for *Death at the Château Bremont*

"This first novel in a projected series has charm, wit, and Aix-en-Provence all going for it. Longworth's voice is like a rich vintage of sparkling Dorothy Sayers and grounded Donna Leon. . . . Longworth has lived in Aix since 1997, and her knowledge of the region is apparent on every page. Bon appétit."
—*Booklist*

"A promising debut for Longworth, who shows there's more to France than Paris and more to mystery than Maigret."

—*Kirkus Reviews*

"Mystery and romance served up with a hearty dose of French cuisine. I relished every word. Longworth does for Aix-en-Provence what Frances Mayes does for Tuscany: you want to be there—NOW!"

—Barbara Fairchild, former editor in chief, *Bon Appétit*

"*Death at the Château Bremont* is replete with romance, mystery, and a rich atmosphere that makes the south of France spring off the page in a manner reminiscent of Donna Leon's Venice. A wonderful start to a series sure to gain a legion of fans."

—Tasha Alexander, author of the Lady Emily mysteries

"Longworth has a good eye and a sharp wit, and this introduction to Verlaque and Bonnet holds promise for a terrific series."

—*The Globe and Mail*

"*Death at the Château Bremont* offers charming French locales, vivid characters and an intriguing whodunit."

—Kevin R. Kosar, author of *Whiskey: A Global History*

"Here's hoping the series lasts for years."   —*RT Book Reviews*

"Your readers will eat this one up."   —*Library Journal*

A PENGUIN MYSTERY

Death in the Vines

M. L. LONGWORTH has lived in Aix-en-Provence since 1997. She has written about the region for the *Washington Post*, the *Times* (UK), the *Independent,* and *Bon Appétit* magazine. She is the author of a bilingual collection of essays, *Une Américaine en Provence,* published by Éditions de La Martinière in 2004. This is her third Verlaque and Bonnet mystery, after 2012's *Murder in the Rue Dumas.* She divides her time between Aix, where she writes, and Paris, where she teaches writing at New York University.

Death in the Vines

A VERLAQUE AND BONNET MYSTERY

· M. L. LONGWORTH ·

PENGUIN BOOKS

PENGUIN BOOKS
Published by the Penguin Group
Penguin Group (USA) Inc., 375 Hudson Street,
New York, New York 10014, USA

USA | Canada | UK | Ireland | Australia | New Zealand | India | South Africa | China
Penguin Books Ltd, Registered Offices: 80 Strand, London WC2R 0RL, England
For more information about the Penguin Group visit penguin.com

First published in Penguin Books 2013

Grateful acknowledgment is made for permission to reprint excerpts from "Esse"
and "From the Rising of the Sun" from *New and Collected Poems: 1931–2001* by
Czeslaw Milosz. Copyright © 1988, 1991, 1995, 2001 by Czeslaw Milosz Royalties, Inc.
Reprinted by permission of HarperCollins Publishers.

LIBRARY OF CONGRESS CATALOGING-IN-PUBLICATION DATA
Longworth, M. L. (Mary Lou), 1963–
Death in the Vines : a Verlaque and Bonnet Provençal mystery / M. L. Longworth.
pages cm
ISBN 978-0-14-312244-9
1. Judges—France—Fiction. 2. Women law teachers—
Fiction. 3. Murder—Investigation—France—Fiction. 4. Aix-en-Provence (France)—
Fiction. 5. Mystery fiction. I. Title.
PR9199.4.L596D46 2013
813'.6—dc23   2012044302

Printed in the United States of America
5   7   9   10   8   6

Set in Adobe Caslon Pro   •   Designed by Elke Sigal

Dedicated to the memory of
Sandra Lorentz O'Hagan, 1946–2012

and

David Ewing Coates, 1929–2012

❧

Death in the Vines

Chapter One

❧

The Angels' Share

*O*livier Bonnard sat on the bottom stone step of his cellar, his hands gathered around his head as if he were attempting to soothe a migraine. He ran his callused fingers up through his thick graying hair and groaned. He glanced over at the embedded fossil in the cellar's stone wall—it was in the form of a scallop shell—and leaned over and carefully touched it. This was his secret ritual; he had been doing it each time he entered the cellar since he was old enough to remember. It was a reminder that millions of years ago much of the south of France had been under the sea, salt water covering the earth where vines now grew. His friends had aquatic fossils in their cellar walls too, in vineyards as far north as the Lubéron and the Rhône Valley, but this perfect little scallop was his favorite. He rubbed his hands through his hair once more and tried not to cry. The last time he had cried was eight years ago, at his mother's funeral.

He sighed and forced himself to look up at the wine racks. He slowly took out a pencil and a piece of paper from his quilted jacket—the cellar's temperature was a constant sixteen degrees Celsius, hence the jacket, even in early September—and began writing. The list included two magnums of 1989 red; one magnum of 1975 white; three bottles of 1954 red (which happened to be Olivier's favorite); two bottles of 1978 white (that was old for a white, and they had probably gone off now); three bottles of 1946 red (the first vintage after six years of war and his father's favorite); and a 1929 magnum that was the very last from his grandfather's first bottling.

He continued his list for some minutes and then put his pen down and stopped: there were other bottles missing, but he needed to take a break. Even though they were his family's wines, Bonnard couldn't begin to put a value on the 1929 or the 1946; both were now collector's items. His insurance agent in Aix would help with the estimates—he had the catalogs from Sotheby's and Christie's wine sales in his office. Paul was an old high-school friend and wouldn't nickel-and-dime Olivier.

Bonnard was devastated by the loss of the wines, many of them bottled by his father and his grandfather, but tears came to his eyes when he realized that the thief must be someone very close to him. Though the cellar was always locked, everyone in Olivier's family knew where to find the key: it hung to the right of the kitchen door, as it had since Olivier was a small boy. Who else knew where the key was kept? He felt himself flush, despite the fact that his hands and feet were almost numb with cold—as he thought of each person's face. Friends, neighbors, acquaintances—he felt awful imagining them as suspects in a police lineup. There was the postman, Rémy, who liked to pull his ancient Mobylette, or, when he was not working, his dilapidated van, right up to the kitchen door; Hélène, the manager of his estate and his chief winemaker—her husband was a policeman, and so he immediately took her off his list; Cyril, his only other full-time paid employee, who helped him year-round at the winery; and Sandrine, a local university student who hosted in the tasting room on weekends and holidays and whom he had hired, if truth be told, more for her beauty than for her wine knowledge or ability to count change. Every year there were a slew of North Africans who picked grapes at harvesttime, but they rarely came near the house, and he felt racist thinking of them as thieves—they were so eager to work during the *vendange,* a backbreaking job that Olivier had gladly done as a student but that nowadays so many young French refused.

Olivier then thought of his immediate family, only their heads weren't in a lineup at the Palais de Justice but sitting around at dinner—not in the bastide's elegant dining room, where his wife liked to eat, but at the long wooden kitchen table before a roaring fire. It was a comforting image and one that usually made him smile, but today it only gave him a knot in his stomach. There could be no reason why Élise, his wife of twenty years, would move the wines. Although she fully supported the Bonnard winery, she was a teetotaler, and her interests lay more in the design shop that she owned with a friend in Aix than in Syrah, Grenache, and Mourvèdre. He couldn't fathom why Victor, his eighteen-year-old son, who had been fascinated by the earth and vines since he could walk, would steal the precious bottles; nor his pride and joy, the thirteen-year-old Clara, always with a book under her nose, and the best student in her class every year since kindergarten. Olivier's father lived with the family, on the ground floor in a separate wing of their large eighteenth-century house. Albert Bonnard was eighty-three years old and though in good physical health was beginning to tire easily and lose his memory. Last week Olivier found his father slowly walking along the rows of vines, talking to the plants, thanking them for this year's generous bounty.

Olivier stood up and stretched his sore legs—he had been sitting on the step, in a daze, for nearly an hour now. He turned around with a jolt as someone came down the cellar stairs. He half expected to come face-to-face with the thief, back to pick up some of the 1960s that he or she—Olivier didn't want to be sexist—had missed.

"I saw the light on; are you picking out some wines for our dinner tomorrow night?" Élise Bonnard asked her husband. "Uh-oh," she continued. "I can tell from that stunned look on your face that you have forgotten all about the dinner with the Poyers!"

Olivier was always pleased to see his wife—even after so many years of marriage—and that afternoon even more so. Though she didn't drink alcohol, she was a fine taster; and she loved to travel around France, and sometimes abroad, with Olivier, on his wine tours. Last year they had been to Argentina, on an exchange between South American growers and French ones. Today, seeing Élise, Olivier realized just how lucky he was, and how much he needed her. His eyes filled up with tears, and his shoulders fell forward and began to shake.

Élise Bonnard looked again at her normally very composed husband, the smile now gone from her face, and she ran down the rest of the steps to put her arms around him.

"*Mon amour?*"

At that moment, every inch of Olivier Bonnard's almost two-meter frame collapsed, and the tears began to flow, interrupted by huge sobs. Élise Bonnard took some Kleenexes out of her pocket and gave them to her husband. Olivier whispered a thank-you, blew his nose repeatedly, and sighed. He breathed in and out a few times to calm himself down, as they had always taught the kids to do when they had fallen or were upset. Only then did Olivier turn his body, revealing the empty racks of wine.

"What the . . . ?" Élise gasped. She walked closer to the racks, as if her eyes were playing a game on her. Four generations of Bonnards had been making wine on this same estate, near Rognes, thirty minutes north of Aix-en-Provence, since Olivier's great-grandfather had purchased the land and the crumbling bastide at the end of the nineteenth century. It was now fully restored and historically listed. Many of their early wines were praised by top wine critics, and Mr. Colter came from America once a year to taste and rate the Bonnard wines. Élise thought for a moment about that critic—famous the world over, and incredibly powerful, as Olivier always reminded her—and yet he was so modest, so easy to talk to, and interested and passionate about everything having to do with their region. Once, he had even asked Élise for her *gougère* recipe.

"How many bottles are missing?" Élise finally asked her husband. She closed her eyes for a second or two and said a silent prayer of thanks. Upon seeing her husband weeping, she had been worried that he had cancer or that they were penniless. The wine couldn't be replaced, it's true—but they would make more, there would be other stellar vintages. What frightened her was that someone had intruded, unseen.

"I stopped counting at twenty-three; some of them were magnums. When I calm down a bit, I'll need to keep going through the bottles. They are randomly missing, that's the weird thing: one bottle here, two there."

"Could someone have left the cellar door unlocked?" Élise suggested.

"It was locked when I came in about an hour ago; and the key was on its hook by the kitchen. Would a thief bother to relock the door and hang the key back up? Besides, I've been working in the yard all morning, trying to fix that damn tractor. The doors are in plain sight from where I was working."

Élise sighed but remained silent. They owned an estate worth millions, and yet her husband still insisted on repairing motors and machines himself.

"But when were you last in this section of the cellar?" she asked.

Bonnard winced. "Good question. I'm embarrassed to admit it, but it's been months." The Bonnard cellars ran for meters and meters under their stone house. Olivier could normally be found in the winemaking section of the estate, located in a series of renovated stables beside the barn. Its vast rooms held enormous stainless-steel tanks and, in the inner chambers, row after row of oak barrels. The *"ancienne cave,"* as they had always called it, and where they now stood, held the family's prestigious wines, and it was located under the kitchen. It had an earth floor, covered in small pebbles, and an old barrel that had been used by Olivier's grandfather and served as a table. Élise had bought four stools from the La Redoute catalog that they used as seating. They had strung white party lights up as well, and had spent many evenings wrapped in woolen sweaters, tasting wines with their friends.

"There must be a reasonable explanation for this," Élise said, her hands on her hips.

"Like what? Evaporation?"

"Listen, honey, I'll call Victor and have him help you take inventory—he's had these bottles memorized since he was five years old." Élise laughed then, and, trying to lighten up the atmosphere a bit, she added: "Victor can't count at school, but in the cellar he's a mastermind!" She turned to go and Olivier stopped her, holding on to her sleeve.

"What is it?" she asked.

"Victor," her husband said, with a look that was half terrified and half as if he would explode in anger. Élise shuddered. The last time she had seen that look also involved Victor—when he was fourteen and had sneaked their car into the village for fun.

Élise now understood her husband's fear. "Victor? You don't think? Why would he take those bottles?"

"Money," her husband said, shrugging. The fear crept back on his face. "I don't like some of those kids from Aix he's been hanging out with; maybe they put him up to it? Maybe he was forced to do it—you know, threatened? He's always been a follower, not a leader." He was careful not to add that Clara was the leader in the family.

Élise bit her bottom lip, as she always did when she was nervous. "I don't much like those new friends either, but Victor hasn't been seeing much of them lately. I think it was a phase. He's going out tonight to the movies with Jérôme and Thomas." Jérôme and Thomas Clergue were brothers, sons of the Bonnards' closest neighbors; the Clergue family also made wine. Jean-Jacques Clergue had bought the land as a gift to himself for his early retirement. He had made a bundle working for Goldman Sachs in London and had "cashed in," as the locals called it, and retired to Provence at the young age of thirty-seven, when his sons were still toddlers. The two families had become instant friends. Élise had been convinced that Jean-Jacques's English wife, Lucy, who had been born and raised in London, would last two months in the French countryside. But it was Lucy who showed Élise how to cook apricot pies with shortbread crusts, and it was Lucy who helped Olivier prune the olive trees every winter. And the best surprise of all: after taking an intensive enology course, Jean-Jacques Clergue made fantastic wines. Clergue, along with Olivier's winemaker Hélène Paulik, and Marc Nagel from the Var, had raised the standards of wines from southeastern France. Other winemakers in the area learned from the trio, and the local appellations just kept getting better and better.

Olivier and Élise froze as a pair of black Converse sneakers came pounding down the cellar steps, leaving a cloud of dust in their wake. "Speak of the devil," Olivier Bonnard muttered to himself.

"Hey! I've been looking all over for you two!" Victor Bonnard said. "When's dinner, Mom? The movie's at eight p.m. in Aix. We have to catch the seven-ten bus." Victor looked at his mother, who said nothing. He then looked at his father, who also remained silent. The boy's first thought was that his parents had been arguing. He felt a lump in his throat. Perhaps they were talking about getting a divorce, like his friend Luc's parents.

His father turned toward the racks of wines and, with a sweeping motion of his hand, invited Victor to look at the partly empty racks.

"What the . . . ?" the boy yelled.

"That's exactly what your mother said."

Victor Bonnard began running back and forth along the racks, as if he were a panicked animal. Élise looked at her husband with raised eyebrows, as if to say, "You see, he's as surprised as we are."

"The 1929 is missing! *Putain!*" Victor yelled as he continued running alongside the racks, bending down every so often to look for bottles. "Does Grandpa know yet?"

"No, he's having his nap. I'm dreading telling him," Olivier replied.

"Who would do this?" Victor asked, of no one in particular.

"That's what I was going to ask you," Olivier Bonnard replied. The minute the words left his mouth, he regretted it.

Victor was stunned. "What do you mean, Dad?" The youth's face reddened, and he banged his fist against the damp stone wall, scraping his hand. "Thanks a lot, Dad!" he yelled, and ran back up the stairs, slamming the cellar door behind him.

"Bravo, *chéri*," Élise said to her husband, rolling her eyes; she too walked up the stairs and outside, into the late-afternoon sunshine.

"*Bon*," Olivier Bonnard said to himself, sighing. He'd go and apologize to Victor; then he would drive into Aix and see his insurance friend. It had been weeks since Olivier had been to town: he had been too busy fretting over an unusually wet late August. He and Hélène had moved their year-old wine, in barrels, to the second-year cellar to make room for the new wines. When that was done, Olivier and Cyril had been moving equipment and clearing space for the crushing and pressing of the new harvest—that is, until the tractor broke down. There was work to do in the cellars, and Bonnard had been topping up the casks, explaining to a bored Sandrine that 5 percent of the wine evaporates through the wooden sides of the barrel. It was normally a job Victor loved, but Olivier had asked Sandrine to help him, hoping that she might gain some insight into the winemaking process. He wanted Victor to concentrate on his schoolwork: they had made a pact that he would, this last year of high school, hit the books so that he could at least achieve a somewhat honorable grade on the Bac—the grueling national exams at the end of the school year. When Victor was a small boy, Olivier had taught him the term for this loss—"the angels' share"—just as Olivier's father, Albert, had taught him. He smiled as he remembered a six-year-old Victor peering at the barrel and walking around it, trying to catch, in his tiny cupped hands, the red wine that he imagined was leaking out.

After Bonnard finished his business in Aix, he would walk over to Jean-Jacques Clergue's house and invite him over—Jean-Jacques would have good advice, and Olivier wanted to drink with a friend, in the cellar, surrounded by what was left of the prized vintages. As winemakers, Bonnard and his fellow *vignerons* were always careful not to overindulge. But tonight he thought he might tie one on. Jean-Jacques was a bon vivant and might even bring along a couple of Cuban cigars—Olivier had smoked one with the judge from Aix the last time he had visited, and he was developing a taste for them. He'd get the silent treatment from Élise, but he didn't care. Olivier Bonnard walked up the stairs, turned off the lights, and closed and locked the door; this time he put the key in his pocket.

Chapter Two

A Final Market Day

It was a typical Tuesday when Mme Pauline d'Arras set out to do her market shopping, the last one she would ever do. The September weather was warm, but she wore a light cotton sweater over her silk blouse. The morning sun was high, and bright; the sky blue; and the closer she got to the Palais de Justice and its square with a thrice-weekly market, the noisier it became. Her dog, Coco, tried to run ahead, excited, sensing that it was market day. Madame tugged on the leash and smiled down at Coco—the little dog loved the market, in particular the traffic policemen on motorcycles.

Mme d'Arras zigzagged her way past the large-scale vegetable sellers and gave them an intentional scowl. Any sellers who had bananas, pineapples, and limes definitely did not grow their own food in Provence: they bought their produce wholesale in warehouses in Marseille. Her favorite seller, Martin, had a small stall at the far end of the market, and he sold organic vegetables that he grew on a farm north of Aix. She squeezed past a group of tourists taking pictures of spices and gave them a good nudge with her basket: *Don't they realize that some people actually have to shop and cook?* Mme d'Arras smiled as she approached Martin's stall, but her smile faded when she saw the queue. *So . . . other Aixoises are catching on to Martin's excellent produce,* she thought. She'd have to wait in line, and lunch would now be at least fifteen minutes late. But if she worked quickly when she got home, and did not stop to have a tea, lunch might be on time. She took one of Martin's plastic bowls, which was sitting on top of a small mountain of red-skinned potatoes, and began selecting vegetables for the pot-au-feu that she would make this afternoon for the evening's dinner: turnips, carrots, potatoes, leeks, onions, and garlic. The beef she would buy at the Boucherie du Palais—*Another queue, no doubt.* She and Gilles would have pork chops and green beans for lunch— that was quick and easy, and Gilles loved them. "So do you, don't you, Coco baby?" she cried, looking down at her dog.

She looked up, startled, when she realized that someone was speaking to her.

"Madame," Martin said, smiling, but his eyes could not hide his worry.

Mme d'Arras composed herself and smiled at Martin. *What lovely big hands he has,* she thought, *but rather dirty. I wonder how long he has been calling my name?* She remembered that she had been talking to Coco, but for how long? She handed Martin her bowl of vegetables. "*Voilà,*" she said.

"Looks like a pot-au-feu this evening?" Martin asked.

"Indeed," she replied. "A delicious dinner, and economical . . . well, except for the beef." She looked over at the Boucherie du Palais, hoping to get a glimpse at how long the queue was, but she could not see inside the shop. A good sign, perhaps: it meant that the line wasn't out the door, as it was on Saturdays.

Martin carefully weighed the vegetables: he knew that Mme d'Arras watched the scales like a hawk. He looked at her perfectly coiffed blond hair and designer eyeglasses: she was one of those Aixoises whose age was indeterminable, somewhere between sixty and seventy-five. Mme d'Arras was a tough old girl, but he liked her. She had been one of his first customers, when he was the only organic seller in the market. He had waited for years to get the okay from the town hall to have a stand, and the down payment had nearly killed him, but now the stand was paying for itself, especially on Saturdays. He usually sold out of his produce by noon.

Madame began speaking to another woman in the queue: they were both making a pot-au-feu that evening and were comparing recipes. Whether or not the two women knew each other was beyond Martin's knowledge; Aix was where he worked and sold the best, but compared with the hamlet he lived in, north of Manosque, this was very foreign—wealthy, privileged—territory. He never knew if Mme d'Arras was genuinely curious, and that's why she was always turning around to chat with someone, or if she was just a busybody. He decided that her curiosity was probably self-centered, and self-serving, but he was worried about her all the same: she was able to get around and do her shopping, and could obviously remember recipes, but she seemed more and more absentminded these past few weeks—she didn't hear him when he spoke to her, and her eyes looked glazed over, almost yellow.

"There you go, Mme d'Arras. That will be seven euros and thirteen centimes, please." He put a handful of parsley into her basket as well, free of charge.

Mme d'Arras carefully took out her Hermès change purse, a gift from her nephew, and slowly counted the money.

Martin smiled and thanked her, and she carried her basket back through the crowd of buyers and sellers, stopping to admire the sunflowers that a farmer was selling. She decided not to buy any, because she was already overloaded with the vegetables—potatoes and onions were heavy—and she continued on to the Boucherie du Palais. Inside the long, narrow butcher shop there was a long queue, and she moved quickly to the back of the shop, where a small second queue had formed, reserved for "preferred" customers, or those in the know. She nodded and smiled to those customers that she recognized, and waited, trying to quiet down Coco, who was now getting impatient. A young American mother was in front of her, busy speaking to her young toddler, who was in a stroller. Mme d'Arras leaned over, pretending to look at the cuts of meat, and began to inch her way past *l'Américaine,* who wouldn't notice or would be too polite to say anything about the old woman's queue jumping. But when Mme d'Arras straightened up, her feet ran directly into the stroller, which the American had thrust in front of her, blocking the way. "*Il faut attendre, madame,*" the young woman said in good, if heavily accented, French.

Mme d'Arras huffed, pretending not to understand, and began talking to Coco; she was perturbed that this young woman not only blocked her way but also knew the shop's secret of the two-line system.

"Mme d'Arras," Henri, the butcher and owner, bellowed when it was finally her turn. "Don't you look handsome today."

Mme d'Arras blushed and replied, "One has to make an attempt to look presentable, no matter what the day."

"Indeed," the butcher replied. "And what is the beautiful madame preparing for her lucky husband?"

Despite herself, she gushed. "A pot-au-feu."

"Well, let me get you one of my select cuts of beef for your pot-au-feu, and some veal as well."

"Veal?" Mme d'Arras stumbled. That would bring the price up considerably. The other butchers in the shop normally gave her only beef.

"Of course . . . veal! But if Madame doesn't agree . . ."

"No, indeed, perhaps you are right . . . a little veal will add wonders to the flavor, *non*?" She didn't want Henri, or especially that busybody Mme de Correz, to think that she was cheap.

Henri, the experienced salesman, smiled and cut a chunk of tender veal and added it to her beef purchase.

Mme d'Arras took her meat and went and stood in yet another line to pay, but she knew from experience that Henri's daughter, who worked the till, was extremely fast and efficient. In no time Madame was walking back up the Rue Émeric David to her apartment. She carried Coco, who was now beside herself with fatigue and hunger. She stopped before she arrived at her apartment, passing by number 16, and scowled. Her neighbor, a young upstart with new money, was outside the Hôtel de Panisse-Passis, speaking to workmen who were setting up scaffolding. Philippe Léridon had bought the grand mansion a few years ago, but it had sat empty—and quiet—while he was living in Morocco, making millions, as Mme d'Arras's husband had informed her, on a luxury hotel chain. He had bought the faded but elegant eighteenth-century mansion on a whim, when he had been in Aix on holiday, and had, earlier this year, sold his hotel chain and moved permanently to Aix. The workmen had been in and out of the mansion for weeks—noise all day long, even on Saturdays—and her apartment had developed cracks in the walls because of their jackhammering. She reminded herself to call her lawyer later that afternoon, and her stride quickened: she was glad—no, proud—that she was able to handle such affairs on her own, without the help of her husband.

Philippe Léridon's "*Bonjour, Mme d'Arras!*" broke her reverie, but she walked on to the Hôtel de Barlet, one building farther north, at number 18. Before putting her key in the door, she turned to Léridon and exclaimed, careful to show him her superior accent, "*Bonjour à vous, monsieur!* My lawyer will be contacting you!"

She vaguely heard Léridon protesting as she quickly stepped inside her hotel's impeccably preserved eighteenth-century entry and closed the door. Her building's carved front doors, though not as ornate as Panisse's, were, to her eye, all the more elegant and better for it. The Hôtel de Panisse's doors were a riot of carved foliage, swords, crowns, and ribbons—loud—just like their new owner, with his thick Midi accent and his oversized foreign vehicle, which could barely fit down the Rue Émeric David.

She stood inside the front hall and sighed, too tired to pick up the mail that the postman had set on the entry's marble console, and slowly walked up the stairs toward her second-floor flat. When she set Coco down, the dog yelped and ran quickly up the stairs. She unlocked the door—it always took some time, since the door had three sets of locks—then she and Coco went inside. Closing the door behind her, Mme d'Arras walked into the kitchen, Coco at her feet, to set her groceries down on the kitchen counter. Wearily she sat down at the little white kitchen table that was just big enough for her and Gilles to take breakfast. Something was bothering her, but she couldn't think what. Was it the queues? No, they hadn't been that bad. Perhaps it had been seeing her show-off neighbor, with his fancy car and new money? She realized that M. Léridon had interrupted her thoughts—she had been thinking of her younger sister, Clothilde, and the small Romanesque chapel where they had sung together as young girls. She could picture the chapel perfectly; its rounded apse was the first thing you saw when you drove into Rognes. Coco yelped, wanting lunch.

"Yes, I'll get you your food," she cooed to the dog, and then, remembering her own lunch, she sat down again and put her head in her hands and began to cry. She had forgotten to buy the pork chops.

Chapter Three

✢

A Worried Husband

*G*illes d'Arras, although he had lived less than a hundred meters from Aix's Palais de Justice for more than forty years, had never set foot inside it. He found himself sitting across from a huge, bald-headed policeman who looked at him kindly and spoke softly. M. d'Arras looked around and saw other police officers typing, or chatting, or walking to and fro, carrying documents. It could have been his office, except that some of the men and women were in uniform. He looked back at the big policeman and realized that he was meant to continue speaking. The words, however, had difficulty leaving his mouth.

"I got home today for lunch at the usual hour, just a little bit past noon. Pauline—that is, Mme d'Arras—usually has lunch ready by twelve-thirty. It's been like that since the day we were married, forty-two years ago."

The officer wrote down the information and then looked up at

M. d'Arras and asked, "Did you argue this morning, before you went to work?"

"No," Gilles d'Arras replied, obviously surprised by the question.

"And that was the last time you saw your wife?"

"Yes. I left for work at eight-forty-five. When she wasn't home for lunch, I began calling our friends and Pauline's older sister, Natalie, asking if she was with any of them. I think she left in a hurry, because Coco—sorry, that's our dog—was left alone in the apartment. She wouldn't do that normally."

"And she isn't answering her cell phone, I presume?"

M. d'Arras shook his head. "She hates them. I tried to buy one for her when they first came out, but she refused."

Commissioner Paulik paused and said, as gently as he could, "I agreed to meet with you, M. d'Arras, because you were so insistent. But I must tell you that you are acting prematurely. Your wife has only been gone the afternoon, and it's now only five-thirty. She could be anywhere."

"That's just it. Anywhere!" insisted d'Arras. "I never would have bothered you had it not been urgent. She could be *anywhere* . . . hungry, hurt, cold. We've eaten lunch together for over forty years. Only once were we not able to, the 20th of March in 1983—I had a meeting in Paris that day. Never, ever, has she not told me her plans for the day. Never."

Paulik felt a shiver on his giant forearms and said, "And you checked the hospitals, Officer Flamant tells me." He couldn't remember the last time he had eaten lunch with his wife, Hélène: they were both too busy. *Ah, the easy life of France's wealthy elderly,* he silently mused.

"Yes. In fact, I checked the hospitals first."

Commissioner Paulik look surprised.

"You see, my wife has been, well, not herself lately. She's become forgetful, and weepy. She has a far-off look in her eyes, like she isn't listening to those speaking to her. It seemed to me like it could be the beginnings of Alzheimer's, but she refused to be tested."

"Ah, *bon*. Your wife is in denial, M. d'Arras?" Paulik noticed that Mme d'Arras was good at refusing things: cell phones, medical tests.

"Yes, denial perhaps. But she had a lot on her plate too. At her last general checkup, our family practitioner noticed a lump in her throat, and she had it tested for thyroid cancer . . . punctured, I think they called it . . . at the hospital, but the results were uncertain. So, last week, we had an appointment with a specialist, who said that, since the puncture couldn't tell us if the tumor was malignant or not, it would be necessary to have surgery. That was very upsetting news for Pauline. She hates hospitals. She's never trusted doctors."

She hates hospitals too, noted Paulik silently. "It's too early to send out a missing-persons alert, but if she hasn't returned home by tomorrow morning, I promise you I will do so. Have you brought a recent photograph of your wife?"

M. d'Arras pulled out a manila envelope from his briefcase. Paulik was impressed—most people forgot to bring a photograph of their loved one who had gone missing, out of sheer panic and stress. Paulik looked at the photograph and noted the unsmiling but distinguished Mme d'Arras. A lover, perhaps? She was undeniably a handsome woman—of a certain age, of course, but well preserved. She'd only been gone for the day, a few hours, really. Paulik was quite certain that M. d'Arras would receive a phone call or, unfortunately, a goodbye letter from his wife soon.

Paulik put the photograph in a file and stood up, indicating that the interview was over. M. d'Arras looked crestfallen and was slow to get up. Paulik moved around the desk, put his hand on the old man's shoulder, and asked, "You'll call as soon as you hear any news regarding your wife?"

"Of course," M. d'Arras replied in a whisper.

"Officer Flamant will see you out." Paulik looked over at Flamant, who was working nearby, and signaled with his eyes and a quick jerk of the head toward M. d'Arras. Flamant jumped up and was at the old man's side in seconds. He took the man by the arm and gently led him past the desks, toward the hallway.

Commissioner Paulik walked past his own desk, heading for the back of the large office, where Mme Girard had a small office. "Is he in?" he asked her, gesturing toward a larger office with a closed black door.

"Yes. I told him you wanted to speak to him," Mme Girard replied. Paulik realized she looked like a younger version of Mme d'Arras—well coiffed, wearing discreet makeup and a designer suit with a short skirt. "Go on in," she said, pointing to the door with her pencil.

"Thanks."

Paulik knocked and opened the door. The judge was sitting at his desk, reading, and, seeing the commissioner, took off his reading glasses and stood up. They shook hands—although they had been working closely together for over a year, they did not exchange *la bise*. Between men, the quick peck on both cheeks was a greeting reserved for very close friends or male family members.

"How are things?" Judge Verlaque asked. "I saw you with that old man. . . . I recognize him, but I can't recall why."

"Ah, he lives just up the street; I vaguely recognized him too. Aix is funny that way, *non*? He came in to file a missing-persons report. His wife has been missing since sometime this morning."

Verlaque looked surprised. "This morning? She could be anywhere. She's probably at Monoprix. Or getting her hair done."

"I know, but monsieur was so distraught. He's afraid that she might have Alzheimer's. I agree, she could be with a friend or a lover, but she may have wandered off somewhere and now can't find her way back. My great-uncle Jean had that."

"What a waste of time," mumbled Verlaque. "Is this what you wanted to see me about?" Only when these words had left the judge's mouth did he realize he had perhaps been insensitive regarding the Uncle Jean in question.

Paulik coughed. "No . . ." He hesitated before continuing. "You will, no doubt, think that this is just as much a waste of time, but right before M. d'Arras came in, I had a phone call from an untypically hysterical Hélène."

"Your wife? Is she all right? Your daughter, Léa?" Verlaque adored Hélène Paulik, a winemaker at a privately owned château north of Aix. Paulik's ten-year-old daughter, Léa, sang at Aix's music conservatory and was, from all reports, a whiz.

"Yes, yes, they're fine, thank you. It's Domaine Beauclaire, where Hélène works. They've been robbed. I know that theft doesn't fall under our jurisdiction, but I need to think out loud."

"Of course. What was stolen? Money?"

"Worse. Wines. But old ones, way back to 1929."

Verlaque whistled and leaned back in his chair, rubbing his stomach. "What a shame. Do they know how much was stolen?"

Paulik shook his head. "They're doing an inventory right now, Hélène and her boss, Olivier Bonnard. Hélène could barely speak, she was so upset, but she said that Olivier hinted that he suspects his teenage son. Apparently, the kid has been hanging out with some local rich kids. . . . Well, that makes sense, because the Bonnards are rich too. . . . Anyway, these teens are into excessive parties with drugs, Champagne . . . *la jeunesse dorée*. There's a nightclub where these golden kids go that costs forty euros just to get in."

"La Fantaisie," Verlaque replied.

"Yes, that's it. Anyway, the poor guy is pained to think that his son may have sold the family wines off just to have money to go to these parties."

"Tell Bonnard not to jump to conclusions. It's no secret that his domaine is the most prestigious winery in Aix. Some thieves do specialize in stealing wines. In fact"—Verlaque paused, putting his reading glasses back on and looking at his BlackBerry—"there's an ex–wine thief who has turned over a new leaf and is now on the police payroll in Paris. I doubt that the theft team here in Aix knows about this guy. He works with Christie's and Sotheby's as well. Quite a character, I understand." He looked at the screen on his phone, scrolling down until he came to what he was looking for. "*Voilà*. Here's the name of the examining magistrate at Saint-Germain. Call him—he may be able to help Olivier Bonnard and get him in touch with the wine-theft expert." Verlaque wrote down the name and a telephone number on a piece of paper and handed it to Paulik.

"Thanks," Paulik replied. "I'm going to call him right now—I hope he's still in the office."

"Come to think of it, I have to go up to Paris tomorrow for family business," Verlaque said. "Get me the name and address of the wine expert and I'll try to pay him a visit. I've been intrigued by this guy for a long time."

"Will do," Paulik said. "Thanks a million."

Verlaque took off his glasses and looked up at Paulik. "So what's your opinion of this Mme d'Arras?"

"Judging by her photo, I'd say she could very well be at the hairdresser's. Hélène once had her hair tinted, on a whim, and it took four bloody hours. She was livid. Mme d'Arras could still be under one of those dome things," Paulik said, gesturing a semicircle with his hands above his head.

"I hope so," Verlaque replied. He resisted the temptation to smile, for when his rugby-playing commissioner had put his hands over his head and made the sweeping circular motion, he had looked vaguely like a ballet dancer.

Chapter Four

❧

Confessions of a Wine Thief

Verlaque had mixed feelings about the neighborhood. He had grown up in the first *arrondissement*, at number 6 Place des Petits Pères, and liked it there: all of Paris was on foot, or at least the areas that he wanted to see. But it was a neighborhood for tourists, and lovers of beauty and grand monuments, and not a residential one. Good butchers and grocers were few and far between in *la première*. People who lived there ate out; or had the servants run around town buying groceries, as his parents had done. He stopped in the Place Vendôme, looked across the cobbled square at the Ritz, and smiled, thinking of a fellow cigar lover—Papa Hemingway—liberating the hotel's bar in 1944.

He continued up the Rue de la Paix, crossing into the second *arrondissement*, and rang at number 15. After some time there came a sharp "*Qui?*" on the intercom, and Verlaque stated his name. When the door buzzed open, he entered the frescoed lobby. The judge began walking up the wide stone staircase, pausing at each floor to read the brass plaques beside the sets of carved wooden double doors. On the third floor he found it—*M. Hippolyte Thébaud, Expert des Vins.* He tapped lightly on the door, and it opened almost immediately. The sight that met his eyes made Verlaque incapable of speaking; the wine expert stepped aside so that the judge could enter. Hippolyte Thébaud was not the middle-aged wine-thief-cum-expert that Verlaque had been expecting. There were no tattoos, no signs of any time spent in prison. In his early thirties, Thébaud was impeccably dressed in a blue velvet jacket and white linen pants with bright-blue leather shoes. His shirt and tie both had blue and white stripes—thick horizontal stripes on the tie and thin vertical ones on the shirt. His hair was blond and wavy and piled artfully on top of his head; his nose was long and thin; his lips were full. Tall and slim, with the wide shoulders of someone who visited the gym regularly, Hippolyte Thébaud was, in a word, beautiful.

They shook hands, and Thébaud motioned Verlaque through the entryway into a salon. Coffee was offered; when Verlaque nodded and mumbled yes, the young man gracefully left the room, almost pirouetting. Verlaque heard water being poured and then the espresso machine thumping into action. As Verlaque was led into the salon, he had been vaguely aware of a riot of bright colors, but now he was able to take some time to look around. The objects that filled the stately room had obviously been bought at different times and in very different places, but their arrangement was completely harmonious. A very long carved sofa covered in a bright-red silk looked Venetian to Verlaque. Beside it was a backless green velvet sofa, also with carved wooden arms and legs, and beside that a blue easy chair whose round frame was made of thin parallel stainless-steel rods that gave the base of the chair a birdcage effect. The chair, though obviously from the 1960s and probably American, stood up proudly against the two centuries-old European sofas. The tables were mostly glass-topped, each one with a different base; some of the table legs looked oddly like bronzed bones. Small sculptures were placed on every available surface, many of them protected—or highlighted—by glass bell jars. The rugs and wall hangings were also in bright colors, save for the curtains, which were white linen with a narrow band of black running along the edge. This was, Verlaque noted, the touch of calm that the room needed.

Hippolyte Thébaud passed Verlaque a demitasse and sat down, crossing his long, elegant legs. Verlaque thanked him for the coffee and added, "Thank you for agreeing to see me on such short notice. As I told you on the phone, Domaine Beauclaire has been robbed, and you are a noted expert on wine theft in France." Verlaque was guessing that compliments suited the young man.

"Wine expert, period," Thébaud replied.

Verlaque raised his eyebrows in obvious disbelief. "Are you not a bit young to be a wine expert?"

"I'm a fast learner," Thébaud replied, smiling.

Verlaque returned the smile and said, "Yes. I read in your file that your first arrest was at age nineteen. Stealing wine from the three-star restaurant where you were a waiter."

"I had *just* turned nineteen. At first I stole them to sell, seeing the ridiculous prices that people were willing to pay for them. I was naïve and didn't know the joy behind a great wine. That sublime feeling that when you taste a Romanée-Conti, you're tasting history and geography and geology in a bottle. That the chalkiness of the soil has as much to do with the taste of the wine as the vintner's hand and head. That an unhappy vintner will make a closed wine, a wine difficult on the palate; and a vintner in love will make an open wine, one that changes as it rolls around in your mouth and then gets better as it slides down your throat." M. Thébaud uncrossed his long, thin legs and laid his left hand on the arm of the sofa, signaling that he was finished speaking.

Verlaque was impressed, almost unable to speak. He drew a breath and asked, "Where did you come across your appreciation for wines?" He had wanted to add "poetry" but now knew that the young man needed no extra compliments.

"Ah. That's the amazing part of the story. I learned all of this without having tasted the grand wines. In jail."

Verlaque raised an eyebrow. "In the jail's library?" He was quite sure that wine tasting was not on the rehabilitation program, whereas creative writing and tennis perfection were.

Thébaud nodded. "I read and read and read. When I had exhausted our library, I asked for books in English, teaching myself that language through the grape. I knew everything about Hungarian Tokays and Italian Super Tuscans without ever having tasted them. I knew how they were made, who made them, and what they should taste like. It drove me to get out of prison earlier, and it gave me strength to go on, despite the filth that went on in there." M. Thébaud made a sour face and shook his head lightly back and forth, erasing the memories of jail.

"And now you're clean," Verlaque half stated and half asked.

The wine expert laughed. "Oh yes. No need to steal wines anymore; I can afford to buy them. When I got out of jail, I knew so much about wine that I was able to buy and sell legitimately and make profits. Because my English was so good, I advised foreign buyers, and because I learned wine before having tasted it, *really* tasted it, I had something unique to offer that no other expert had."

Verlaque tilted his head. "You had no biases?"

"Exactly, my dear judge. You're one of the few people ever to have understood that. I didn't have a great love for one region over another. For me it was a numbers game, and one I was good at. Since then I've changed, naturally, and now have preferences. But back then I didn't."

"Fascinating," Verlaque said with complete sincerity. He loved stories like this one—where against all odds someone makes something out of his or her life—a story that he thought very un-French, given the French preferences for the right schools, the right accent, the good families. Hippolyte Thébaud was a wine expert who didn't grow up in a Bordeaux wine family, didn't attend the right schools, and certainly had no connections, having begun his career as a waiter. "You could write your memoirs," Verlaque said.

"Oh, but I have already!" Thébaud mused. "We're just hunting around for a good title."

Verlaque wasted no time in answering: "*Confessions of a Wine Thief.*"

Thébaud beamed. "Wonderful! That's exactly why, when you walked through the door, I knew I had to tell you my story," he said, drawing his legs up under him.

Verlaque paused, unsure how to respond to the exaggerated compliment. Thébaud was a salesman, first and foremost, and wine expert and consultant to the police second. He decided to say nothing, and instead he plunged straight into Olivier Bonnard's wine theft. He gave Thébaud the details and ended the story by saying, "We believe that the thief is someone who knows the family and the winery."

Thébaud sat back and put his hands behind his head. "Why so?"

"Because the lock hadn't been tampered with, and the key was found in its usual spot, beside the kitchen door."

"Classic!" Hippolyte Thébaud cried out. "Vintners are *so* imaginative! They hide the keys to their cellars—whether in Argentina, Alsace, or Adelaide—all in the same idiotic place. Any fool could have slipped in and made a copy. I've done it before, while pretending to check the electricity meter. Next!"

"Okay. The thief didn't take all of the premier crus; he or she took different wines, here and there, regardless of their age or quality."

Thébaud threw his hands in the air. "They're stealing my moves! I did that once or twice, to make it look like an in-house job. The second time, I went back for more while the Bordeaux police were on the premises, busy interviewing family and staff. Ha!" He had such a look of divine pleasure on his face that Verlaque thought, very briefly, that the handsome young man might be stealing again. Seeing the judge's look, Thébaud said, "Don't worry. I was telling the truth when I said that I don't need to steal anymore."

"So what's your opinion?" Verlaque asked.

"They'll be back for more," Thébaud answered. "Would you like another coffee?"

Verlaque, uncharacteristically, had decided to take the metro to the train station, knowing that over the lunch hour taxis would be few and far between. After sitting on a bench in the Tuileries for a few minutes, admiring the top-heavy, rounded women sculpted by Maillol, he got on the number-1 metro line. At the next stop, Musée du Louvre, the train sat in the station for four minutes before the doors finally closed and the train lurched forward. Verlaque breathed a sigh of relief, glancing at his watch, realizing that he had underestimated the time it took the number 1 to snake along downtown Paris, parallel to the Seine. At the next stop the train had been in the station for more than seven minutes when, finally, an announcement came over the PA that a passenger had met with "an accident" farther up the line and it would be some time before the train could leave. Passengers began mumbling about a suicide and then, slowly, began filing out of the carriage. Verlaque followed the crowd out of the station and up to the Rue de Rivoli, where he battled with others for a taxi, all of which were already occupied. Lunchtime in Paris . . . Verlaque cursed under his breath. He walked up to the next street—Rue Saint-Honoré—where traffic flowed in the direction of the Gare de Lyon, moving as quickly as he could, at the same time checking over his shoulder for a vacant cab. All were full. By the time he got to the next metro entrance, at the busy Châtelet, he looked at his watch, seeing that he had missed the twelve-forty-nine to Aix. He could risk taking the line 14 from Châtelet, which was automated, or keep walking. He kept walking, trying to admire Paris and be philosophical about the missed train. It had been a profitable day. He had gone over the family's finances with his parents—a twice-yearly obligation—and obtained good information from Hippolyte Thébaud. Thébaud was the quintessential *dandy*—a word that had no translation into French, so the French had taken it on as one of their own. Verlaque couldn't wait to tell Marine about the wine thief.

He whistled as he walked, and arrived at the train station in time for the one-fifty-three train, showing his ticket to the controller and explaining the delayed metro.

"You'll still have to buy a new seat."

"What?" Verlaque exclaimed. "It wasn't my fault. There was a suicide at one of the metro stations."

"That's what they all say. You have to allow yourself extra time for things like this. That will be ninety-five euros for a new ticket, in second class."

Verlaque handed him his credit card and cringed at the thought of sitting on one of the narrow seats in second class. "There will be plenty of empty seats, don't worry," the controller said. "You can pick any one."

The controller was right: the train was only half full, and Verlaque was able to have to himself four seats facing each other, spreading out his books and papers. He looked around for an outlet to plug in his laptop, but this car didn't have one. He hoped he had enough battery power. The countryside whizzed by, in the full, glorious sun of an Indian summer day, and Verlaque felt as happy as he had ever been. He had begun to draft some e-mails that he had been avoiding when a terrible noise, as if some teenagers had pelted the train with rocks, or the train had run over some fencing, was heard. His fellow passengers stopped what they were doing, setting down books and magazines and removing headsets. The noise continued for a few awful seconds. The train slowed down and finally came to a full stop, while the passengers let out a communal moan. "We've hit something," the man across the aisle said to himself.

"No," an elderly woman said, "it was more like the sound of something being thrown at the train. Like rocks."

The car had remained silent for a few seconds when two young girls came running through, looking for the controllers. "There's a broken window in our car."

The passengers again moaned, not knowing how the window came to be broken, but knowing that this would mean a delay, possibly for hours. Verlaque was about to text Marine and tell her to eat without him when one of the TGV's staff—a short, thick woman with spiked white hair—came through the car, her face as pale as her hair. "We hit someone," she said, resting her hand on the back of Verlaque's seat. "Suicide. Three hours' delay, at least." Verlaque texted Bruno Paulik about the delay, since the commissioner had offered to pick the judge up at Aix's TGV station. He would be getting in too late for that now, and would take a taxi or the shuttle bus into Aix. He leaned back and closed his eyes. A few of the passengers got back to work, unperturbed by the delay: they had work to do, and there was nothing anyone could do. Others pressed their faces against the glass, trying to see a bit of blood or scoping out the possibilities of slipping out for a quick cigarette. A woman behind Verlaque called home, instructing whoever it was who answered about which leftovers to heat up for the children and not to forget that *petit Charles* did not like zucchini but was to eat it anyway.

Verlaque looked out at the sunny day, feeling the warmth of the late-afternoon sun on his forearms. He suddenly missed Marine, terribly. He felt saddened, not by the delays and the fate that seemed to rule this day, but by the desperation that led people to take their own lives. It was a threat that Monique had used to use on the young Verlaque: "If you don't come, I'll do something drastic." Verlaque closed his eyes, angry at himself for allowing the ghost of Monique to reappear. He hadn't thought about her in months.

The emergency teams arrived, and passengers began talking among themselves and inviting each other to the bar car for coffee or beer. Two hours later, they were still there, in the middle of a flat but pretty countryside, and a farmer drove by on a parallel farm track. Verlaque looked up and watched the farmer as he drove, dust flying up behind the tractor, and noted that he did not turn his head to see why police and firemen were gathered around a stopped TGV. Work to be done. Or perhaps the farmer had seen this sort of thing before? The fields on either side of the train tracks were planted with some kind of fruit trees, Verlaque now noticed, and the yellow wildflowers that lined the tracks began waving in the breeze.

Chapter Five

❧

An Attack in Équilles

*T*he TGV pulled into Aix's contemporary wood-and-steel station four hours late, at 9:15 p.m. A sigh of relief swept the tired passengers as they reached for their coats and bags. "Well, have a great evening, everyone," joked a middle-aged man as he tucked his laptop into his briefcase.

"Yeah, it's been a blast," answered a student, putting his headphones and iPod in a tattered backpack. The woman behind Verlaque was once again on the phone as she made her way up the aisle—it seemed that *petit Charles* had indeed eaten all of his vegetables, but he was now refusing to go to bed until Maman was at home.

Verlaque smiled at the elderly woman who had been sitting across the aisle and let her pass in front of him. "We have been inconvenienced," she said, admiring her handsome fellow passenger with the dark, sad eyes. "But that's nothing compared with the poor desperate soul who ended his or her life today."

Verlaque nodded. "Yes, madame, we are inconvenienced, but fortunate." He didn't bother telling her that it was his second suicide of the day. "Would you like me to help you with your suitcase?" he offered, seeing that she had a large brown suitcase on the luggage rack as well as a carrier bag.

"That's very kind," she replied. "Yes, I would. My son-in-law should be waiting for me on the platform."

Verlaque lifted her suitcase and followed her out onto the lit-up platform. A man in his late thirties was there, arms outstretched, to greet her. She embraced her son-in-law and thanked Verlaque, and they wished each other well. It was the first time on any of his TGV journeys that he had made an acquaintance. The shock of the suicide had been great, he realized.

Verlaque looked out into the night sky and saw a full moon over Aix. He stood there for a few seconds, wondering if he should drag himself to the other side of the station and down several flights of stairs to where the shuttle might or might not be waiting, or simply walk out the door and take one of the taxis that were lined up just a few meters away. But he didn't have to make that decision: Bruno Paulik came quickly through the automatic doors that led from the parking lot to the tracks. "I'm sorry I'm late," the commissioner said.

"I only just got here. Bruno, you certainly didn't have to come and get me. I assumed that when I texted you with the train's delay you would just go home."

"I was at home, but at eight p.m. I got a call from the Palais de Justice, and I drove to Éguilles," Paulik answered. "Here, get in," he said, opening the door of his older-model Range Rover for Verlaque.

"I want to thank you for going up to Paris to speak to that wine expert," Paulik said as he pulled up to the parking gate and paid. "Hélène and Olivier too. They send their greetings."

"I had some papers to go over with my parents this morning, and our wine expert, Hippolyte Thébaud, lives around the corner," Verlaque answered. "He gave me some useful information, including the fact that he's sure the thief will be back."

Paulik groaned. "I was afraid of that. Okay, I'll warn Olivier." He got onto the highway and then looked quickly at the judge. "Are you hungry?" Bruno Paulik thought often of food.

"Not really, thanks. When we stopped to change trains in Valence, we were given boxed emergency meals. I was half expecting to find a toy inside."

Paulik laughed. "They had to change trains?"

"Yes. The front of the train was too damaged to go any great distance. We limped along to Valence."

"The poor soul," Paulik quietly said.

Verlaque nodded, then realized that the commissioner had been called back into the Palais de Justice after being comfortably at home in Pertuis, twenty minutes away. "So, tell me, what was the call about that made you drive back into Aix and wreck your evening?"

"That's partly why I'm picking you up, sir," Paulik replied. "I thought I could fill you in, and I wanted to beat Roussel to it."

Verlaque didn't say anything. He didn't need to—Yves Roussel was Aix's hyperactive prosecutor. "What happened in Éguilles?" he asked.

"A young woman was raped early this evening," Paulik replied. "She was badly beat up and then strangled, but she didn't die. She's at the hospital, fighting for her life."

"Oh my God." Verlaque buried his head in his large hands and breathed deeply. He looked up and saw the city lights of Aix in the distance. "This morning the world was looking like a rosy place," he said, still looking out of the window. "But, then, I always think that when I'm sitting in a park in Paris."

"Her name is Suzanne Montmory," Paulik continued. "She's twenty-eight years old and lives by herself in an apartment in Éguilles. The immediate neighbors didn't hear anything except her television; we'll be interviewing more tomorrow morning."

"Was it a break-in?" Verlaque asked, getting interested in the case.

"The lock wasn't damaged."

"So perhaps she knew her attacker?"

"It looks like that; most women do. The place was trashed. Mlle Montmory put up a good fight, it looks like."

"What time did it happen?"

"Sometime after four-ten and before seven-thirty p.m. Mlle Montmory's co-workers—she works at a branch office of the Banque de Provence in Éguilles—said that she was complaining of a sore throat and left a bit early. She left the bank just before four p.m., and it's only a ten-minute walk."

"Who found her at seven-thirty?" Verlaque asked.

"A colleague was worried and went to check on her. He knocked a few times, and when she didn't answer he said he thought he'd try the door, which was unlocked. He found her and called emergency right away."

"Check him out."

Paulik sighed. "That's exactly what Roussel said, and when I left the two of them, Roussel was raking the kid over the coals."

"Good."

Paulik looked surprised. The judge was usually more compassionate and prone to thinking about the big picture.

"I've had a day of death," Verlaque said, looking over at the commissioner. "Why would this guy go and check on a co-worker who just has a sore throat? People have sore throats all the time. I don't believe him."

"He says he has a crush on her, so he used the sore throat as an excuse to pop by. He was going to ask her out to dinner."

"That's a little more believable. What do you think?"

"I believe him," Paulik said, turning the car off the highway and into Aix. "He couldn't stop crying. Sobbing, actually. And then he got mad, really mad. His emotions were all over the place. He's a Sciences Po grad, and this is only his second job."

"Going to an elite university doesn't exempt him from a crime, but you're right, his emotional response isn't that of a killer," Verlaque said as they drove into the downtown, down the narrow Rue de la Mule Noire. Verlaque looked out the window at the golden light that lit up Aix's stone façades. This was the only positive thing to come out of the train's delay, he thought: he always preferred to come home to Aix at night, for the town was at its best then. "This woman . . ." he said.

"Mlle Montmory," Paulik answered.

"Thank you. If she lives, she'll be able to identify her attacker."

"Exactly. I put two officers on patrol at the hospital, and two are watching her apartment."

"Good."

"Should I take you home, sir?" Paulik asked. They were at a fork in the road where turning right would take the judge home, to his fourth-floor apartment overlooking Aix's cathedral, and turning left would take them to the Palais de Justice.

Verlaque turned to the commissioner and asked, "What do you feel like doing?"

"Flamant has been putting together a file on Mlle Montmory. I thought we could look at it. But if you're tired, we could call it a night and start early tomorrow morning."

"Is there any cold beer in the building?" Verlaque asked.

Paulik laughed. "Yes, I think there may be some left over from Flamant's *pot*."

"What was the *pot* for?" Verlaque asked. He hadn't heard about the celebration, but maybe he had received an e-mail and disregarded it.

"It was last night. He's engaged." Paulik coughed. He wasn't sure if Antoine Verlaque had been invited. Perhaps he should have mentioned it, but he was never sure if the other policemen liked his boss. He turned left and said, "We'll do a little work, then. I'm up for it."

"So am I. The delayed journey home somehow gave me a second wind, or at least didn't exhaust me the way I thought it would."

They parked Paulik's car in the underground garage of the Palais de Justice and walked into the common room to look for something to eat. As Paulik had predicted, there were leftover cans of beer in the fridge, and not-quite-stale potato chips and pretzels sitting out in bowls. They grabbed four cans and the chips and pretzels and made their way upstairs to Verlaque's office. As soon as Verlaque called Marine to apologize, they sat down with the file Flamant had prepared and left on Verlaque's desk.

Verlaque put on his reading glasses and leaned over the desk, his forearms resting on the glass surface. "Tell me what you have."

Paulik opened the folder and began reading through the papers that Flamant had assembled. "Mlle Suzanne Marie Montmory. Born in Avignon on July 18, 1978, which means she just turned twenty-eight. Single, never married. Lives alone, no pets."

Verlaque said, "Go on."

"She's worked at the Banque de Provence since she got out of community college eight years ago. She was hired back then by her current boss, the director, Kamel Iachella. He's married with four kids and lives in Éguilles. Flamant has made a note here that Iachella was 'in shock' at the news of her attack."

"He must have been, given that he gave Mlle Montmory her first job," Verlaque said. "They would have been close."

"Given the late hour, it was agreed that we'd go to Éguilles tomorrow morning and interview her colleagues at the bank," Paulik continued. "They're closing the bank until noon."

Verlaque took a sip of beer. "What about this kid who has the crush on her?"

Paulik turned a page and leaned in to read. "Gustav Lapierre, age twenty-five, graduated from Sciences Po Lyon three years ago. This is his second banking job; he wants to be an investment banker, apparently."

"Working his way to the top, is he?" Verlaque asked. "If he graduated from one of our best schools, what's he doing working in a rinky-dink branch office of a so-so bank?"

"Good question," Paulik answered, sipping his beer. "One of my cousins graduated from Sciences Po and immediately moved to Paris and got a great job at the Ministry of Culture."

"Bruno, just how many cousins do you have?" Verlaque asked. Bruno Paulik was reared on a farm in the Lubéron and came from a very, very large family.

Paulik grabbed a handful of pretzels and began eating. "First cousins? Only forty-two. Second cousins? More than two hundred."

Verlaque smiled. "Any more information?"

Paulik turned the page and came to the end of the file. "Nope."

"Let's call it a day, then. I'll meet you at the bank tomorrow morning?"

"Yeah. It's in downtown Éguilles, near the *hôtel de ville*. Just before nine a.m.?"

"Great."

They threw their beer cans in a recycling bin near Verlaque's office. "By the way," he asked, "is there news on that missing woman?"

"Mme d'Arras, yes, I meant to tell you. It was just as you had predicted, sir. She was indeed at Monoprix and then decided to get her hair done. She seemed confused after the appointment, so one of the hairdressers walked her home, where M. d'Arras was waiting for her. I'm sorry to have wasted your time with it, sir."

"Don't worry about it, Bruno," he said, remembering Bruno's uncle Jean. He put on his jacket and decided that he would sleep at his place tonight, texting Marine with a promise that they would see each other the next evening, when he'd cook dinner. He thought of *his* cousins—he had two—whom he hadn't seen in years, perhaps decades. His father had been an only child, and his mother had two brothers, one of whom had never married, the other a widower with two sons. The older cousin was a heart surgeon in Geneva; the last Verlaque had heard, the younger one had given up his job as a high-school history teacher and now lived somewhere in the Massif Central, rearing sheep.

"Is everything all right?"

Marine thought she had properly hidden the disappointment that she wouldn't see Antoine that evening. But she had never been very adept at hiding things from her father. "Antoine's back from Paris, but he's working late," she said, hanging up the phone. Because of the rain, her father had driven her mother to choir practice at Saint-Jean de Malte, and so his visit had been unplanned but very welcome. Marine wished that it happened more often. "Care for a glass of wine?" she asked. "Or herbal tea? I know that you and Maman are crazy for that stuff."

"I have, late in life, deleveped a love for herbal tea, it's true,"

Anatole Bonnet told his daughter. "But I'll have a glass of wine to keep you company."

"I have some cheese in the fridge, and olives," Marine called from the kitchen. She came back into the living room carrying a platter of cheeses: a pyramid of chèvre from the Loire, a slice of Stilton, and a Saint-Marcellin that was so runny it could only be served with a small spoon. She went back into the kitchen for the wine and glasses, and when she came back, her father was leaning over the coffee table, a small knife in hand, anxious to cut into the pyramid.

"A Pouligny Saint-Pierre," he said, beginning to cut into the cheese, its inside as smooth and white as marble. "I haven't had this in years." Marine smiled, watching her father cut a generous slice of her favorite cheese.

"There's a new cheese shop on the Rue d'Italie," she said. "The owner worked for twenty years in high tech and gave it all up to follow his passion." She thought that if she told her father where the shop was he might go and buy some cheeses for himself. Her mother had always done the grocery shopping—buying food for the price and convenience, instead of the taste and quality—even though both parents had busy careers. But it was her father, a general practitioner, who was the *gourmand* in the family. This was one of the things he shared with Antoine Verlaque.

As if on cue, Dr. Bonnet asked, "How is Antoine, anyway?"

It didn't surprise Marine that her father asked about Verlaque at the same time that she had been thinking of him. The mental telepathy between her and her father happened all the time. "Busy," she answered. "There's been a wine theft at Domaine Beauclaire. And this thing tonight—I don't know—but, judging from Antoine's voice on the phone, it sounds serious."

Her father quickly took a bite of the Saint-Marcellin before it ran off the bread. "I like Antoine," he said, as casually as if he had said that he liked the cheese.

Marine felt her heart could burst. Her father's opinion meant so much to her. "I'm glad," she said, trying to sound equally casual.

"And anyone who can make your *maman* laugh the way he did the other night must be okay."

Marine laughed, remembering what she had feared would be an awkward family dinner the previous week. Antoine had hosted it—he and Marine had cooked a leg of lamb together—and the evening had been a success. Not rip-roaring fun, but passable. "I wasn't sure how Maman would take a religious joke," Marine said. Mme Bonnet was a retired professor of theology.

"Oh, your mother loves a good joke that involves a priest, a rabbi, and an imam in an airplane together." He took a sip of wine and made a sound of delight. "What's this we're drinking?"

"A Burgundy, from Givry," Marine said. "Do you like it?"

Anatole Bonnet took another sip. "Just to recheck," he said, smiling. "It's very good. Where did you buy it?"

"Antoine orders it from the vintner, by the case," Marine replied.

"Fancy that," her father said. "Do you think he could order me a case, next time there's a delivery?"

"Of course." Marine took this new interest in fine wines as further proof that her parents—or at least her father—approved of Antoine.

"And how's your pal Sylvie?" Dr. Bonnet asked.

"Great. She just called from Mégève—it's already chilly there— they'll be back just before school starts."

"Just before school?" he asked. "Poor little Charlotte will need more time to get prepared. . . ."

"Papa," Marine warned, "they're used to doing it that way.

They'd rather stay as long as they can with Sylvie's parents and brothers and sisters in the Alps. . . ."

"Without a father . . ."

"Papa!" Marine bit her lip to stop herself from getting angry. Her best friend, Sylvie, was a photographer and art historian, and the single mother of nine-year-old Charlotte, Marine's goddaughter.

Anatole Bonnet realized that he had been out of line, so he pointed to the Stilton. "And what kind of cheese is this? It doesn't look like any blue I've ever seen."

"Stilton," Marine replied. Before he could protest, she put up her hand. "Try it."

Chapter Six

❧

An Alsatian Tries
to Understand Provence

I t took Jules Schoelcher two tries to close the car door. "*Scheiße,*" he whispered, trying to close the door with one hand while holding on to his police hat with the other. Roger, his partner today, looked over and laughed.

"It's just a mistral," Roger said. "It will cool things off."

Jules shrugged and tried to smile, but the truth was, he was missing home. How could a twenty-seven-year-old policeman tell a fellow officer that? He knew when he signed up for the police force he could be sent anywhere in France, but he hadn't counted on this desperately hot place, still over thirty degrees Celsius even in September. At least the wind—this mistral, they called it— cooled things down. But he couldn't stand Provence: the wind, the dry heat, and his fellow officers with their big hugs and *bise* (real men in Alsace did not give each other the *bise* unless they were family); and their clichéd Provençal nonstop jokes and loud laughter. Everything was "*mon ami*" this and "*mon pote*" that. Was there never any calm? Alsatians didn't have to bark when they spoke, or didn't feel the need to be the loudest in the room, nor did they jump queues, as Jules had already seen countless times at the post office and bank. Perhaps people in the south didn't respect the queues because there weren't any, just roughly formed huddles, as if they had no idea how to form a straight line. And if there were two bank machines open, or two windows at the post office, what did the Provençals do? They didn't form one single line in the middle, as one did in Colmar or Strasbourg; they formed two lines and then switched back and forth until they were at the front.

Jules ran into the hospital and held the door open for Roger, who was taking his time strolling across the parking lot, smiling like an idiot. "Slow down," Roger said, taking a pack of cigarettes out of his pocket. "We're ten minutes early. Time for a ciggie."

"You go ahead and smoke your cancer stick," Jules said.

Roger laughed out loud. He hadn't heard anyone refer to cigarettes as cancer sticks since fifth grade. Come to think of it, he thought that was when he had started smoking: fifth grade. "Hey, Jules, did I ever tell you about the time we played hooky from school and went out to sea with some old fisherman?"

Jules sighed. "No, but I'd love to hear all about it, another time. I bet you caught a fish this big, eh?" He held out his hands a yard apart.

"Yeah! It was about that big!" Roger said. "But we've fished the Med clean now; they don't make fish that big anymore."

Jules laughed, not believing his good luck at trapping this Marseillais into the biggest stereotype of all. The French made fun of Provençals, especially those from Marseille, for their habit of exaggerating stories. An eight-inch-long fish became a yard long; the wind blew not thirty-five miles an hour but fifty-five. Jules waved goodbye and walked up the hospital's cheap linoleum stairs, still chuckling to himself. Well, Roger could be late if he wanted to—typical for the south, always five or ten minutes late, even on the job—but he would be on time.

Roger in turn watched Jules skip up the stairs. "What a geek," he whispered under his breath, lighting his cigarette and smiling at a passing nurse. Jules had hardly spoken to anyone Tuesday night at Alain Flamant's *pot*, except for some of the female officers and a couple of the secretaries. Roger had overheard Jules saying that he didn't drink pastis and that he only liked white wines—preferably Rieslings. Most of the officers had changed into civvies for the party, and one of them had nudged Roger and pointed to Jules's jeans—ironed, with two big pleats running down either leg. Jokes about ironing abounded, until no one listened anymore to Roger and the other policeman, so they poured each other another pastis and consoled each other over the Marseille soccer team's losing streak.

Jules was thinking of this moment as he came down the brightly lit hallway toward Mlle Montmory's room. He had heard the ironing jokes and knew that they were referring to his jeans, but none of the other policemen had paid attention to them, and Commissioner Paulik had even smiled at Jules and rolled his eyes.

Jules could see Officer Flamant standing at the end of the hall-way, speaking to a young red-haired policeman whom Jules knew by sight only. The young man was a rookie and always seemed nervous yet willing to please, and to work hard. Unlike Roger, downstairs smoking. Jules walked up to both men and shook their hands, and was briefed on Mlle Montmory's condition (critical) and told that only hospital staff, with badges, were to be permitted into her room. In the late afternoon, the girl's parents would be allowed to visit. Flamant had a photograph of them, which he passed to Jules.

"Where's Roger?" Flamant asked.

"He'll be up in a minute," Jules answered. "Um . . . he forgot something in the car."

A doctor wearing a white lab coat emerged from Mlle Montmory's room and stopped when he saw the two officers. "Hello," he said, shaking hands with them. "I'm Dr. Charnay. Glad to see that Mlle Montmory's room is being guarded."

Jules Schoelcher read the doctor's name tag and studied his face; the young officer wanted to try to memorize the names and faces of all hospital personnel who visited Mlle Montmory's room. "I'm a specialist," the doctor said, seeing that the younger policeman had studied his name tag. "Have a nice evening," he said, looking at his watch. "I hope the evening isn't too dull for you. You can always bug the nurses if you get bored," he added, laughing.

"Goodbye, Doctor," Flamant said. The doctor waved and said something to the nurses; Jules saw one of the nurses roll her eyes as he walked out of the ward. Roger suddenly appeared, smelling of smoke, and Flamant sighed and repeated what he had just told Jules. "You'll be relieved at five p.m.," Flamant told the two officers. "It goes without saying that you'll spell each other off when one has to eat or do other business. I want one officer here at all times."

The young redhead began moving from side to side, and Flamant realized that he probably had to relieve himself in the men's room. "You may leave," he said. "Get a good sleep, and see you tomorrow."

Roger laughed as the rookie raced down the hall. "Will Commissioner Paulik pass by today?" he asked.

"Probably," Flamant answered. "He's at the bank now, interviewing the employees. He may stop by with Judge Verlaque."

"Ahhhh," moaned Roger. "Christ!"

"I beg your pardon?"

"Good thing he wasn't at your *pot*, eh, Alain?" Roger went on, slapping Flamant's arm.

Jules stared in disbelief. He hadn't met the judge, but couldn't believe that Roger would speak of a superior this way.

"That's enough," Flamant said. "Careful what you say, Roger." Alain Flamant said goodbye to the men and walked down the hall, thinking of his fiancée, whom he would see this evening, and Judge Verlaque. What was it about him that others thought irritating? Was he really that much of a snob? The judge hadn't been at his *pot*, but had he been invited? Flamant felt bad—he didn't like to see anyone left out. He stood at the top of the stairs and looked down the hall, its walls painted in what he thought was always a hospital color—mint green. There was the young Alsatian policeman, standing at attention at Mlle Montmory's door, and Roger, famous at the Palais de Justice for his Marseillais bravado and jokes, chatting with the nurses at the front desk. Flamant sighed and ran down the stairs, anxious to get back to the Palais de Justice to do research. He wanted to find out anything about Mlle Montmory's life that might shed light on her attack, and attacker.

The square that held both the town hall and the church of Éguilles had always pleased Verlaque. From the edge of the Place Gabriel Payeur there was a magnificent vista south; cypress trees dotted vineyards as they did in Tuscany, and Verlaque thought that the square reminded him of Cortona's, especially the view. He turned around and looked at the imposing four-story goldenstone town hall, built in the Renaissance for a wealthy local family. It seemed too big to be the *mairie* for a town of only eight thousand inhabitants. The church was dwarfed by its neighbor.

The Banque Populaire was around the corner—he had passed

it on the way into the town but had parked his car in the square so he could admire the view. He walked to the bank now, head bent against the mistral wind. When he looked up, he saw Bruno Paulik locking the door of his Range Rover.

"Salut, Bruno," Verlaque said.

"Good morning," replied Paulik. "*Merde ce vent!*"

"You never get used to it?"

"I never have!" Paulik shouted over the wind. "And I was born here! I spoke to Olivier Bonnard last night and relayed the information your wine expert . . . contact . . . told you. He's taken the key to the cellars off the hook and now has it with him at all times, and he's doing an inventory of the wines with his son."

"The inventory is a good idea, but the thief may have taken an imprint of the key to be copied."

"I know; I told him the same thing."

"Is there someone who copies keys in Puyricard, or Rognes?" asked Verlaque as they crossed the street.

"No, unfortunately," said Paulik. "Because a key maker in a small town like Rognes might remember a face."

"Well, there must be a dozen key makers in Aix, and with an attempted murder on our hands, there's no way we can spare the manpower to go and talk to every one of them."

Paulik nodded. "I know."

They arrived at the front doors of the bank, its metal shutters closed. A note had been firmly taped to them: "We regret to inform our customers that due to the attempted murder of one of our staff we will remain closed this morning and will reopen at 2 p.m."

"Wow," Paulik said, turning to Verlaque. "That's direct."

"Yes, isn't it? Let's walk around to the back door, since they're expecting us."

They moved along the side of the bank and waved to a woman through an office window; she motioned to the back. When they arrived, she opened the door and ushered them in. "We were watching for you," she said. "We couldn't open the front door, because then we'd get a crowd of customers wanting in. I'm Charlotte Liotta, the assistant manager. Please come in." She held her hand out and shook the men's hands. Mme Liotta was in her mid-fifties, and she wore a crumpled pink silk blouse and a gray polyester pantsuit. Her hair needed another rinse: about a half-inch of her gray roots were showing, creeping down into her bright-red curls. Verlaque imagined her being the mother figure to the other employees, making them tea and coffee when they felt down or too harried. He realized that they didn't have anyone like that at the Palais de Justice. Mme Girard would think it below her to perform such tasks.

Mme Liotta walked quickly down a hallway, past a few offices whose doors were open and a very untidy kitchenette. She glanced at the kitchenette and said over her shoulder without slowing down, "Sorry about the mess. We're all in shock here. But I'd imagine you've seen much worse." She stopped and turned around. "On the job, I mean, of course. Not at home." They came into a small lobby, where the rest of the staff had gathered, some sitting and drinking their coffee, others pacing. Verlaque took a quick count; there were, including Mme Liotta, five employees.

"Okay, everyone, listen up," she said. "The examining magistrate and commissioner are here to talk with us. We'll be interviewed until noon and then will reopen for business at two p.m. sharp." She put her hands on her wide hips and nodded in the direction of Paulik.

"Thank you, Mme Liotta. I'm Commissioner Paulik, and this is Judge Verlaque. What happened last night was terrible, and we'll need to try to think of any connection, any reason why you think this may have happened to Mlle Montmory. We'll . . ."

"Is she going to be okay?" a young man broke in, his voice cracking.

"She's in critical condition," Paulik said. "But the doctor I spoke with this morning was optimistic."

The group murmured their relief, and a gray-haired North African man, who had been pacing back and forth, patted his forehead with a handkerchief.

"Wearing out the carpet won't make Suzanne better, Kamel," Mme Liotta said to him.

"You're M. Iachella, the branch manager?" Verlaque asked.

"Yes. I beg your pardon," he said, crossing the room to shake Verlaque's and Paulik's hands. "I'm completely distraught. Forgive me."

"I'll get you a tea, Kamel, with lemon and honey," Mme Liotta said. Verlaque was pleased that he had guessed correctly as to Mme Liotta's caregiving nature.

Paulik continued. "We'll speak as a group, then we'll conduct private interviews with each of you. For now, I'd like to begin by asking you if Mlle Montmory has said anything to any one of you this past week about her private life, anything at all . . . any worries she may have been having, any boyfriend trouble, anything."

The group looked around at one another until a young woman wearing a short, tight skirt stepped forward. "Suzanne was superquiet. Never spoke of her private life, and she'd never come out with us, right?" The woman looked around at her co-workers, who nodded.

"That's because you weren't nice to her, Sharon," the young man said.

"That's so not true, Gustav!" she returned. "Sorry, Officers. I'm Sharon Pallard. Sharon, as in Sharon Stone."

Verlaque was thankful that Paulik had stepped forward to shake the woman's hand, because Paulik's wide shoulders temporarily hid his grin. Mlle Pallard may have been wearing a short skirt, but with her black hair held up in a ponytail and her large lips painted bright pink, she had little in common, at least physically, with the actress.

"Mlle Pallard," Paulik said, "why do you think Mlle Montmory was quiet?"

The young woman pulled at her skirt and shrugged. "Dunno. Just shy, I guess. Or maybe she thought she was better than us, eh?"

"She isn't dead, so stop referring to her in the past tense. I'm Gustav Lapierre," the young man said to Verlaque. "Suzanne isn't at all a snob. She just doesn't mix work and her private life."

"You found her, didn't you?" Verlaque asked the young man, who wore a pressed suit and shirt and tie. He looked young to be already working in a bank, and then Verlaque remembered that he was a recent Sciences Po graduate.

"Yes," Lapierre said, looking down at the worn carpet. "I was at the Palais de Justice last night."

"Fine. We'll talk about that later, in private," Verlaque said. "Who has known Mlle Montmory the longest?"

Kamel Iachella and Charlotte Liotta raised their hands. "We—I mean, Kamel—hired Suzanne, but I was already working here," Mme Liotta said, having just come back into the room with her boss's tea. "I've been here almost twenty years."

"That's right," M. Iachella said. "Suzanne started here just a few months after I did. She had just completed a B.T.S. in finance and was the first employee I hired."

"Is she from Éguilles originally?" Paulik asked.

"She grew up in Aix," M. Iachella answered. "So she was thrilled to find full-time work so close, here in Éguilles."

"And does she have friends and family in Aix?"

"Oh yes—family, at least," Mme Liotta replied, for M. Iachella had sat down and was mopping his brow again. "Her parents live north of the downtown, and she has a brother and a sister, both older and both married. No nieces and nephews yet, though!" Mme Liotta looked to the rest of the group, and Gustav Lapierre rolled his eyes.

"No boyfriend?" Paulik asked.

"No," Mme Liotta said.

"No, that's right," Gustav Lapierre confirmed. "She told me so."

Sharon Pallard guffawed.

"Sharon! Hold your tongue!" Mme Liotta said.

Verlaque glanced at Paulik with an exasperated expression, and Paulik said, "It seems that private interviews may be more revealing. We'll begin now. Both of us will speak to M. Lapierre, and then we'll speak to each of you individually. Where can we hold the meetings?"

"In my office." Mme Liotta spoke up. "I've already prepared it for you. Would you like coffees?"

"Yes, please," Verlaque and Paulik answered in unison.

They entered Mme Liotta's office with Gustav Lapierre and closed the door. Verlaque sat in Mme Liotta's chair, and the other two men sat opposite. "I know you met Commissioner Paulik last night."

"Yes," Lapierre said.

"I'm sorry to have to ask you some of the same questions and go over what happened last night, which must have been traumatic, to say the least."

Lapierre nodded, and his eyes welled up with tears. Verlaque glanced over and saw a box of tissues; he wondered whether Mme Liotta had put them there especially for today's interviews or if they were always there.

"I've never seen anything like it. 'Traumatic' isn't a strong enough word," Lapierre said. "'Harrowing' might be better."

Verlaque stared at the young man, impressed. "Is there a front-door buzzer?" he asked.

"Yes," Lapierre said. "I rang it, but of course there was no answer. I was about to leave when a neighbor came in from work and she let me in."

"What time was it?" Paulik asked.

"Just before seven-thirty. I left the bank around six-thirty, at the same time as M. Iachella, and then I drank a beer at the bar across the street. To get up my nerve, as it were."

Verlaque looked at Paulik, who nodded and took notes. The murderer could have also been let in by a neighbor. It was unfortunate that none of those neighbors had heard anything.

"The attacker could have got in the same way I did, or he might have known Suzanne and she buzzed him in," Lapierre said. "I just thought of that."

"Right," Verlaque answered. "Tell me about Suzanne. You seem to know her well, and respect her."

"As I said last night," Lapierre said, looking in Paulik's direction, "I was heading over there not so much to check on her health—it was just a sore throat—as to ask her out for dinner. It seemed impossible to do it here, at work. You've seen a bit of the atmosphere . . . with Mme Liotta babying us, and Sharon being the prima donna in her tacky short skirts. . . ."

Verlaque noted Lapierre's disgust at Sharon's short skirts.

Lapierre reached across the desk, took a tissue, and blew his nose. "The more I worked with Suzanne, the more interested I became in her. She was mysterious in a way, not like other girls I've met. She was pretty and wore trendy clothes, but she talked about knitting and watching those costume dramas on television that my mom likes to watch. She was different. Do you get it?"

The two men nodded. They were both in partnerships with women whom Gustav Lapierre would have considered "different," even "mysterious." Verlaque thought of Marine, curled up on the sofa, drinking single-malt whiskey and reading Jean-Paul Sartre's memoirs. Paulik thought of Hélène, wearing the blue cotton overalls worn by agricultural workers around the world, kneeling on the rocky ground of Domaine Beauclaire, snipping leaf samples from the vines, then bringing them home and checking on them daily. "I'm watching them for parasites," she told her husband. "When there are more of the black spiders, life is good. Too many red spiders, I'll have to spray."

"Go on," Verlaque said, leaning back on Mme Liotta's swivel chair.

"So . . . I walked over there to ask her out; that's all. But you may as well know now, before that policeman I spoke to last night tells you first . . ."

"Prosecutor Roussel?" Paulik asked.

"Yeah, that's him. He asked me how I knew where Suzanne lived. I could have looked up her address here, at the bank, but I followed her home one night last week. I was curious."

Both men looked at each other. Verlaque raised his eyebrows; Paulik took notes.

"And when you found her last night?" Verlaque asked.

"I didn't touch anything," Lapierre answered. "I've seen enough crime dramas to know I shouldn't, plus I could see that Suzanne was badly hurt. I pulled my cell phone out of my pocket and called an ambulance right away. She looked awful."

Gustav Lapierre drew his arms in around his waist, leaned down, and began to sob. Paulik looked at Verlaque; the judge put his hands on his head, rubbed his thick black hair, and stayed silent.

Chapter Seven

꙳

Lemon Cake

Kamel Iachella, although not sobbing, seemed as distressed as Gustav Lapierre had been. The bank manager's eyes were puffy and watery, and he moved Mme Liotta's box of tissues closer to him as he sat down opposite Verlaque.

"I'm sorry you have to meet me, and my small but very efficient staff, under these circumstances," he said quietly.

"So am I," Verlaque answered. "Mlle Montmory seems to be a quiet, reserved young woman."

Iachella nodded. "She is. She was so quiet during my first interview with her that I had to ask her to speak up. But I could see that she was bright."

"Do you know anything about her personal life?" Verlaque asked.

"Not anything more than Gustav could have told you. I know that her parents and siblings live in Aix. I should know more about her; I feel bad about that, you know? Especially now."

"I understand," Verlaque said. "Did she seem upset recently? Out of sorts?"

Iachella shook his head back and forth, looking surprised. "No . . . no. I wish now I had been more observant. But she seemed like the same quiet Suzanne. It's unfortunate, but as a manager I tend to deal more with the employees who are having problems or are dissatisfied. The quiet, hardworking ones just get on, don't they?"

Both Paulik and Verlaque smiled.

"And that day, when she left early?" Verlaque asked. "Normal?"

"She was behaving normally, yes," Iachella answered. "As the day went on, we could all hear that she was losing her voice. Mme Liotta was worried that it was a sinus infection coming on, and sent her home around four p.m."

Verlaque thought silently that if she was losing her voice she wouldn't have been able to call out for help. A team of policemen were spending the day interviewing the tenants of Mlle Montmory's three-story apartment building. Perhaps one of them had unintentionally let in the attacker?

"What time did the rest of you leave the bank?" Verlaque asked.

"We close at six p.m. and usually have the place tidied up—I mean the financial transactions, not the housekeeping—by six-thirty. I left at six-thirty, with Gustav. The others had gone before us, between six and six-thirty."

"Thank you," Verlaque said. "That will be all."

"You'll keep us informed?" Iachella asked, his eyes watery. "Mme Liotta tried calling the hospital this morning, but they wouldn't give out any information."

"They were told not to," Verlaque said. "We'll keep you informed, yes. Goodbye. You can send in Mme Liotta now."

When Iachella had quietly left the room, Paulik turned to the judge. "The attacker must have known her working hours. But he wouldn't have known that she'd be home earlier than usual unless he works here. So I think the attack took place closer to seven-thirty p.m."

"So do I," Verlaque answered. "If she left the bank daily between six and six-thirty, and it's a ten-minute walk home, he could have been waiting for her. But it's risky, isn't it, an attack like that in broad daylight? Why not wait until evening, when no one will see you entering the building?"

"A family man?" Paulik suggested. "Or he worked nights?"

"Or he wasn't worried about anyone seeing him?" Verlaque asked. "Because he's respectable. No cause for worry. Wearing a suit and tie."

"A banker?"

"Or any professional. Nice-looking. Handsome people have an easier time in this world. People are more trusting of them."

Paulik nodded. The commissioner had a bald, scarred head; a pug nose; and one ear that was beginning to "cauliflower" from too many rugby scrums. He looked across the desk at Verlaque, whom, although he was not classically good-looking, women thought of as handsome.

There was a knock at the door, and Mme Liotta came in, carrying a tray. "Funny to knock at my own office door," she said, setting the tray down. On it were placed three cups of coffee, a bowl of sugar with three spoons, and three pieces of cake. "I baked the lemon cake last night, after Kamel phoned me with the news of Suzanne's attack. I needed to keep busy." Smiling, she served each of the men a coffee and a slice of cake, without asking them if they wanted the cake. As she sat down, she adopted a more serious expression—her stint as mother hen had been completed. "I don't know very much about Suzanne's private life," she began, uninvited. "But I do know that, about two years ago, she dated a young man from Aix. I gathered that it had become quite serious, for Suzanne at least, until he up and left."

"Left?" Verlaque asked.

"Yes, he moved to Montreal. With hardly a warning. Suzanne told me that one morning, when I made her a coffee and sat her down. I could see she had been crying."

"He couldn't have just moved to Montreal like that," Verlaque said. "It takes a few months, if not a year, to get the paperwork together to immigrate."

Mme Liotta nodded. "That's just it. He had already done all the paperwork, without telling Suzanne. It was her opinion that he had been using her." She leaned in and whispered, "For his own benefit."

"What do you mean?" Verlaque asked. "For sex?"

"Oh no," Mme Liotta said. "Suzanne told me that she thought she had been courted by him to impress his family. She cried in my arms when she said she believed he had asked her out only so he could have a charming date for two family weddings that summer."

"Did they part on good terms?" Verlaque asked.

"No," replied Mme Liotta. "They fought, Suzanne told me, and she also told me—in the strictest confidence—that he was awkward . . . um, in bed. . . ."

Verlaque glanced at Paulik, who was writing in his notebook. Mme Liotta now sat back and ate some cake, her eyebrows arching in delight at its taste.

"Can you at all remember his name?" Verlaque asked.

"His first name was Edmond. Unusual, old-fashioned name, quite bourgeois. Perhaps her family would know his surname? I do know that he worked in logistics, at the Marseille airport. Suzanne said that the Canadians were hiring French with experience in those sorts of jobs."

"Thank you, madame. Is there anything else you can tell us about Suzanne's life outside the bank?"

She set her cake down and wiped her hands clean on a paper napkin. "No. Suzanne's a quiet girl. I was surprised that morning when she told me so much about Edmond. Since then, there's been nothing."

"Her routine is fairly consistent?" Verlaque asked.

"Yes, except yesterday, when she left early, and once last week, because she had a doctor's appointment. Routine, she told me. I didn't pry."

"Do you know the name of her doctor?" Verlaque asked.

"I can't remember, but Patricia, our loan officer, will be able to tell you. She was the one who suggested that Suzanne see him, because she was looking for a doctor here in Éguilles."

"Thank you, Mme Liotta. And thank you for the cake. I'll try it now."

As Mme Liotta left, the judge and commissioner leaned over the desk, both quickly eating their cake.

"This is very good," Verlaque said. "Too bad Mme Girard doesn't bring in food like this."

"That would be against her dietary rules," Paulik said, his mouth full. He used the last bit of cake to pick up the remaining crumbs.

Verlaque smiled. "Make sure you get all the bits."

"Don't worry."

"Let's bring in this loan officer and talk to her next," Verlaque said. He stuck his head out of the door and called for the loan officer.

Patricia Pont was an elegant woman in her mid- to late thirties. Slim, of medium height, she was dressed conservatively in a pale-blue suit that, unlike Mme Liotta's crumpled polyester, was made of good-quality linen. She had a long face with bright-blue eyes and wore a touch of pale-pink lipstick. Her necklace suggested that when she was not at work she dressed with panache—the necklace was unusual, made of large transparent glass beads, worn close to her neck like a choker.

"I work here part-time," she said, wasting no time. "And part-time at a slightly larger branch in Ventabren, where I live."

"And do you know Suzanne Montmory well?" Verlaque asked, but he was already sure of the reply.

"No, since I'm sort of in and out. No."

"You have the same doctor, I'm told," Verlaque said.

"Yes, Dr. Vilion, Jean-François. His practice is just up the street, at number 46, on the second floor, above yet another new real-estate agent in town. That makes four now, I believe."

Verlaque said, "I used to think that hairdressers outnumbered all other services in Provence. But you're right, I believe now it's Realtors. Why did Mlle Montmory need a new doctor?"

"Her doctor retired."

"What was wrong with her?" Verlaque asked.

Mme Pont flinched for a second but answered his question. "Stomach flu."

"What else do you know about her?" Verlaque asked.

Mme Pont smiled. "Other than sharing the same general practitioner, I can't say that I know much about Suzanne. I have three children, so when I leave work I switch off my banking mind."

"I couldn't help hearing the antagonism in Sharon's voice whenever Suzanne Montmory was mentioned," Verlaque said.

"Oh, that Sharon," Mme Pont said, sighing. "That's not a big story. Sharon and Suzanne were up for the same promotion, and Suzanne won. I think Sharon's jealous, that's all."

"That may explain it," Verlaque said. "Thank you. And if you think of anything at all unusual about Suzanne's recent behavior, or moods, you'll call us?"

"Certainly," Mme Pont said. "By the way, did you see my note on the door?"

"You wrote that?" Paulik spoke up. "It's very direct."

"Yes, and I wanted to add 'raped' on it, but Kamel wouldn't let me."

Verlaque nodded and stayed silent. He agreed with the bank manager's decision.

"I have two daughters," Mme Pont went on. "This man has to be caught, for all of us."

"He will be," Verlaque replied. "I promise."

Mme Pont quietly left the room, but Verlaque and Paulik had no time to debrief: Sharon Pallard was already at the door.

"Hello, hello," she said, quickly walking into the room and taking a seat. "I'm ready! Fire away."

Couldn't she even pretend to be shocked by the attack on Mlle Montmory? Verlaque thought to himself. Irritated, he said, "You don't like her, do you?"

If Sharon Pallard seemed surprised by his directness, she did not show it. "Um, I wouldn't say that," she answered. She paused for a few seconds and added, "And I am sorry about what happened to her. Can you *imagine*?"

"No, I cannot," Verlaque said. "Did she ever confide in you?"

Mlle Pallard laughed. "No! We stay clear of each other!"

"Why?"

"Well . . . we just have nothing in common, that's all."

"So you don't know anything about her? Even though you're both women, and the same age?"

"I'm older," she said, tugging at her skirt and sitting straighter. "Um . . . you know . . . I know just little things about her. Like, she lives this totally boring life, and watches old-fashioned movies, and sucks up to M. Iachella and Mme Liotta."

"Really?"

"If you must know, we were up for the same promotion last month, and she got it. I have more experience, I'm older, and she still got it. You should see her with the customers! So sober and serious! I chat them up, you know? Make them happy about their day. Ask about their children and grandchildren. That sort of thing."

Verlaque smiled, glad that Mlle Pallard didn't have access to his bank account. "Are you angry with her for getting promoted?" he asked.

"Hey, wait a minute! You're putting words in my mouth!"

"I didn't have to," Verlaque said. "You told me about it."

Mlle Pallard shifted in her seat. "I didn't hate her guts."

Paulik wrote the words down exactly as she had said them, and put a star in the margin. His ten-year-old daughter, Léa, would use those kinds of expressions. Or had, when she was seven or eight.

"You may go," Verlaque said.

The young woman got up noisily, huffing and smacking her gum as she left. "Okay," she said at the door. "See you later."

Paulik closed the door, then turned to the judge and said, "Suspect?"

Verlaque sat back. "I don't know. She didn't hide her contempt or jealousy of Mlle Montmory, which a guilty person would have. She's quite thick, and hopping mad. But mad enough to arrange a brutal attack on a co-worker?"

Paulik shrugged and closed his notebook. "Should we go to the hospital or the Palais de Justice?"

"Let's go to the Palais and see how Alain's research is getting on. We can check up on the ex-boyfriend too. Finding the surname of someone named Edmond who worked at the Marseille airport shouldn't be too difficult. You don't have a cousin who works there, by any chance?"

Chapter Eight

·

I Am, She Is

Marine Bonnet shifted from foot to foot, angry that she was having to line up at the post office on the sole day when she didn't have to teach. She had prepared the large manila envelope ahead of time, but the two automated machines that weighed and stamped parcels were both out of order. She was pleased with her essay on the relationship, and admiration, that Honoré Mirabeau—Aix-en-Provence's famed politician and man of letters—had shared with Thomas Jefferson. She even thought that the paper could become a chapter in what she thought should be a new, sorely needed more modern biography of Mirabeau. Biographies were her favorite genre of literature, and she was much teased by Antoine Verlaque because of it. "Voyeur," he had called her the other night as she lay in bed reading a biography of Eleanor of Aquitaine.

"It's not so much that I love to peek into other people's lives," Marine had answered. "Which I do, by the way. But I love biography because it's a genre that encompasses so many disciplines—

politics, history, art, science, religion, gender politics, and so on and so on."

"I get that," Verlaque answered, getting into bed with his own book, his reading glasses perched at the end of his nose.

"Aren't you interested in the poets' lives?" she asked, seeing that Verlaque had not, for once, an anthology of Philip Larkin poems, but one of Czeslaw Milosz.

Verlaque laughed. "Not at all. I think I'd be disappointed by their lives."

"That's a shame," Marine answered. "I think it would help you understand their poetry."

"I don't think that one's life has much to do with one's art."

Marine set her book on her lap. "I'm not so sure about that. What about that English poet who composed his poems while walking in the Lake District with his sister?"

"Ah, Wordsworth."

"Didn't the fact that he walked all the time, in the mountains, affect his poems?"

Verlaque leaned over and kissed Marine. "You're right; I suppose it did. Would that ever tempt you?"

Marine laughed. "Surely you don't mean walking in the mountains and writing poetry?"

"No!" Verlaque answered, laughing. "Writing a biography."

"With my teaching schedule?"

"Anthony Trollope wrote in the early mornings, before he went to work at the post office."

"Well, then, your Mr. Trollope was much more talented than I will ever be."

"Marine," Verlaque continued, "you do have about five months off each year from the university."

"Yes," she answered. "And that's when I research and write papers."

"So forget about the papers and write a book instead. Take a sabbatical."

"Mmm. You may be on to something. But on whom?" As much as Mirabeau tempted her, she wasn't sure that his life thrilled her enough to spend what could be years writing a book about him.

"You'll think of someone."

Now, standing in the small stuffy post office on the Place de l'Hôtel de Ville, she was waiting to mail her essay to the French department at Cambridge for a symposium on the history of French law. She drew the envelope to her chest, wishing herself good luck. She could have e-mailed the essay but had decided against it, imagining that a university such as Cambridge might prefer paper copies. Seeing that the line had not budged in the past five minutes, she was regretting her decision. Marine Bonnet, even on her day off and wearing jeans and a pale-pink Petit Bateau T-shirt, was a striking figure, and some of the people in the line looked at her, admiring her curly auburn hair and green eyes. She in turn looked at some of the people around her, trying not to pay attention to how quickly the other lines were moving.

"We'll just have to be patient, Coco," a woman said behind her. Marine turned around and smiled, not surprised that Coco was not a Labrador or another big dog but a poodle. "I just have to buy stamps," the woman said. "That takes no time at all."

Marine forced a smile, knowing that the woman was hinting for Marine to let her pass in front of her. "Me too," Marine said. "I just have to mail this . . . letter. It's a shame that both of the automatic machines are down."

The woman, who had immaculate golden hair and a Chanel suit that Marine thought would be too hot for early September, sighed, making a clicking noise with her teeth. "Oh, what lovely envelopes," the woman said, moving ahead, pretending to look at a display of cards and envelopes decorated with regional photographs that the post office produced.

"Oh, here goes," Marine whispered under her breath, for she could see the woman inching her way toward the front of the line at Marine's right.

"Madame," a young black teenager said to the old woman, "I'm sorry, but this is a queue."

"Bravo, jeune homme," Marine whispered under her breath.

Mme d'Arras continued looking at the postcards. She quickly selected one and, ignoring the young man, walked to the front of his line, taking advantage of the fact that the two young girls who were at the front were busy chatting. One of the girls then noticed and looked at the old woman. "Hey," she said to her, "were you always in front of us?"

Her friend looked up from her iPod, just as surprised. "We were in front, weren't we, Eugénie?"

"I was most assuredly in front of you two," the old woman answered, and then began speaking to her dog.

"I don't think you were," the girl named Eugénie repeated.

"No, she wasn't," said a middle-aged woman ahead of Marine, who, like Marine, had been watching. The young black boy sighed and put his earphones on, not wanting to be part of a conflict.

A deep voice with a thick Midi accent then bellowed throughout the post office, and a hand was put on the old woman's small shoulder. "Mme d'Arras," the man said, "how lovely to see you here at the post office. Nice postcards, eh?" He looked down at her, smiling.

The woman was so flustered that she dropped the postcard and waved her hands in the air as if she had just been attacked. The two young girls laughed, as did the black youth, who had removed his earphones to listen.

"M. Léridon!" the woman squeaked. "Whatever on earth are *you* doing here?"

M. Léridon laughed. "Buying stamps, like everyone else, Mme d'Arras." Marine looked at him, relieved that her line was finally advancing. He was handsome in a movie-star sort of way, or in the way that some sports stars are after their sporting career has finished and they find themselves in front of the camera as commentators. He had thick black hair—probably dyed, Marine thought—and too-perfect white teeth. He wore linen pants and a shirt, and his tanned feet were tucked inside of an expensive pair of light-brown Italian moccasins. Marine looked down at her bright-green Nike running shoes and grinned, thinking of her best friend, Sylvie, embarrassed, making Marine walk behind her. Marine turned back to the couple, realizing that she had missed part of their conversation.

"Don't think I don't know what you're up to in that house of yours," Mme d'Arras said. "The Hôtel de Panisse-Passis has seen lots of owners over the years, but none as active as you are during the evening, M. Léridon."

Marine, and the woman in front of her, exchanged looks. Marine thought that the *hôtel*'s name rang a bell. She was sure it was on the Rue Émeric David. Come to think of it, d'Arras was a family name she knew as well.

"What do you mean?" M. Léridon said, now not looking so friendly.

"All hours of the night, walking around your back garden with a flashlight . . . people coming and going. I've heard from trades-men that you have secrets. . . ."

M. Léridon shifted from foot to elegant foot. "I didn't realize I was being watched in my own home," he said sternly.

"I know everything," Mme d'Arras continued. "Don't I, Coco?"

"I've offered to pay for any damage that my renovations have done to your home, madame, as I explained to M. d'Arras." His voice became softer, as if he was making an effort to be civil and perhaps charm the old woman.

"Anything dealing with the house is my department, *cher* M. Léridon," she said. "I've always prided myself on that. Most women have their husbands do everything. . . ."

"I wish!" the woman in front of Marine whispered, and then winked.

"But I insist on making all household arrangements," Mme d'Arras went on. "Which is why, as I already told you, my lawyers will be contacting yours." With that she picked up Coco, who had begun to bark, and left the post office.

"*Merde! Quelle chiante dame!*" M. Léridon said. "The earth should be rid of women like her!" And he too left.

"Exactly as I would have described her," the woman in front of Marine said.

"Yes," Marine agreed, "she was a perfect pain in the ass."

"They both forgot to buy their stamps," the woman said.

"You're right!" Marine answered, laughing. "Oh! It's your turn!"

Finding an Edmond who worked at the Marseille airport had been easy for Alain Flamant, as was finding Edmond Martin's phone number and address in Montreal. Understanding the young man's roommates on the telephone had not. He held his hand over the mouthpiece and said to Verlaque, "I'm sorry, Judge! Their accent is too thick! It doesn't sound like any French I've ever heard. Would you mind talking to them?"

"No problem," Verlaque said, taking the telephone. "Hello," he said in English, and the conversation switched into English.

"They also speak English in Montreal?" Flamant asked Bruno Paulik.

"I think so," Paulik said, not very sure if all Québecois were bilingual or if the judge had just been lucky.

Verlaque went on talking, but neither the commissioner nor the officer was able to understand. Verlaque raised his eyes a few times, and once shook his hand back and forth, Italian style, as if something the Montrealer had told him was surprising, or even shocking. After five minutes, Verlaque said goodbye and set the receiver down, then pulled up his chair closer to Flamant and Paulik.

"Edmond Martin's roommate tells me that M. Martin is out of the country at the moment, on vacation."

"Where?" Paulik and Flamant asked in unison.

"Here. The roommate also said that Martin was strangely secretive about the trip."

Paulik whistled. "Let's contact his family."

"What if they're protecting him?" Flamant asked.

"If we speak to them in person, it should be obvious that they're lying. Most people are terrible at it," Verlaque said. "Martin flew out of Montreal last Friday, to arrive Saturday. He's due back at work in Montreal next Monday."

"I'll go speak to the family right now," Paulik said. "They own a winemaking château in Puyricard, not far from where Hélène works. It's on my way home."

"Perfect. Try to get an idea of where he is and who he's with," Verlaque said.

"I'll do my best." Paulik grabbed his jacket and cell phone, said good night, and quickly left. Almost immediately there was a knock at Verlaque's office door.

"Come in!" he said.

It was Mme Girard. She stood awkwardly in the doorway, playing with a long pearl necklace. Verlaque and Flamant looked on, surprised. Mme Girard was usually so composed.

"I've just had a phone call from Officer Schoelcher at the hospital," she said, her voice cracking ever so slightly.

"Go on, Mme Girard," Verlaque said. He shifted in his chair, feeling uncomfortable. Flamant, obviously feeling the same way, got up and stood by the bookcase, where he pulled out a book at random.

"It's bad news," she went on. "Mlle Montmory went into cardiac arrest and died about an hour ago."

Flamant sat back down, and Mme Girard left, quietly closing the door. The young officer looked down at his knees and stayed silent. Verlaque took the opportunity to look at Flamant, someone he liked more and more every day. Alain Flamant was of medium height and build, but was lean and strong. He had begun his career on a bicycle, riding through Aix's narrow streets, until a recent promotion had brought him under the wing of Commissioner Paulik. Flamant had brown, saddish eyes, and his light-brown hair was receding very quickly. But he had high cheekbones and good teeth, and Verlaque imagined that he had good luck with the ladies. He then remembered that they had just held a *pot* to celebrate Flamant's engagement.

Verlaque leaned back in his chair. "This is bad news."

"Yes, it is, sir. Shocking, even."

"Could you please call the officers who were guarding the room and have them come here first thing tomorrow morning?"

Flamant looked surprised. "But it was a heart attack."

"Yes, Alain. But even so, we need to know who was in and out of that room."

Flamant looked at his watch. "Their shift has just ended. I'll quickly call them."

"Good. I'll call the commissioner on his cell phone and update him."

When Flamant had left, Verlaque got up and looked out of his window onto the yellow-walled prison, wishing whoever had attacked Suzanne Montmory was already in there.

Antoine Verlaque couldn't remember a time when it took so long to walk the few streets home. On the Rue Rifle-Rafle he had caught himself staring absentmindedly in the window of a chocolate shop until he moved on, crossed the Rue Paul Bert, and made his way up the tiny Rue Esquicho Coude—Provençal for "scraped elbows," it was more of a sidewalk than a street—toward his apartment. In the entryway of his building, he emptied his mailbox—usually full of bills, but today there was a postcard—and then he walked slowly up the stairs, feeling as if someone had punched him in the stomach. At this unusually slow pace he was able to discern just how much the paint was peeling off the three-centuries-old walls and how many of the tomette floor tiles were cracked or loose.

Thankful that he had asked Marine to pick up the steak for tonight's dinner, he entered his apartment and emptied his pockets of cash and his BlackBerry onto the kitchen's white Carrara-marble counter. Just then his cell phone beeped—a text from Marine—"Running late; post office a nightmare! Will be there in half an hour, with the steak and dessert from Michaud!" Verlaque's apartment was three times as long as it was wide, and he walked back to his bathroom, separated from his bedroom by a large glass wall, and began to run a bath. In the bedroom, he looked at the giant black Pierre Soulages painting and then turned and looked out one of the two windows that gave onto a silent and tree-filled courtyard. The only noise was that of the birds, and he was thankful that he had been persistent and lucky enough to find this apartment in the middle of the city. He undressed and sank into the tub, plugging his nose and dunking his head under the hot bathwater three times, hoping that when he came back up for air, somehow, miraculously, Mlle Montmory would still be alive.

Verlaque reached across to a small Provençal cane-seated stool where a stack of thick white towels lay and looked at the postcard he had brought in with him. Its bright, almost fluorescent colors made it look as if it had been printed in the 1960s. A field of tall green plants with fat leaves filled the foreground; in the background was a thatched drying-hut, beside it a straw-hatted farmer bent over, picking the plant. Verlaque smiled, recognizing immediately the famed tobacco fields of Viñales in western Cuba. He turned the card over and read: "Doing as you instructed and visiting your tobacco-growing friends. Enormous men! They really are the salt of the earth. I can't believe their strength, and pride, and generosity. I feel so spoiled. Back to Havana tomorrow, where I hope, by miracle or lots of rum, to perfect my salsa dancing at the Casa de la Música! OX Arnaud."

Smiling, Verlaque got out, drained the bath, dressed in jeans and a polo shirt, and walked back into the kitchen, where he put Arnaud's postcard on the fridge. Arnaud, at the young age of eighteen, wrote as well as he spoke, and Verlaque felt the tiniest bit of pride that he had given the boy odd jobs to help fund his epic adventure before beginning his serious studies. Arnaud and his mother—who was a widow—lived downstairs in the same building.

Opening the cupboard, Verlaque selected one of his grandfather's Baccarat cut-crystal tumblers and poured himself some of the whiskey that his friends Jean-Marc and Pierre had brought him from Dublin: Writers Tears. He sat down in a club chair and opened his humidor, which sat on a table beside the chair, and looked at his selection of cigars, touching them to feel their moistness. When he finally selected a robusto from Hoyo de Monterrey, he smelled it, snipped off the end, and slowly lit the opposite end with a new torchlike lighter that he had just bought at the tobacconist's. Puffing, he leaned his head back and closed his eyes. Lying beside the notebook was the hardbound copy of Czeslaw Milosz's poems, and he grabbed it, opening it at random. He imagined that a real scholar would read all the poems one by one, in the order in which they had been selected and edited, but he never read poems that way. He realized that he read poems in order to find ones that reflected his mood at that time.

The first poem he came to was about Europe and its postwar citizens; although there were some lovely lines, it didn't suit his mood this evening. He turned the page and saw a poem titled "Esse," written in 1954. Today had been a day of women, he thought: Mlle Montmory; the women at the bank; Mme Girard; even Flamant's fiancée, who he imagined was a kindergarten teacher, or even a nurse: a caregiver to match the gentle Alain Flamant. And now the poet's Esse, whoever she was. Smoking, he read the poem once, then twice. Marine had said the other night that it might help to understand a poet's work if one knew about his life. Verlaque still wasn't convinced of her argument. Did it matter who Esse was? Was she even a real person? And couldn't he enjoy the poem just as words on a page? He found himself forgetting about his cigar and whiskey as he reread the lines toward the end of the poem four or five times over. He grabbed his notebook and wrote them down:

"And so it befell me that after so many attempts at naming the world, I am able only to repeat, harping on one string, the highest, the unique avowal beyond which no power can attain: I am, she is. Shout, blow the trumpets, make thousands-strong marches, leap, rend your clothing, repeating only: is!"

"'I am, she is,'" Verlaque repeated aloud. "'I am, she is.'" He closed the book and smoked his cigar, taking tiny sips of his single malt. He had to make a conscious effort not to fall asleep, for the night before he had tossed and turned. He had dreamed of Monique, only in the dream her name was Suzanne. He had been thankful that Marine had not been beside him, however much he missed her, for he was sure he had said Monique's name aloud, and then woken up, sweating.

The intercom buzzed and he jumped up, running barefoot to answer it. "Come up!" he said, realizing that he had almost yelled. He couldn't hear her high heels on the tile steps and became concerned. Perhaps it was a delivery? But then her auburn hair became visible through the wrought-iron balustrade—even though she was still two flights down—and he could hear her familiar humming. He stood in the doorway, anxious to see her. She arrived at the last step, and he saw why she hadn't made any noise: she was wearing bright-green sneakers. He lurched out of his doorway and stood on the landing, then ran across it to greet her. "I love you," he said, holding her as tight as he could without hurting her. He was grateful that Marine had the good sense not to speak, just to hold him back.

Chapter Nine

❧

Jules's Little Notebook

*I*t was a warm September morning as Jules Schoelcher left his small apartment on the Rue du Cancel, making his way toward the Palais de Justice. The mistral had cleaned the air and left a clear blue sky, and he knew that his hometown of Colmar was already covered by low gray clouds and would stay like that well into the new year. His mother had telephoned the previous evening to keep him informed of family news and the weather in Alsace: cool and drizzling, as was most of northeastern France at that time of year. Jules realized that somehow he was becoming acclimatized to the dry heat of Provence, and he began whistling as he walked through the giant Place des Cardeurs; at 9 a.m., its cobblestone surface was empty of the restaurant tables that would fill it up at noon.

He went under the Tour d'Horloge, ducking to get out of the way of a tourist who was taking a photograph of the sixteenth-century golden stone clock tower. After passing by the town hall, he descended into the Place Richelme and decided that he had time for a quick espresso at a small café that he had recently discovered, the only one in Aix to roast its own coffee beans. He went in and ordered an espresso with a glass of water and sat himself down at one of the outdoor tables, watching the fishmongers across from him chat with each other and their customers, many of whom they greeted by name. It surprised Jules that, although the café's tables were within reach of the rows of fish stacked neatly on ice, there was almost no smell. He looked over and smirked to see a statue of a wild boar that looked anything but wild.

The sun felt good on his forearms. He reached into his pocket and put on his Ray-Bans, smiling at the pretty waitress as she brought him his coffee and water balanced on a small tray. "Not bad, this September weather, eh?" she said, passing Jules a demitasse with a small piece of chocolate set on the edge of the saucer.

"Glorious," Jules found himself saying. "I'm from Alsace," he added, opening a sugar packet and slowly stirring it into his coffee.

"Oh la la," she said, laughing. "Different weather up there! Do you have all of this in Alsace?" She made a sweeping gesture with her hand, indicating the market, its tables laid out with colorful displays of fruit and vegetables, fish and shellfish, honey and soaps, mounds of spices, and tubs of olives.

Jules shrugged. "A little less colorful. More potatoes and turnips."

"Ha!" She laughed again. "Still, it must be nice up there. I've never been to Alsace. In August it's too hot for me in Aix, and I was born here."

Jules smiled, taking in her petite figure and big brown eyes. "Yes, I suffered this summer too, especially at work."

"What do you do?" she asked, clearing the next table and putting the empty cups on her tray.

"Um, I'm a policeman."

"Oh! I'll let you know if I ever need assistance!" she said, laughing once more. "You've been here before, haven't you?"

"Yes, usually on my way to the Palais de Justice."

"You're not wearing a uniform," she said.

"I'm supposed to be off today," he answered, "but I have to go into work for a quick appointment."

"Next time wear your uniform," she said, winking.

"Hey, Magali!" the fishmonger yelled from across his display of freshly caught Mediterranean fish. "Stop flirting with the customers!"

Jules and Magali—he was glad to know her name—laughed, and the fishmonger, encouraged and now with an audience, continued. "You have a half-dozen customers inside dying for their first coffee of the day! They need to get to work and make some money! The European economy is going to crash, thanks to you!"

"Oh, Anne can serve them!" Magali called. "The customers on the terrace take priority at the moment!" She looked at Jules and winked again.

"Yeah, I can see that!" yelled the fishmonger. "I'll have espresso, whenever you think you have the time! Sometime between now and noon!"

Magali laughed. "Coming right up!" she said. "But you'll be lucky if you get a piece of chocolate!"

"See you around," she said to Jules, and he nodded and gave her a salute. When he finished his coffee, he put 1,50 euros on the wooden table and hurried off; the fishmonger was now busy, showing a customer his spiky purple sea urchins and instructing the buyer on how to prepare them.

Jules walked to the Palais de Justice on autopilot, thinking of Magali, and almost ran into Roger Caromb on the way in the front door.

"Wakey wakey!" Roger said, stubbing out his cigarette butt on the sidewalk.

"There are garbage cans for that," Jules said.

"Oh! Miss Prim!" Roger said. "Remind me next time to sweep the sidewalk for Your Royal Highness!"

"It's just that if we all acted like you, Provence would be even dirtier." Jules looked at the sidewalk, where a few pieces of newspapers floated by, accompanied by a crushed-up pack of Marlboros and an empty Orangina soda can.

Roger looked around him. "Provence is dirty?"

Jules sighed and held the door open for his partner. "Forget it."

"Say," Roger said as they walked up the stairs toward Verlaque's office, "what's this meeting about?"

"They're firing you," Jules replied.

"Ah, such a kidder!" Roger said, slapping Jules on the back.

Verlaque and Paulik were already in Verlaque's office when the two young policemen arrived. "Sit down," Verlaque said. "That was terrible news about Mlle Montmory's death yesterday, and even though it was cardiac arrest, I'd like to know the names of each hospital staff member who went into her room."

Roger looked at Jules and then at Verlaque. "We looked at their name tags, Judge, but didn't memorize their names."

Verlaque sighed. "You didn't write them down?"

"I did, sir," Jules said, thankful that he had remembered to bring his little orange notebook with him. He pulled the book out of his jacket pocket, opened it to the appropriate page, and passed it to Verlaque. "Mlle Montmory's parents were the only nonhospital people who went into her room."

"That's right," Roger quickly added. "We looked carefully at each nurse's and doctor's name tag."

"And the orderlies'?" Verlaque asked.

Roger looked at Jules, bewildered.

Jules said to Roger, "Those big guys who came in to help move Mlle Montmory for the nurses. Yes," he went on, now looking at Verlaque, "we checked everyone; the cleaning staff too."

"Thank you for writing the names down, Officer . . ."

"Schoelcher. Jules Schoelcher."

"Can you make us a photocopy, please?" Verlaque asked.

"I'll do it," Paulik said; he took the book and left the office.

"And nothing seemed out of the ordinary?" Verlaque asked.

"Of course not," Jules replied. "Like Roger said, except for the girl's parents, only hospital staff went in and out. Quite a few doctors and nurses."

Roger glanced at his partner, relieved that Jules was sticking up for him, and doubly relieved that Jules had thought to record names in the little notebook that Roger had suggested contained girlfriends' phone numbers.

Mme Pauline d'Arras enjoyed the view from the bus windows. She couldn't remember the last time she had been on a bus, and she was thankful that she had had enough money in her change purse for the fare. The high-school students at the back of the bus had been making quite a racket during the first part of the trip, but now most of them were sitting back, listening to music with little white earphones. She folded her long, beringed fingers across her lap and looked out of the window at the passing bright-green vineyards, heavy with big bunches of red grapes. There were so many more houses now, ugly sprawling bungalows built in a Provençal style with bright-yellow walls and new, cheap-looking roof tiles. They had none of the charm of her beloved Hôtel de Barlet in Aix, or her family home, the Hôtel Bollène, a large seventeenth-century manor house that was just outside of the village where she was now headed. She wasn't sure if she would be able to find the Hôtel Bollène. It had been in the Aubanel family for centuries, until it was sold after the death of her father. In fact, she couldn't remember why she had come, but it had seemed important. She couldn't get the image of her former home, and the village chapel, out of her head. At any rate, she had the time, and she was happy with her decision to take the bus. Why, she was getting a sightseeing trip out of this as well. She missed her sister Clothilde, and looked forward to the next time she would see her, so that she could tell her all about her neighbor, the show-off with the vulgar car and his little secrets. Clothilde would know what to do.

She looked up and saw a man in a uniform looking down at her. "Yes?" she asked him. "Is there a problem, young man?"

The man wearing the white shirt and blue tie coughed. "It's just that we're at the end of the line, madame. This is the last stop."

Mme d'Arras looked around her. The students had all gone, and the bus was no longer moving. What had she been doing? Ah, she had been enjoying the scenery. So few people did that these days. She picked up her pink Longchamp purse from the seat beside her and got up. "Excellent," she said.

"Do you need some assistance?" the man asked her.

She realized that he must be the bus driver. She certainly did not need any help from someone who drove a bus for a living. "No, thank you, young man. I just didn't recognize the"—she looked out the window and saw the village wine cooperative—"the wine co-op. I'll pop in and buy a bottle of wine to take to my friend . . . Philomène. Perfect."

"Very well," the bus driver said. "*Bonne journée, madame.*"

She got off the bus and walked across the street to the wine cooperative. Why had she lied? But the name Philomène had rolled easily off her tongue, and she thought of her childhood girl-friend, from this same village, her jet-black hair and loud, hearty laugh. She had told Philomène the Aubanel family secret, late one night when they were supposed to have been sleeping. They must have been twelve, perhaps thirteen. Pauline had immediately re-gretted it, and for a while lived in fear that Philomène would spread the secret, but she never did.

"I just got off the phone with Dr. Bouvet," Verlaque told Paulik after Officers Schoelcher and Caromb had left. "He says it's pos-sible that Suzanne Montmory's heart attack was induced by one of the hospital staff."

"I hate to think that," Paulik said. "Certainly it could have been natural, *non*?"

"Yes, but she was doing so well earlier in the day," Verlaque said. "Even that young officer from Alsace said so. He said he saw Mlle Montmory open her eyes and squeeze her father's hand."

Paulik closed his eyes for the briefest of moments. "Let's talk to each staffer, then. I'll put in a request to the family to let Bouvet perform an autopsy."

"Good. We also need to find Edmond Martin as soon as pos-sible," Verlaque said, "although it's next to impossible that he could have disguised himself and got the name tag of one of the hospital staff."

"The Martin family was genuinely surprised that he was in Provence," Paulik said. "As far as they were concerned, he was coming home for Christmas, not before. They were shocked."

Verlaque got up and began pacing around his office. "Why not tell them that you're coming home?"

"Because you were coming home to rape and try to kill your ex-girlfriend?" Paulik asked.

"Innocent before proven guilty," Verlaque said. "Although he's also my number one suspect. And if he *really* is on vacation, why keep it a secret from the family?"

"Because he's with someone they would disapprove of?"

Verlaque nodded. "That could be it. Do you mind if I have a cigar?"

"No," Paulik said, smiling. "I won't tell anyone."

"I'll open the window, but if Mme Girard gets a whiff of this . . ." Verlaque sat down and pulled a double corona out of its leather holder and lit it. "What kind of woman would be 'not their type'? You met them last night."

"A working-class girl wouldn't do," Paulik said. "The Bonnard family knows the Martins, and Olivier warned me that they are real snobs; that was confirmed at our meeting last night. Plus, their wine isn't that great."

Verlaque laughed. "I know. I bought it once, and then never again. Zero finish. How about an older woman? Or a married one?"

"Possibly," Paulik replied. "Alain is on the phone right now, trying to get access to Edmond Martin's bank records, so we can try to find a purchase record of hotels, rental cars, etc."

"And this list of names," Verlaque said, smoking and looking down at Jules Schoelcher's photocopied list. "Edmond Martin may or may not have raped his ex-girlfriend, and she may or may not have died of natural causes, but we still need to talk to every-one on this list. Can you pull that kid from Alsace off the beat and onto this case? His first task can be organizing the hospital staff for interviews."

"Will do."

Someone knocked on the door. "Come in," Verlaque said, hid-ing his cigar under the desk and waving the smoke toward the open window.

"Smells nice," Alain Flamant said as he came into the office. "Don't worry, Mme Girard isn't at her desk."

"Thank goodness," Verlaque said. "Were you able to understand the Québecois police?"

"This time, yes. One of the guys emigrated from Paris a few years ago; he didn't have that accent yet. But they are sticklers for rules and didn't want to give me any information. Said we have to go through the 'proper channels.'"

"*Merde*," said Verlaque. "So what did you do?"

"Bypassed them and called Edmond Martin's bank directly."

Verlaque looked up at the officer, his eyebrows raised. "How did you know his bank?"

"I called the roommate back, and he told me, only too willingly. Martin is behind on the rent. I managed to understand him this time."

Verlaque and Paulik laughed. "Bravo, Alain," said Verlaque. "So what did you get out of the bank?"

Flamant stepped forward and handed the judge a few papers that he had just printed. "Edmond Martin's on a cruise that left Toulon on Sunday, September third. They get back tonight."

Verlaque squeezed the edges of his glass desk with both hands and looked at Paulik.

"Hard to be on the Mediterranean and in Éguilles at the same time," Paulik said.

Flamant coughed. "Unless you board farther down the coast—at the stop in Genoa, for example, on Wednesday evening."

Chapter Ten

❧

Judy Cruises

*R*ight," Verlaque said. "Alain, can you stay here and call the captain of this cruise line and have them hold on to Edmond Martin until we get to Toulon? Guilty or not guilty, Martin needs to be told of Suzanne Montmory's death."

"Yes, sir."

"Let's get one of the officers to drive us," Verlaque said to Paulik. "It's at least an hour's drive to Toulon, and the ship's due to dock in an hour and a half." He looked at the papers that Flamant had printed for him. "We'll take these with us. You'll have to print out more for yourself."

"No problem," said Flamant, already on his way out the door.

"Judy Cruises. What a strange name," Verlaque said, reading the papers with his reading glasses. "Aren't they usually called Sunset, or something to do with the color of the sea?"

They walked out and saw Jules Schoelcher. Paulik pulled him aside and told him to arrange interviews at the hospital for Monday morning.

"Who can drive us?" Verlaque asked. At that moment, he and Paulik saw Roger Caromb standing by the coffee machine, obviously—judging by his hand gestures and their laughter—telling a joke to three or four other officers who were gathered around him.

"I have another one!" Roger said. "How do blondes . . ." He saw Verlaque approaching and stopped.

"Officer Caromb," Verlaque said, "how fast can you drive?"

Roger Caromb sucked in his stomach and puffed out his chest. "Like the wind."

"Let's go, then. We need to be in Toulon by two-thirty p.m."

Roger Caromb, once he found out where they were going, did not have to drive quickly or dangerously; his grandmother lived in Toulon, and he knew not only where the port was but how to get there by the back streets. They arrived at the port as the ship was coming into the harbor, and parked the car in front of the Coast Guard office. Verlaque had called ahead from his cell phone, and the harbormaster was waiting for them, a tall, tanned man who looked as if he spent much time outside. "The captain has notified me that the young man in question will be the last off, with the captain and first mate," he said.

"Thank you," Verlaque said.

The men stood in front of the office's picture window and watched the ship get closer to the port. "It's massive," Paulik said.

"Actually, the *Judy* is a small cruise ship," answered the harbormaster. "She holds only seven hundred passengers. The big cruise ships pack in as many as three thousand."

Roger Caromb squinted and then pointed out the window. "Colorful ship," he said, smiling. "I like the rainbow on the stern side."

The harbormaster smiled. "It's always a bit of a lark when the

Judy comes into port," he said. "They're a great bunch of . . . guys . . . and gals, I shouldn't forget! We're in the twenty-first century, aren't we? I didn't know what to think the first time she set sail from here, oh, back four years ago now. But, like I say, they're a great bunch. Never had any problems."

Verlaque looked at the harbormaster, perplexed. He glanced at Paulik, who looked equally confused and then shrugged.

The ship came into port, blowing its horn. One of the port's crew came running into the office and yelled, "*Judy's* here! Let's go!"

The harbormaster turned to the three Aixois and said, "Let's hope they're still dressed up! They usually are!"

"Dressed up?" Roger mumbled to himself. They walked out of the office, down a flight of steps that ran alongside the building's exterior, and out onto the pier.

The ship blew its foghorn again, and a loud cheer went up from the ship's passengers, who were gathered along the upper deck, waving. The passengers slowly began filing off, some still cheering and others singing. The sun shone in Verlaque's eyes; he held his right hand up to his head to shield them.

"Cheerio, mate!" a sailor said as he walked by, returning Verlaque's salute.

"Sorry, I wasn't saluting . . ." Verlaque began to reply to the sailor, but then stopped. He realized that the sailor was not a sailor but a passenger in disguise, for dozens more sailors came down the plank, arm in arm with priests, bishops, football players, firemen, and policemen. Roger Caromb saw the policemen and waved excitedly. Paulik and Verlaque burst out laughing.

"The *rainbow*," Verlaque said.

Paulik laughed. "*Judy*."

"Garland?" Verlaque asked.

"Yeah, she's a gay icon," Paulik replied.

"I didn't know that."

Most of the passengers were men, but some women disembarked too, arms linked with other women, some dressed in costume and some hardly dressed at all. Verlaque nudged Paulik and they looked over at Roger Caromb, who was now staring straight ahead, watching the crowd, his mouth open. Once again they burst into laughter.

"That's why Edmond Martin didn't tell his parents," Verlaque said, wiping the tears from his eyes. "This is a gay cruise."

Both men coughed, in an effort to get serious quickly, before speaking to Edmond Martin. When they scanned the crowd, they thought they recognized the young man from photographs; he was dressed as a monk, walking ahead of two uniformed men, who they assumed were the captain and first mate, not fellow passengers in disguise.

"Should we go back up into the office?" the harbormaster asked, now standing beside them. "I see the captain and first mate now; the man dressed as a monk must be your M. Martin. You may use my office."

"Thank you," Verlaque said. A scantily clad man, wearing a chef's toque and apron but not much more, walked by and winked at him.

A few minutes later, they were in the office, with Edmond Martin standing before them.

"What's going on?" Martin asked, wringing his hands, the sleeves of his long white cloak swaying as he did so.

"I'm afraid I have bad news," Verlaque said. "Please, sit down."

"My family?" Edmond Martin asked, jumping up out of the chair.

"No, no," Verlaque assured him.

Martin sat back down and stared at Verlaque with what looked like terror in his eyes. "What is it, then?"

"It's Suzanne Montmory."

"Suzie?"

"Yes. I'm sorry to have to tell you that Mlle Montmory died yesterday afternoon of heart failure."

Edmond Martin's face went white. "But that's impossible," he said. "She's so healthy." He shook his head back and forth. "No," he repeated. "It's absolutely impossible. You must have the wrong girl. Suzie's in great shape."

Paulik looked at Verlaque. "It's more complicated than that," Paulik said, leaning over the harbormaster's desk toward the young man. "On Wednesday night, sometime between four and seven-thirty p.m., Mlle Montmory was raped and viciously attacked in her flat, left for dead. She survived overnight in the hospital, but unfortunately slipped away on Thursday afternoon."

"Oh my God!" Martin tried to yell, but only a hoarse whisper came out of his mouth, for he had begun weeping. Verlaque reached across the desk and passed a box of Kleenex to Martin, at the same time looking at Paulik with an expression that said, "There's no way he did it."

"I'm sorry, Edmond," Verlaque said. "Will you be all right?"

"Yes," the young man said, wiping his tears and blowing his nose. "Thank you. I have a lift back to the Marseille airport with some friends from the cruise; they're waiting for me in the parking lot. We all fly out early tomorrow morning, so we're staying in an airport hotel tonight."

"Your parents have been trying to get hold of you in Montreal to give you the news, and Commissioner Paulik visited them yesterday."

"You did?" he asked, looking frightened.

"I had to find out where you were," Paulik said.

"I was a suspect?"

Paulik nodded.

The ship's captain then stepped forward and handed Verlaque a sheet of paper. "I can testify that M. Martin boarded the ship last Sunday here in Toulon and did not step off it, except for an afternoon's shopping trip in Cannes, until today."

"Thank you," Verlaque said.

"You won't tell my parents that I was on this cruise?"

"No," answered Verlaque. "But they now know you were in Provence, so perhaps this is a good time to tell them . . . your news."

"No," said Martin. "I'd be disowned."

"You may be mistaken," Verlaque said. "I'm sure they would get over it."

"No, not them."

"Wouldn't you sleep better at night?" Verlaque asked.

"Perhaps," Martin replied. "But I'd have no more family, and no inheritance."

Chapter Eleven

❧

A Changed Village

*I*t was strange, Pauline d'Arras thought, that a village could look as familiar as it had fifty years previously, and yet so very different. The buildings themselves were still the same, all made of the local golden stone quarried just outside of town; the quarry and its porous yellow stone had given the village its wealth. The main road hadn't changed either; it still veered eastward at the *cave* cooperative and then descended gently northward out of the village, until it reached the vine-covered plains outside of town. Of course, it was rather hard to change buildings and roads unless war destroyed them, thought Mme d'Arras as she sat on a bench under a plane tree. Or as the earthquake had. Its date came to her easily: 1909; fourteen villagers killed.

A young mother walked by, dressed in what Mme d'Arras considered a "risqué" outfit, the skirt much too short for a woman of her short and stocky build. The woman spoke impatiently to her son—who looked too big to be in a stroller, and too big to have a pacifier in his mouth. He had an Anglo-Saxon name, although they were clearly French. That was what had changed, Mme d'Arras now realized: the people, and the shops. Fifty years ago, even thirty, she could have sat on this bench and known almost everyone in the village. And they her: the villagers would have passed by and bowed their heads and said, "Good afternoon, Mlle Aubanel." They might have even chatted about the hot September weather, and passed their hello on to Pauline's sisters. Natalie was two years older than Pauline, and Clothilde two years younger.

"Good Clothilde," Mme d'Arras mumbled to herself. It was time she got to the chapel and made inquiries as to where Clothilde was these days, because she couldn't remember. In the church there would be some relief from the heat, and Pauline d'Arras was glad that she had made this trip. She got up off the bench and walked down the main street toward the church. With its rounded Romanesque apse, it was one of the first buildings one saw when coming into the village from the south, from Aix. By the time she got to the chapel, she was tired and regretted buying the bottle of wine at the *cave* cooperative; she didn't have a taste for wine, so Gilles always chose it. She set her purse down at her feet and looked at the chapel. It was unadorned—Mme d'Arras liked that—and a tall cypress tree was planted on either side of the building. There were no sculptures or adornments of any kind; the only ornamentation was a bell in a small tower at the top of the church's pediment. The wooden front door was unlocked, as Mme d'Arras had assumed it would be. She didn't realize that most village churches in France were now locked during the day— for fear of vandalism and robbery—but the church's cleaner was inside and had left the door open.

The Aubanel family pew had been near the left front, in the third row, and Mme d'Arras went there now and sat down. The cleaner looked up from where she had been mopping the altar, nodded, and continued her work. Inside, the chapel was drastically different from its rough-hewn stone exterior—the whitewashed walls were smooth, and the ceiling was painted a bright blue that early-twentieth-century restorers seemed to prefer. Mme d'Arras leaned forward and played with the little brass hook that used to hold their hats and her mother's purse; it slipped from her hands and snapped back against the wooden pew in front of her with a loud bang. The cleaner looked up again, and Mme d'Arras quickly got to her feet, made the sign of the cross once she was in front of the altar, and left.

From the chapel it would be an easy walk to her childhood home. She reached into her purse and set the bottle of wine against the church's stone wall. Either she could come by and pick it up later or a villager, or the cleaner, would take it. Let them have it: she had only purchased it because of the bus driver.

The path that led from the church toward the Hôtel Bollène was shaded; large bunches of valerian lined the path, and butter-flies circled in and out among the hearty purple flowers. At the bottom of the path she frowned, and stopped. On the other side of the street should have been her friend Philomène's house—a pretty 1920s house built after the Great War, where Philomène had lived with her mother and two maiden aunts. They had become friends when singing in the choir. Beside the house was a footpath that Pauline and her sisters had always taken to their family home. She hadn't been there in years, and the last time Gilles had driven, and she mustn't have been paying attention, because Philomène's house and the path were gone, replaced by a string of detached modern bungalows with small alleys—used for parking—paved between them. Poor Philomène, thought Mme d'Arras. A radio or television—she wasn't sure which—was blaring from one of the

tacky little houses, and she shuddered, moving on. She didn't remember that Philomène had married one of the Joubert boys and
they had moved to Aix shortly after their marriage, and that
Philomène still sang, but in the choir at Saint-Jean de Malte.

Mme d'Arras walked up the street a bit, but the new houses
went as far as she could see. She was suddenly very tired, and it
was still hot. She had no idea what time it was, but she knew that
she should go back to the bench and wait for the bus if she was
ever going to get home before dinner (it was, in fact, already 7:15
p.m.). She had turned around, deciding that she would visit her
childhood home another time, when the loud music stopped and
the front door of one of the little houses opened (she made clicking sounds with her tongue as she noted that its yellow trim badly
needed touching up). She jumped back and, out of instinct, held
her purse close to her chest.

"Hello," a man said quickly, closing the door behind him.
"What a surprise."

"Well, it shouldn't be," she replied. "This is my village."

"Oh, is it?" he asked.

"I grew up here," she went on. "And this was Philomène's
house."

"Oh, was it?" He tried to smile. "Have you been standing here
long?"

Mme d'Arras sighed. "Of course I haven't. Why would I, when
Philomène obviously no longer lives here?" She was angry at this
man, angry that her village had changed so much (and without her
knowledge or consent), angry that Philomène's house was gone and
that she no longer saw her old friend (truth was, Pauline d'Arras
was too much of a snob to socialize with Philomène Joubert, a
woman who for forty years had proudly worked as a secretary in
one of Aix's high schools, her husband a printer).

He took a step forward, and Mme d'Arras stepped back, alarmed. "I'm only opening the car door," he said. "Did you drive here?"

"Of course not. I don't drive."

"Let me take you back to Aix, then," he said, motioning to the passenger seat. "We must go quickly or we'll be caught in traffic." He noticed that she was fanning herself with the back of her hand. "The car's air-conditioned," he added.

"All right," she said. "I have to get back to make our dinner."

"Of course," he said, looking at his watch. "Let's hurry along, then." He gave her his elbow, walked her around to the passenger side of the car, and helped her in, holding her purse as she swung her legs into the car. Now he moved swiftly around the front of the car to the driver's side, got in, started the car, and backed out—too quickly, and without even looking, thought Mme d'Arras. "We can take the scenic route, through the forest," he said. "The *route nationale* will be too busy."

Mme d'Arras was too tired to contradict him. Because he barely slowed down at the stop sign, she had to tilt her head to get one last look at the chapel and its rounded apse. She glanced over at him; he was no longer smiling, just looking straight ahead, both hands firmly on the steering wheel.

Chapter Twelve

✤

Too Bling for Me

What do you think?" Marine asked. She was standing in her living room, hands on hips, wearing a blue silk wraparound dress with green high-heeled sandals.

"You look so great, perhaps we should just stay in this evening," Verlaque replied, setting down his book, the better to concentrate. "Are you sure you want to do this?" he asked. He got up off the sofa and walked over to Marine to kiss her on her forehead, having almost to get on tiptoes to do so.

"Of course I do," she answered. "I said so."

"And you won't mind a dozen or so cigar smokers?"

Marine laughed. "A dozen cigar smokers outside, on a warm late-summer evening? No. It will be better than getting stuck with you smoking in your Porsche with the windows rolled up."

"Hey! That's unfair," Verlaque said. "I always open the windows."

Marine smiled. "You're right. It was only once, and that was because it had started to rain. Well, you've promised me good food and fine wines this evening, so let's get going before I change my mind. The other wives and girlfriends will be there, right?"

"Twice a year it's permitted," Verlaque answered. "But only twice a year. And Pierre and Jean-Marc will be there, of course."

"But they're a couple! Isn't that unfair?"

"No, because Pierre and Jean-Marc are both *members*," Verlaque said, getting his jacket from the coatrack in the front hall. "Besides, I'm not sure if the other guys have figured out their relationship yet."

Marine put on some lipstick before the front hall's mirror. She pinched her lips together and said, "I'm sure the other guys have figured it out. They're not thick." She smiled at Verlaque, and he laughed, knowing he was being teased. When he had been told, by both men, of their love for each other, it had come as a complete surprise. "Who's hosting the cigar club's dinner tonight?" she asked.

"Jacob," Verlaque said. "He's part Egyptian, part French. And he works in the City in London."

"London? Why so far away?"

"You'll see."

Fifteen minutes later, Verlaque pulled his Porsche through a set of tall black gates that had been left open for the party.

"This is beautiful," Marine said, sticking her head out of the open window. "It seems like a silly thing to say, but I *love* this driveway!"

Verlaque smiled and rolled down his window. He loved Marine's enthusiasm, even for a driveway. Birds were singing, flying between the plane and pine trees that lined the drive. "You're right," he said. "I've been here before, but only at night. Now I see what you're talking about." The driveway wasn't paved; two narrow strips of paving stones guided the car's wheels. Between the strips and on either side was bright-green grass, so that the overall effect one saw when approaching the house was not concrete, or stone, but *verdure*. Something about the cicadas' chants, the warm evening, and the hazy greens made Verlaque's eyes water. The car slowly bumped along the path until it stopped at the end of the drive, in a large graveled parking area.

Pierre's meticulously cared-for Deux Chevaux was dwarfed by much larger cars, mostly German-made, and three or four SUVs. Pierre and Jean-Marc were just getting out of the little blue car; they walked over to Verlaque and gave him the *bise*. The three men peered into the front seat of a new silver Porsche Cayenne. "Whose car is this?" Pierre asked. "I don't recognize it."

"It's Christophe Chazeau's," Verlaque replied. "He told me about it when I bumped into him at the Café Mazarin."

Jean-Marc toured the car. Marine watched the men and smiled. "You're like teenagers," she called. Pierre shrugged and said, "They're beautiful objects, what can I say?"

Verlaque kicked at some mud on the left rear hubcap. "Christophe needs to get his new beauty washed."

"Hey, what's wrong with Marine?" Pierre asked.

Verlaque turned around and saw Marine staring up at the house.

"Marine!" Jean-Marc called. "Cat got your tongue?"

"Shhh!" Marine said, walking toward them. "They'll hear!"

"You like houses, we like cars," Verlaque said.

"Impressive place, isn't it?" Pierre said.

"Yes, impressive, but not imposing," she answered. "I think this is the most beautiful house I've ever seen."

The three men turned instinctively away from Marine and

looked up at the three-hundred-year-old *mas*. The farmhouse, despite its size—Pierre mumbled that it must have twelve bedrooms—was unpretentious. It looked as if it had begun as a small *manoir,* or the farmhouse of a wealthy farmer, and been enlarged over the decades and centuries in a most harmonious way. The stone was rough, exposed, the shutters all painted a light gray. The plants were Provençal: a myriad of greens and grays, dotted by tall, skinny cypress trees. The foursome made their way around to the back of the house, where they could hear music, laughter, and voices. A dozen or so couples were gathered around a long, sleek swimming pool. The north end of the pool was protected from the wind by a five-foot-high stone wall; above the wall rose hills that were covered in vineyards. To the west was another, steeper hill, this one terraced with plants: small rounded box hedges, rosemary, thyme, lavender, and here and there Mediterranean flowers that loved the sun, weren't picky about soil and rainfall, and could withstand Aix's cold winters.

"They're all white," Pierre said, looking at the plants with Marine. "The flowers, I mean."

"You're right," she said. "That's what makes the garden so pleasing, so easy on the eye."

"And tasteful," Pierre said, winking.

"Well, well, well," said Fabrice, the cigar club's president and the owner of plumbing stores that stretched across Provence, as he approached Pierre and Marine. "Lovely to see you, Marine." He switched his large drink from his right hand to his left so that he could shake Marine's hand.

Marine instead leaned over and gave him the *bise.*

"Is your wife here?" Pierre asked.

"No," Fabrice replied. "Our eldest daughter is about to go into labor any day. My wife won't leave the house until she gets the phone call. How about you, Pierre?"

"What do you mean?"

"Come here with anyone special?" Fabrice asked. He leaned over and poked Pierre's side with his elbow. "Any nice young girl you'd like to introduce to us? Eh?"

"I came with Jean-Marc," Pierre said calmly.

Fabrice nodded and looked perplexed, but then smiled. "I knew that."

"Hello, Fabrice," said Verlaque, who had just come up and slipped his arm around Marine's waist.

Fabrice leaned forward and said excitedly, "There's a guy making mojitos in the pool house. They're even better than mojitos I've had in Cuba!"

"Sounds great. Let's go and get some," Verlaque said to Marine.

Fabrice took one last loud sip from his straw and said, "I'll join you! Looks like I need another one."

On the way to the pool house, they met Jacob and his wife, Rebecca. Introductions were made, and Rebecca said, "Help yourself to anything—the apéritif is self-serve, but we'll sit down to dinner. Now, if you'll excuse me, I have to run in and get some more tapenade."

"She makes it herself," Jacob said, beaming.

"Really?" Marine asked, impressed. She had tried making tapenade only once; she found pitting the olives too tiresome.

"Here's this evening's first cigar," said José, another member, as he handed Verlaque a small square wooden box. "It's a Limited Edition Upmann."

Verlaque introduced Marine. "My wife, Carmé, wants to meet you," said José. "She's over there, wearing beige pants and a white blouse. She teaches Spanish at the university, and I told her that you teach law."

"That would be great," Marine said. "Tell Carmen I'd love to gossip about the university."

José and Verlaque laughed. "I'll tell her. By the way, it's 'Carmé,'" José repeated. "That's Catalan for 'Carmen.'" José left to serve more cigars. Verlaque snipped off the end of the Upmann and, patting his jacket pockets, realized he didn't have a lighter. As he turned to his right, he saw a flame approaching his cigar, held by a man he didn't know.

"Thank you," Verlaque said, lighting his cigar. "I don't think we've met. I'm Antoine Verlaque."

"Hello," the man said, shaking Verlaque's hand. "Philippe Léridon."

"This is Marine Bonnet," Verlaque said.

"Very pleased to meet you," Léridon said, smiling. "Do you smoke cigars too?"

"Oh no," Marine answered. "I'm here as part of the wives-and-girlfriends club."

Léridon laughed.

"And you?" Marine asked. She tried not to stare, but she recognized him. From where? Aix was so small, it could just be that they once stood in the same line at Monoprix.

"I was invited this evening by Christophe Chazeau," Léridon said.

Verlaque said, "Listen, you two stay here and chat, and I'll get us some mojitos before Fabrice drinks them all."

Marine didn't show her frustration at being abandoned, forced to make small talk with someone that she and her best friend, Sylvie, would have classified as a "*kek*." Philippe Léridon was very much a Mediterranean male: too much gold jewelry, too tanned, and showing off his abdominal muscles by wearing a very fitted white shirt unbuttoned too far down. Her awkwardness was cut short by the arrival of someone she had once met briefly at the Café Mazarin. "Hello, Christophe," she said. "Nice to see you here." Then it clicked; she remembered where she had seen Philippe Léridon. It was in a queue, but not at Monoprix—at the post office. "Nice to see you too," he said, giving Marine the *bise*. She noticed that both men wore thin Hermès belts, which she had always disliked. She listened while they spoke of Christophe's new car.

Verlaque returned with two mojitos, one already half finished. Marine laughed, and Verlaque shrugged, smiling. "How goes it, Christophe?" he asked.

"So-so," Chazeau said. "Family troubles."

"Join the club," Verlaque said. "Is everything okay?"

"My aunt Pauline has been causing us all grief. She keeps wandering around Aix and having to get taken home hours later by a kind stranger."

"Is *that* your aunt?" Verlaque asked. "Pauline d'Arras?"

"The same."

"Your uncle came into the Palais de Justice claiming that she was missing. I was told that she turned up a few hours after, safe and sound."

Chazeau nodded. "Yes, that's about the whole story. And I just found out tonight that she's been giving my buddy Philippe here a hard time."

"*Ah bon?*" Verlaque asked.

"We're neighbors," Léridon explained. "I've been doing *extensive* renovations on my house, and I'm afraid it's been making a lot of noise. Plus, the jackhammering has caused some *minor* cracking in Madame's kitchen walls, which I've offered to repair."

Marine looked at Léridon, annoyed at the way he had emphasized the words "extensive" and "minor." "Where's your house?" she asked.

"It's the Hôtel Panisse-Passis, on the Rue Émeric David," Léridon said. "Do you know it?"

"Oh yes," she answered. "I'm a native Aixoise." She tried not to show her disappointment; it had always been one of her favorite *hôtels*, very faded and elegant. "But your insurance will cover her damage, right?"

"Yes, of course. But Mme d'Arras still won't speak to me; and when she does, she threatens to sue me." Now it all clicked for Marine: the old woman in the post office, the queue jumper, was Christophe's aunt, and she remembered Madame's heated conversation with Philippe.

"Is she capable of that?" Verlaque asked.

"Oh yes," her nephew answered. "My aunt is a very sour person, and misery enjoys company."

"That's a funny thing to say about your aunt," Marine put in boldly. Verlaque finished his drink with a loud slurp, and she looked crossly at him.

"I know that it sounds unkind, but the truth is, we're all a little fed up with her at the moment," Chazeau went on. "She calls my mother late at night, accusing her of all sorts of nonsense that went on long ago. My mom gets off the phone and is really shaken up. I think that the only person who can stand my aunt right now is her husband, and of course Coco, her dog."

Dinner was served in the dining room, which Marine estimated was bigger than her living room, dining room, and kitchen combined. Some village girls had been hired to help serve, and hovering between the kitchen and dining room was a middle-aged couple that Rebecca told Marine had been with the family for more than thirty years. "They're like family," Jacob said over coffee on the terrace after dinner. "They helped us raise our three graces—that's what we call our daughters. Wherever we go, Tony and Margritte come with us. We would be lost without them."

Marine smiled, warmed by the obvious affection Jacob had for the couple.

After dinner, Verlaque and Fabrice sat on chaises longues, smoking cigars. Fabrice fussed with his chair's back, trying to get the angle just right. "There we are," he finally said, crossing his outstretched feet and putting his head back to smoke. He took a sip of Tony's homemade limoncello and smacked his lips, looking over at Verlaque. "That new chap, Léridon, seems like an okay guy."

"You think so?" Verlaque asked. "Too bling for me. I'm not sure we should vote him into the club."

Fabrice glanced at Verlaque. "You're too hard on people. Give the guy a break."

Verlaque stayed silent.

"Did you know that Pierre came with Jean-Marc this evening?" Fabrice asked.

Verlaque puffed on his cigar. "I know; we ran into them in the parking lot."

Fabrice uncrossed his legs and put a foot on either side of the chair, shifting it with his legs to get closer to Verlaque, trying not to spill his limoncello.

"Would you like me to hold your limoncello while you do that?" Verlaque asked, laughing.

Fabrice handed Verlaque his liqueur glass, struggling to move his chair sideways. Verlaque in turn struggled to hold both limoncello glasses and his cigar at the same time.

"You know what I think?" Fabrice asked when his chair was next to Verlaque's. He leaned in as close as he could to the judge without having his chair capsize.

"No, what?"

"That they're a couple."

Verlaque took a sip of his limoncello. "I think you're right, Fabrice. Very astute of you."

Verlaque stayed silent, waiting for Fabrice to speak next, unsure what the club's president would think of a gay couple in their midst. He could trust Fabrice Gaussen with his life, but he also knew that Fabrice came from a Marseille working-class family, and in his professional life among plumbers and construction workers had probably never come across homosexuals. The cigar club was also, Verlaque had to admit (remembering the expensive cars in the parking lot that evening), fairly macho. But there were many exceptions to the cliché that cigar smokers were rich, conservative men; the proof was Pierre and Jean-Marc, and the club's sole female member, Virginie, a pharmacist, who was absent from this evening's party.

"And do you know what else?" Fabrice asked.

Verlaque gave out a long, exaggerated sigh. "No, what, Fabrice?"

Fabrice looked across the terrace at Jean-Marc and Pierre, who were deep in conversation with Marine and Carmé. "I think it's great that we have a . . . gay . . . couple . . . in our club, and for that reason we can have some bling guys too. It takes all kinds, right?"

"It takes all kinds to do what, Fabrice?" Verlaque asked, laughing.

Fabrice tapped Verlaque's chair with the bottom of his shoe. "You know what I mean! It . . . it . . . takes all kinds of fish to make a bouillabaisse!"

Chapter Thirteen

✌

Philomène Arranges the Flowers

Victor Bonnard lay in bed, his hands behind his head, and looked up at the ceiling. When he was nine years old, he and his father had pasted glow-in-the-dark stars all over the ceiling. He looked up at the Big Dipper and wondered when he should take the stars down; he was eighteen years old, after all. Someone knocked on the door. "Come in," he said, not taking his eyes off the ceiling.

"I realize it's not yet ten a.m.," Olivier Bonnard said, walking through the door and sitting on the edge of the bed. "But you didn't get to go out clubbing last night, so you should be in fine shape."

Victor lay still and looked at the stars.

"Did you know that when I was your age we also went to La Fantaisie? I'm sure it still looks the same inside; only the music has changed."

"Yeah, no more Beatles."

Olivier playfully cuffed his son on the side of his head. "I'm not *that* old!" Bonnard looked at his son, admiring the fine aquiline nose, high cheekbones, and freckles the boy had inherited from his mother. "Still mad at me?" he asked.

"Yup."

"I'm really sorry for what I said the other day."

"You should be."

"What was I to think?" Olivier said to his son. "Not many of us have a key to that cellar. I was in shock."

Victor turned his head so that he could look at his father. "All right, then. But you must know that I would never, ever take your . . . *our* . . . wine."

"All right," Olivier said. "And if you needed money, for whatever reason, you would ask us. Right?"

"Of course!"

A vehicle pulled into the estate's graveled courtyard, and both Olivier and Victor jumped up to look out of Victor's bedroom window. "Ah, it's just Rémy, coming to get Dad for his *boules* game." Both men watched Albert Bonnard walk quickly to the postman's battered van, cradling a leather duffel bag in his arms.

"He sure loves those *boules*," Victor said, laughing. He fell back onto the bed and pulled the covers up to his chin.

"Don't get too comfortable," Olivier said, sitting back down on the edge of the bed. "Hélène's husband, Bruno, called me yesterday. You remember him, don't you?"

"Yeah. Big scary-looking, rugby-playing cop."

"Policeman," Olivier said. "Yes, that's him. He told me that his boss, Antoine Verlaque, visited a wine thief in Paris and got some information that may help us."

Victor sat up. "Really? Cops—policemen—visit wine thieves these days?"

"He's a reformed thief, actually, and now helps the police solve cases when expensive wines have been stolen."

"And what did this guy say?" Victor asked.

"That the thief will be back." Olivier Bonnard stood up and put his hand on the doorknob. "So get up and get dressed."

"Are we going on watch or what? I need to eat breakfast. What's the rush?"

"Because I just checked the cellar," Olivier said. "And more wine is gone."

Marine knew that she was a lousy Catholic. She sometimes wished that she could have the unquestioning faith that her parents had; she liked the mystery of the church, and the ceremony, but wasn't a big enough believer to attend Mass on a regular basis. Was this just an excuse? Was she just too lazy to get out of bed on Sunday mornings? No, she thought not. She disagreed with the pope's stand on birth control and abortion. The irony was that she felt so good in churches. She loved their stark stone walls; the golden light streaming in through high windows, as it did this Saturday morning; and she loved the song and the time to meditate. She had been half relieved when Verlaque said he was going into the Palais de Justice to work this morning; she knew that she would come to Saint-Jean de Malte straightaway. Shiny brown chestnuts had fallen from the trees in the square, and she gently kicked them aside as she walked toward the church. There were new all-glass entry doors, and Marine vaguely remembered her mother telling her about their cost and the trouble the monks had had finding exactly the *right* kind of door. The inside of the church smelled of incense, as it always did, and the beauty of the church took her breath away. Everything was golden, she realized, as she sat down and looked all around the church. The stone walls were gold, as were the light shining in from the south windows, the gilded pulpit and statues of Mary, the polished brass contemporary light sconces, even the woven cane seats. She twisted around so that she could see the new organ, largely funded by wine sales that her parents had organized: it too was golden, sculpted from a pale-blond wood—perhaps birch?—with shiny stainless-steel pipes that soared up toward the ceiling. She realized that the triumph of the church lay in its being beautiful in its entirety. No one object stood out—say, a famous painting or an exquisite sculpture. The whole church, the package, was perfect.

A rumbling noise made her turn around again; the church was now busy, with elderly women bringing in armloads of flowers and excitedly whispering to one another. Of course, thought Marine, it was a Saturday in early September: there would be a wedding or two today. She got up off her chair and walked over to a small chapel to light a candle. The south chapels had always been too humid and in disrepair, and Marine noticed that the walls looked even more crumbling and cracked than the last time she had been in the church. She put a two-euro coin in the brass slot and heard the coin fall with a bang. Bending her head and closing her eyes, Marine prayed to whatever spirits she thought might listen to her. She raised her right arm and lightly pressed the far side of her left breast. The bump was still there, like a hard pea, or perhaps a little bigger, an almond. She stood still for some minutes, watching the flames flicker, and tried to drown out the noise in the church behind her. Modern medicine would help her now, not the saints, but she was glad that she had come. She turned around and watched the women rushing about the church, half envious of their Saturday-morning obligation. How nice it must be for them to have this sureness, and routine.

"Well, well," a male voice behind her said, "if it isn't Marine Bonnet."

She turned around and saw Père Jean-Luc smiling at her. "Hello, Father," she said, and shook his hand. She stopped herself from adding, "It's been a long time," although the smiling abbot didn't seem in the least angry that she hadn't set foot in the church since Étienne de Bremont's funeral. The monk was discreet enough not to have asked Marine what she was doing in the church, for he had seen her lighting a candle.

"How do you like it?" he asked, looking up at the organ, which took up most of the mezzanine above the front doors.

"It's wonderful," Marine said. "My parents said it was big, but I had no idea how big."

"Your mother had to be convinced that selling wine, a special Cuvée Saint-Jean de Malte, would help pay for the organ," he said. "But once she set her mind on it, she was one of our best sales-women!"

Marine laughed. "I bought a few cases, as did many of my friends."

"It was a good rosé, wasn't it?" he said. "I'm not much of a rosé drinker—I prefer a cold beer when it's hot out—but that rosé was very fine indeed."

Marine smiled and nodded, delighted that a monk would voice an opinion on wines to her.

"Well, I must go," he continued. "As you can see, we have a busy day today."

"Yes, I see, Father," she said, taking his hand. "Have a nice day."

"You too, Marine. It was lovely to see you." She watched him walk toward the altar, then turn right and head back into the sacristy—perhaps hoping for a little lunch before the wedding rush hit the church.

"Is that Mlle Bonnet?" came a woman's voice from behind her.

Marine turned around and saw an elderly woman with white

hair, a tanned, healthy-looking face, and clear blue eyes. "Ah, Mme Joubert," Marine said, smiling. "How are you?"

"Oh, busy!" Philomène Joubert replied, fanning herself. "We have three weddings today, so we are busy with flowers, as you can see! *No*, Constance, *not* the lilies *there*!"

Mme Joubert was Marine's neighbor; they shared views of each other's apartments over the courtyard that separated Marine's street and the Rue Cardinale.

"How is M. Joubert?" Marine asked.

"Seventy-three years old and still working!" Mme Joubert replied. "You couldn't get him out of the printing shop for all the tea in China. And to think that *some* people in France want to retire at sixty!"

Marine smiled, knowing that Mme Joubert meant the Socialist Party and voters. This was one of Antoine Verlaque's pet peeves as well.

"If M. Joubert is still working, it's a good thing that you're busy with the church, and the choir," Marine said.

"Oh! This church! I know it as if I had made it."

Marine smiled at Mme Joubert's curious use of the old Provençal saying. "Were you baptized in Saint-Jean de Malte?" she asked.

"Oh, heavens no! Far from Aix, let me tell you!"

"In the north?" Marine suggested.

"Yes! Rognes!"

Marine concentrated as hard as she could, trying not to laugh. Rognes was a village about a thirty-minute drive north of Aix. When she had suggested "north," Marine had been thinking Normandy or Brittany.

"Came to Aix when I got married," Mme Joubert continued. "*Constance!*" Philomène Joubert watched, hands on her thick hips, as her co-volunteer put the wrong bunch of white roses in front of the lectern. "I have to go, Mlle Bonnet," she said. "Maybe some Saturday we'll be doing your flowers, eh?"

Marine made a valiant attempt at smiling. She tried not to think of the lump in her left breast, and of Antoine Verlaque, who hated the institution of marriage. "Perhaps," she said quietly.

"I think I'll try an Ethiopian this time."

"Branching out from your usual Italian, are you?" Magali asked.

"I'm feeling wild today," Jules answered, enjoying the low-cut T-shirt that Magali wore and her slim-fitting jeans. He was getting used to the dark look that she seemed to be a fan of: extra-dark eyeliner, black nail polish, and extra-dark-red lipstick. Jules contemplated the tiny diamond stud in her left nostril and came to the conclusion that it suited Magali's long, thin nose. His mother wouldn't like it, but they were hardly at that stage in their relationship. For now the conversation revolved around the weather, and coffee.

"Working day?" Magali asked, pushing the sugar bowl toward Jules.

"Yep," he replied. "But I have Sundays off. Do you?" Jules hoped that he sounded casual enough.

"Yes, we're closed Sundays. A good thing too, 'cause that's when I go to Mass."

He stirred a packet of brown sugar into his coffee and stared at Magali, unsure of what to say next.

Magali laughed and moved on to the next table. "They sure are gullible in Alsace!" she yelled over her shoulder to Jules. When she had taken the next order, she went back into the café winking. He finished his espresso and waved goodbye, leaving money on the table, then walked down the Rue Chabrier. Sundays would be a good time to ask Magali out, he thought; they could go to the beach or to an exposition in Marseille. He had no idea what she liked to do. He walked to the Palais de Justice, mulling date ideas over in his head; by the time he got to the front doors, he had convinced himself that he couldn't ask her out—they hardly knew each other.

Jules could hear loud voices and what sounded like sobbing as he approached the large second-floor office space shared by six officers, Commissioner Paulik, and Mme Girard, the judge's secretary. He quickened his pace. When he came through the double glass doors, he saw Roger bending down over an elderly man who was sitting on a bench against the wall. "Your wife will be back today, I guarantee it," Roger said. He looked at Jules and rolled his eyes. "Just like the last time." Roger winked at Jules.

"She was gone for a few hours last time," the man answered. "Not overnight."

"Overnight?" Jules asked.

Roger motioned him off with a raised palm. "Everything's fine, Officer Schoelcher," he said in a deep voice, much too polite and professional for the usual Roger Caromb.

Jules ignored Roger and bent down so that his face was parallel to the old man's. "When did your wife go missing?" he gently asked.

The man breathed deeply and replied, "From what I can tell, she left shortly after lunch yesterday. I left the apartment at one-forty-five to return to work, and when I got back, at five-thirty, the dirty lunch dishes were in the sink. Pauline always does the dishes right away."

Jules shifted his weight from one leg to the other, trying to ignore Roger's exaggerated sigh. "And your wife has never done this before?"

The man looked at Jules with reddened, swollen eyes. "No, of course not," he said quietly.

Jules stood up and put a hand on the man's shoulder. He whispered to Roger, "This is serious." Suddenly an office door opened, and Roger shot Jules a glance that read "Oh no!" Verlaque walked out of his office and said to the officers, "I was on the phone and thought I heard sobbing. What's going on?"

Roger grimaced and nodded down in the direction of M. d'Arras.

"M. d'Arras," Verlaque said, also bending down on one knee to speak to the old man. "I'm Judge Verlaque. What's wrong? Is your wife missing again?"

M. d'Arras nodded, relieved to be in the presence of the *juge d'instruction*. "*Oui*. She left, from what I can guess, sometime yesterday afternoon. She hasn't come back. She has her purse; it's a big pink Longchamp one that I bought her for her birthday. And that's all she took; our suitcases and overnight bags are all still in the closet. The neighbors said that Coco—our poodle—was barking most of the afternoon."

"And you gave Commissioner Paulik a photograph of Mme d'Arras, didn't you?"

M. d'Arras nodded. Verlaque rose to his feet and said to Roger, "Please find that photograph of Mme d'Arras; phone the commissioner at home if you have to." He reached out a hand to help M. d'Arras up and ushered him into his office, closing the door behind them.

"A *juge d'instruction* helping out an old guy whose wife has walked off?" Roger whispered to Jules. "*Incroyable!*"

"He has his reasons," Jules answered. "Let's find that photograph."

"After I slip out for a ciggie," Roger replied.

Verlaque's door opened, and he stuck his head out. "Officer

Schoelcher, you'll head this investigation. I'm surprised to see you both still standing there. Go find that photograph and get on the phones: hospitals, bus and train stations . . . the usual."

"Yes, sir!" the two officers replied.

Verlaque went back into his office. "We'll begin a department-wide search for Mme d'Arras, beginning now," he told the old man. "Does your wife drive, M. d'Arras?"

"No, she never has."

"*Bon*," Verlaque said. He sat down opposite M. d'Arras. "I'm a friend of your nephew Christophe's."

M. d'Arras looked up. "Ah, that's why a judge is helping me."

Verlaque ignored the comment and said, "I saw Christophe at a party last night. He's concerned about the state of his aunt's mental health. Does she have Alzheimer's, M. d'Arras?"

The man nodded. "She shows every sign of having the early stages, from what I've been able to learn from reading. But she refuses to go to the doctor. She thinks all doctors are in a medical conspiracy, out to make money from unnecessary operations. She even said that to a specialist who checked a lump in her thyroid."

Verlaque breathed deeply. "I see. Where do you think she might go?"

M. d'Arras shook his head. "I just don't know. She doesn't drive, and she doesn't like traveling. But she's been speaking of wanting to see her sister Clothilde."

"Where does Clothilde live?" Verlaque asked.

"In the southwest, at Jonquières, near Narbonne."

"Jonquières?" Verlaque asked. "Isn't that a medieval abbey?" He remembered his grandmother Emmeline telling him about a visit she had made to the abbey.

"Yes," M. d'Arras answered. "Clothilde is a cloistered nun."

Chapter Fourteen

꒦

Les Enfants d'Amour

Hippolyte Thébaud stepped gently out of his rented Clio, not wanting to get his shoes or pants dusty. Olivier Bonnard heard the car and came out of the house, wiping his hands on a tea towel (Élise was doing inventory at her design shop in Aix, and it was Olivier's turn to cook lunch for the kids and his father, Albert, who was anxious to get to his *boules* game on time). He tossed the tea towel over his shoulder and shook the young Parisian's hand. "How do you do," Bonnard said. "Thank you so much for coming."

"*Pas de problème,*" Thébaud answered. "I have friends in Gordes and was due for a trip. Plus, I enjoy your wines."

Bonnard smiled. "Thank you. That's a compliment, coming from such an expert. Our wines in the south may never be comparable to a Côtes de Nuit, but . . ."

"Ah! A Côtes de Nuit! As if!" Thébaud burst out, laughing.

Bonnard looked at the young man, imagining how he could describe Hippolyte Thébaud to Élise later that evening. He was no good at remembering the names of movie stars, so he couldn't compare Thébaud's face to another man's. He knew that the wine expert's pale-blue eyes, high cheekbones, and full lips were beautiful, but it was his thick mop of curly blond hair and elegant clothing (a pale-green linen suit with a pink polka-dot bow tie, and white patent-leather brogues) that Bonnard found so striking.

"So the thief has returned," Thébaud said, looking up with visible admiration at Bonnard's manor house and extensive outbuildings.

"Yes, and we were all here," Bonnard said. "I noticed the theft early this morning, and my son and I have tried to do an inventory of what was taken. It's just like the first time—odd bottles here and there, and not necessarily our best."

"Really?" Thébaud asked. "Usually, the second time around the thief is more selective." Thébaud looked behind him at the property's massive wrought-iron gates and the high stone wall that surrounded the courtyard. "Do they come and go on foot?"

"That's my guess. My wife and I are both light sleepers and so would hear a vehicle. That said, we obviously didn't hear the thief taking bottles out of the cellar."

"How do they get over that wall?" Thébaud asked.

"Ah, I think they come through the vineyard. There's a small gate beside the house that leads to an old vegetable garden, and beyond that are the vines, open to the road. The lock on the gate has been broken for years. I just remembered about the gate this morning and had my son put a padlock on it."

"Are the police coming to check for prints?"

"Today, in fact. It surprised me that they'd dust for prints for stolen wine."

"Wine theft has become big business, and it's surprisingly common. Every day I read reports of wine thefts, ranging from hundreds of bottles to a couple here and there. It's amazing what people will do for grape juice." Thébaud smiled at the irony of his statement, given that he had spent five years in prison for wine theft.

They walked across the graveled courtyard of the domaine, and Thébaud took in the graceful proportions and yellow stone of the manor house and the outbuildings that flanked it.

"People will steal just a few bottles?" Bonnard asked.

"Sadly, yes," Thébaud replied. "One of France's top diplomats was just fired from his Hong Kong post last month for sneaking away from a private club with two bottles of old Bordeaux worth more than five thousand euros. I guess he figured he had diplomatic immunity. At least he had good taste." Thébaud laughed at his own joke. "But most wine thieves are professionals—upmarket criminals like those who steal old masters and antiques, to order. They usually know what they're going to steal beforehand and then go in and do it—if not the first time, then the second. Your break-in doesn't sound like that." Thébaud frowned, as if he was disappointed in the amateur nature of Domaine Beauclaire's theft. "Lead me to the cellar and I'll have a look, but if I were to guess right now, I'd say that your thief isn't a thief at all."

Verlaque watched Marine hunched over his dining-room table, writing. She had been oddly silent all weekend, and this morning had joined her parents for Mass at 10:30 a.m., something he could never remember her doing. She said something about wanting to hear the new organ, but her voice didn't sound convincing, and as soon as she got home she had called Sylvie on her cell phone from Verlaque's bedroom, with the door closed. But that was not unusual—Sylvie must have a new boyfriend, he finally decided. He hoped.

"I'll make dinner," he said, putting down his book.

"Pardon?"

"I said I'll make dinner tonight," he repeated. "You have an early class tomorrow morning, right?"

Marine turned around to face him. "Yes, Mondays I start early. Thank you."

"Is everything all right?" When he returned yesterday from the Palais de Justice, they had quickly dressed for a fiftieth-birthday party for one of Marine's colleagues and had not had the chance to speak before falling into bed, exhausted, at 2:00 a.m. That morning, while Marine was at Mass, Verlaque had slipped out to the market on the Place Richelme and bought figs, fresh chèvre, and bacon, which he planned to roast in the oven.

Marine nodded and then turned back around to her writing. "Yes, everything's fine. How are your cases going?"

"We're interviewing hospital personnel tomorrow," Verlaque answered. "Those who were in and out of Mlle Montmory's room. And Mme d'Arras has gone missing again."

"Christophe's aunt?"

"Yes. She's been gone since Friday afternoon."

"*Mon dieu!* That's terrible. Do you have any leads?" she asked.

"No, not yet. I've put a young officer from Alsace in charge of the case, and he has sent her photograph and description out to hospitals, train stations, and so on." Just then Verlaque's cell phone rang, and he saw the name of Jules Schoelcher on his phone's screen. "It's that officer from Alsace I was just talking about. Excuse me, Marine."

Marine crossed her fingers for good luck and continued reading, but she couldn't concentrate. A few minutes later, Verlaque came back into the living room. "A bus driver recognized her photograph," he said quickly.

"That's a good start."

"That officer had the good sense to include a description of what she was wearing that day, including a big pink purse. The bus driver remembered the purse: A few months ago, he went into Longchamp on the Cours Mirabeau, looking for a present for his wife. He did a double take when he saw the prices and walked right out, but he remembered the pink purse."

"Thank goodness for elderly fashion victims," Marine said, pouring herself a glass of water. "So where did Mme d'Arras go?"

"Rognes."

"Really?" For a minute Marine couldn't remember who had spoken of Rognes, but then remembered the bustling gray-haired Mme Joubert, arranging flowers in church.

"Officer Schoelcher is sending out a team to ask the villagers if they've seen her, but since it's Sunday that will be difficult—none of the shops will be open. The bus driver says that Mme d'Arras crossed the street and went into the *cave* cooperative, to buy wine for a friend. The bus driver remembered that the friend's name is Philomène. I've only ever seen that name in nineteenth-century novels."

"Philomène? But it was my neighbor, Philomène Joubert, who spoke about Rognes yesterday. She grew up there."

"How old is she?"

"My guess is between sixty-five and seventy-five."

"So they could be friends. Could you talk to Mme Joubert? This afternoon, even?"

Marine set her glass down on the kitchen counter. "I'll go right now." She was happy to leave the apartment and try to walk off her anxiety. Why she hadn't told Antoine about the lump—the "pea," she secretly called it—she didn't know. Over the telephone, Sylvie had suggested reasons for Marine's silence: that Marine didn't want to be weak, especially in front of Verlaque; that Marine was a martyr and preferred to suffer through this on her own; that Marine was avoiding facing her own *angoisse* by not telling Antoine. . . . But Marine didn't agree with Sylvie's ideas, except for the martyr one, which she didn't dare admit to. She had learned to trust her instincts, and her instincts had told her to keep it a secret just a little longer.

"Thank you for taking the time to talk to me," Marine said.

"Oh, it was obvious that you have something on your mind," Philomène Joubert said. "I'm good at reading faces." She smiled kindly and poured Marine a cup of coffee. "What is it, dear?"

"It's Mme d'Arras," Marine replied. "Pauline, your old friend."

"*Ah bon?*"

"She's been missing since Friday afternoon."

Mme Joubert made the sign of the cross.

"She took the bus to Rognes. . . ."

"Rognes?" Mme Joubert said quickly. "That's where we grew up!"

"Yes, and she told the bus driver that she needed to buy wine for her friend . . . Philomène."

"*Moi?* But that's crazy. We haven't had a meal together in years. Decades, even. I do see her around Aix from time to time, naturally."

Marine nodded. She couldn't step out of her front door without running into someone she knew from the university, or her childhood, or from other social contacts. "So you didn't see each other on Friday?"

"No, of course not." Mme Joubert pushed her coffee cup toward the middle of the table and crossed her thick, muscular arms. "But where could she be? *La pauvre!*"

"That's what the police, and M. d'Arras, would like to know. Do you have any ideas? Does she have family in Rognes?"

Mme Joubert shook her head. "No. Her sister Natalie lives here, in Aix, as does Natalie's son, Christophe. The third Aubanel daughter—they were beauties, they were—is a nun near Narbonne. A Carmelite."

"M. d'Arras thinks that his wife has Alzheimer's, but she refuses to be tested. Is there something from her past that would make her want to return to Rognes?" Marine asked.

Mme Joubert stayed silent for a few seconds, looking at Marine. Then she leaned toward Marine and whispered, "Perhaps you should speak to her sister Natalie."

"Christophe's mother?" Marine asked. "I know Christophe; in fact, I saw him on Friday night, at a party. He mentioned that Pauline d'Arras was phoning her sister—Christophe's mother—and upsetting her."

Philomène Joubert sighed. "Poor Natalie. As if her life hasn't been hard enough. Pauline was always such a pest. I now know, looking back, that I played with Pauline because she was rich, and pretty. I was honored to have such a fancy friend. But later, when we were in our early teens, I learned not to trust her. We stopped seeing each other when I met my husband; I was eighteen."

"What does Pauline say to Natalie that's so upsetting?" Marine asked. "Why has Natalie's life been difficult?"

Mme Joubert sat back. "Clothilde and Pauline Aubanel were beauties. Their most striking features were their white-blond hair and clear blue eyes, just like their mother's and father's. They were petite, and graceful, and we all wanted to be like them. They were like little dolls."

"And Natalie?" Marine asked. "She wasn't like them, I take it."

"Have you noticed your friend Christophe's hair?"

Marine nodded. "Jet black."

"As is his mother's, and mine, before it went gray," Philomène said, touching her head. "Natalie Chazeau has big brown eyes. And she's tall, and strong. I'm not saying she was fat, but she was a big girl, not at all what you'd call petite."

"Mme Joubert, are you saying that Natalie had a different father?" Marine asked. "Siblings can look very different, even when born of the same mother and father."

Mme Joubert again made the sign of the cross. "But we all knew that wasn't the case. Natalie was clearly her mother's favorite. I always thought it was because Natalie was the oldest child, but one day when I was home in bed with the flu, I overheard my mother speaking with a neighbor in our kitchen. The neighbor had lived in Paris during the war, working as a maid, and Mme Aubanel—her name was Francine Lignon at the time—was at the Sorbonne in Paris. It was before she came back to Rognes and married M. Aubanel, who had been her childhood sweetheart. They were to be married when they finished *lycée*, but Francine got cold feet. She broke off the engagement and moved to Paris to study after high school. That was in 1939, and then the war began. . . ."

"And Paris was invaded," Marine said.

"Yes, and so Francine was stuck, so to speak, in Paris. But she came back to Rognes, in 1943 . . ." Mme Joubert leaned in. "*Enceinte.*"

"Pregnant, with Natalie," Marine suggested.

"Yes." Mme Joubert sat back and allowed Marine to take in this fact that she so obviously thought was shocking.

"But that happened all the time, didn't it?" Marine said. "Francine had an affair with a soldier, and then perhaps he died."

"He died all right, and he was a soldier. But he wasn't one of ours. *Sale boche!*"

"A German? But the black hair . . ."

Mme Joubert laughed. "I guess not all the Germans in Paris were blond and blue-eyed. Just last year, my husband and I took our first airplane ride, to Venice—it was a gift from our children, God bless them. And do you know what? The Italians there are blond and blue-eyed. Some are even redheads. Not with jet-black hair, as the Italian immigrants have here in Provence. I'd look more like an Italian than they would."

"And how do you know that Natalie's father was a German?" Marine asked. She was careful not to use the word *boche*. The war was so long ago, and it bothered her to hear that expression.

"Our neighbor, the one who was visiting that day, was a maid for one of the German headquarters, in a mansion that they took over near the Parc Monceau. This German officer was a bigwig, and she saw him with Francine all the time. . . . They were very cozy together, if you get my drift."

"And you're sure it's true?"

"Confirmed by Pauline Aubanel when we were young girls. She told me everything. She had snooped around her mother's wardrobe and found letters and a photograph."

"That's when you knew not to trust her," Marine offered.

"Yes."

Marine closed her eyes. "That story is heartbreaking."

"Hmmph!" Mme Joubert said, banging the table with her fist.

Marine didn't try to argue with the elderly woman. "But why would Pauline bother her sister Natalie over something that happened to their mother?"

Mme Joubert shrugged. "Pauline had a nasty streak. I have no idea why, but she was just like that."

Neither woman finished her coffee, which had gone cold. They chatted for a few minutes about the weather and the new shopping complex at the bottom of the Cours Mirabeau that had just been built and that both women detested. On the way back to Verlaque's apartment, Marine walked as if dazed. Since it was a Sunday, the streets were quiet, except for the odd person window-shopping, or tourists wandering with guidebooks in hand, looking at the fountains or oratory statues that were built into the corners of Aix's medieval and Renaissance buildings. Marine thought of Sylvie, still away on holiday, and missed her. One night in July, she and Sylvie had stayed up late, after Sylvie had tucked Charlotte into bed, and watched a documentary—*Les enfants d'amour*—children born to French mothers and German fathers during World War II. Both women had cried during the program, Sylvie finally putting a box of Kleenex between them and pouring two generous tumblers of whiskey. The program's host, a famous historian, explained that more than two hundred thousand children were born in France of these liaisons, most of them out of love, and that a million people now descended from them. "That would be Christophe," Sophie whispered to herself as she went up the Rue Gaston Saporta.

Chapter Fifteen

❧

Oh Voleur, Oh Voleur!

*B*runo Paulik held open the doors for Jules Schoelcher. "Is it an unwritten rule that there's never enough parking at a hospital?" he asked.

"I was just thinking the same thing, sir," replied Schoelcher. "While my mom was upstairs giving birth to my youngest sister, my dad was cruising around the hospital parking lot, trying to find a parking spot. My mom was hopping mad. It's become one of their favorite stories."

Paulik laughed. "How many are you?"

"I'm the second oldest of six."

"So am I."

They approached a busy reception desk, and Paulik leaned over the counter to speak to the receptionist. "We're here to meet with Dr. D'Almeida. I was told to report here first, since she wasn't sure where she would be this morning."

Without looking up, the receptionist began talking. Paulik

looked at Schoelcher and shrugged; he hadn't noticed that she was wearing earphones and had someone on the phone. She arranged for the appointment and then took another call while the two policemen waited. After she took a third call, Paulik began to look around for another secretary. A woman came behind the reception area, carrying files and loudly chewing gum. "Excuse me, I'm Commissioner Bruno Paulik, and we were told to report here to find out where our interview room is," he said to her. The woman looked at him, bored, said nothing, and, setting the files beside the phone receptionist, turned on her heel and walked away. The phone receptionist ended her call, and Paulik reached over and gently removed her headset.

"Hey, what do you think you are doing?" she asked.

"Surely someone who is physically present, less than a meter away from you, takes precedence over someone on the other side of town on the telephone. I'm Commissioner Paulik—"

"And I'm Carla Bruni."

Paulik ignored her comment. "My colleague Officer Schoelcher and I were told to report here. We're to meet with Dr. D'Almeida."

"And what am I supposed to do for you?" she asked, reaching for her headset.

Paulik put his large hand on the headset. "You're supposed to tell us where to go to meet the doctor. This is a big place."

"I wasn't told about this."

"Could you please make a phone call to find out where the doctor is?"

The receptionist sighed as the gum-chewing woman came back behind the reception desk with another stack of files.

"Hey, Odile," the telephone receptionist said. "Could you tell these guys where to go?" She smiled at her play on words and then answered the telephone.

Odile rolled her eyes, but she did slowly pick up another telephone and walk away from the counter with it. In a few seconds, she was back. "She's up on the third floor, geriatric wing."

One elevator was being repaired and the other had an orderly with a stretcher waiting for it, so the two policemen took the stairs. They followed the signs for the geriatric wing, zigzagging down halls and through doors.

At the reception area, a duplicate of the one on the ground level, two similar-looking receptionists stood behind the counter, chatting.

"Excuse me," Paulik said, "we're looking for Dr. D'Almeida."

"She's not here," the taller one answered, and then turned to her colleague and continued talking.

An elderly man approached the counter. "Excuse me, I'm waiting in the waiting room for my wife to have an exam, and there's a woman in a wheelchair who needs to visit the toilet."

The two receptionists looked at each other and said nothing.

"Um," the man continued, "do you think you could help her?"

"Us? You need a nurse."

"Oh, I'm very sorry. Of course."

Paulik looked at the woman in disbelief and was about to speak when a tall black woman wearing white approached them.

"Mme Fournier in the waiting room needs to go pee-pee," one of the secretaries yelled.

"Then call a nurse right away," the handsome black woman answered shortly. "And in future, Marie-Pierre, please say that the patient needs to use the toilet, and in a quieter voice." She turned to Paulik and Schoelcher. "I'm sorry about that. I assume you're the police. I'm Dr. D'Almeida." They shook hands, and she said, "Please come this way."

"The receptionists here are a far cry from professional," Paulik said as they walked down the hall. "At least the four we've just had to deal with."

"I know," the doctor answered. "And they're planning to go on strike, so it's been even worse. I'm afraid that the brunt of the workload will fall on the shoulders of the underpaid nurses, as usual." She opened the door to a small office with a desk and four chairs, and a small potted plant in the corner. The room's drabness was balanced by the view through the window: downtown Aix and the steeple of the Cathedral.

"Please sit down," she said. "We were devastated by the death of Mlle Montmory. We did everything we could."

"I'm sure you did," Paulik answered. "Officer Schoelcher was here, guarding her room, and he said as much."

"I thought I recognized you," Dr. D'Almeida said, smiling for the first time. "You're out of uniform today. I'm sorry I didn't notice."

"It's no problem," Schoelcher replied.

"I can only assume that you are both here because you want to ask about the possibility of foul play," Dr. D'Almeida said.

Paulik nodded. "Mlle Montmory's attacker is still out there somewhere. If she had lived, she could have identified him. We're fairly certain that the attacker was someone she knew."

"As Officer Schoelcher can verify, only authorized hospital staff were in and out of Mlle Montmory's room," the doctor said. "We're in the business of saving lives here, not killing people."

"I understand. Call it professional paranoia if you will, but I need to cover all the angles. Was there anyone present in the room when the young woman went into cardiac arrest?" Paulik asked.

Both the doctor and Schoelcher shook their heads.

"We all came running," Dr. D'Almeida said, "when we heard the alarm of her life-support machine go off."

"Who was there?" Paulik asked.

"Well," Dr. D'Almeida replied, "myself, the head nurse, an intern . . . and . . ."

"Dr. Franck Charnay," Schoelcher said.

"Yes, that's right," Dr. D'Almeida said.

Paulik looked over and saw that Schoelcher had read the name from a little orange spiral-bound notebook. He silently noted the young officer's thoroughness. He said, "We'll speak to Dr. Charnay today." He hoped that Verlaque would have had time to visit the doctor at his office in downtown Aix.

"You'll find him cooperative, I'm sure," Dr. D'Almeida replied.

"As you've all been," Paulik said. "And if there was foul play . . ."

"How would it have been done, do you mean?" the doctor asked. "A murder?"

Paulik nodded.

"Smothering the patient with a pillow would be the quickest and quietest way, but her life-support machine would have alerted us immediately, thus trapping the murderer."

"And by drugging her?" Paulik asked.

"Yes," answered Dr. D'Almeida. "By putting any number of drugs into her IV, such as potassium. That would be almost an instant death."

"And a not-so-instant method?" Paulik asked.

"Air."

"Excusez-moi?"

"Air injected into the veins with an empty syringe. It stops the heart from pumping. That could take ten minutes or so."

"Long enough for the murderer to get into his car and drive away . . ." Paulik said.

"But we checked . . ." Schoelcher said.

"As did we," Dr. D'Almeida agreed.

"And those drugs could be traced in an autopsy?" Paulik asked.

"Yes, traces could be in her blood. But there're ways to hide that, even from an autopsy—for example, just by slightly increasing the doses of what she was already being given by IV."

"So an autopsy could shed some light, but not necessarily."

"And I'm not sure her parents would agree to it," replied Dr. D'Almeida. "They're in great shock, and are strict Catholics. And as I said, the only people who had access to her room were hospital employees and her parents, and I have a hard time imagining any of them doing such a thing, as you would with your own staff at the Palais de Justice."

Paulik nodded, and briefly turned his head to look at the Cathedral's steeple.

"The head nurse wept," Dr. D'Almeida continued. "We were greatly saddened, especially since it seemed that Mlle Montmory was out of danger. But in medical school we were always told never to assume that."

Hélène Paulik and Victor Bonnard walked together through the vines, stopping every so often to look at them, or to hold a heavy bunch of grapes in their hands. "The harvest will be soon, won't it?" Victor asked.

"Yes, your dad and I would like to hold out just a few more days. After all that surprise rain at the end of August, the grapes just need a little more sun."

"Rain and sun equals weeds," Victor said, leaning down to pull a bunch out of the dry, rocky ground. "I've never seen so many."

"Nor have I," Hélène answered.

"What if there's more rain in the next few days?" Victor asked. "Shouldn't we pick now?"

"That is a danger, and we used to do what you say . . . but we were picking too soon. The right moment to pick is when the sugar and acid are in balance; pick too soon and they'll be out of whack."

Victor looked up at the clear sky. "But if it rains . . ."

"September rain can bring rot, but that can be fought with fungicides. I prefer to take the risk."

Victor saluted Hélène. "Okay, boss!"

"We'll test the sugar content with the Cinsault grapes first, and let's hope it will later give us twelve or thirteen degrees alcohol," Hélène said. "Why am I worried about the Cinsault?"

"Because they're on the northeast slope, down by the road, and so get the least amount of sun."

"Right," Hélène said, smiling. "You have the syringe? Although I suppose I should have asked you that when we started off."

Victor patted the backpack that was on his back. "And we'll check the Syrah next?"

"Yep. I'm not too worried about them, because they're on the southwest hill. But we don't want too much alcohol either. Fifteen degrees alcohol content is too much for my taste."

"More bang for your buck," Victor said, laughing.

Hélène laughed. "I'm glad you're able to help out today," she said. "Thank goodness for teachers' strikes."

"I'd much rather be here than at school, believe me," Victor said. He was careful not to add, "be here with you." He had always followed Hélène Paulik around the vineyard like a puppy, but he had recently been keeping his distance, for he had become completely infatuated with the petite brunette. It wasn't just her looks—thin, muscular, big brown eyes—or her loud laugh. It was her knowledge, and the fact that she never talked down to him. At breakfast that morning, his father had asked Victor to help Hélène in the vines, and although Victor had been reluctant—afraid that he'd show his crush—he was now happily, and easily, walking with her and chatting. He also knew that his father wanted to tour the cellars with that dandy from Paris, who was coming back, and that the cigar-smoking judge would be with them as well.

"You don't much like school, do you?" Hélène asked.

He shook his head and kicked a rock.

"It could come in useful, down the road," Hélène suggested.

"What good is Molière to me when all I want to do is make wine?"

"*Oh voleur, oh voleur!*" Hélène called out, and the two laughed.

"*À l'assassin!*" Victor cried, lunging forward with an imaginary sword. They went down a small hill, between the narrow vines that were still hand-picked. They could hear traffic on the departmental road that went between Aix and Rognes.

"Let's start here," Hélène said, stopping. "This bunch looks good." She held some grapes in her hand while Victor took off his backpack. "They've already started to shrivel slightly. That's good."

"Lovely Cinsault," Victor said. He squatted, getting their equipment out, but then quickly jumped up. "What the fuck?" he said. "Excuse my language, Hélène."

"What is it, Victor?" Hélène asked. "Too much Molière?"

"There's a pink purse lying over there."

"What?"

He bent down to pick it up but quickly recoiled. "Oh my God!" he yelled, stepping backward and almost falling into Hélène's arms. He turned and fell down on his knees and retched.

"Victor!" Hélène said as she knelt down and rubbed his back.

"Don't look at it, Hélène," he mumbled. She took a Kleenex out of her pocket and gave it to him, then stood up, craning her neck over the thick four-foot-high vines to try to see what lay beyond the pink purse. "Dad, go get Dad," he mumbled.

"What in the world is it?" she asked as she walked to the end of the vine and back up around the other side. "Oh my God." Hélène Paulik held her hand to her mouth and turned around, looking at Victor.

"What happened to her?" he asked, his voice cracking.

Hélène shook her head. "I don't know, I don't know." Her mouth was dry; she kicked herself for not bringing a bottle of water, especially for Victor.

"I can't leave her alone," Hélène replied.

"Why not? She's . . . dead."

"That's why," Hélène said. She came back around the vine and sat down beside Victor. "Out of respect. She's an old woman. Can you go?"

Victor got up and brushed the red dirt off his pants. "Yes."

"Are you sure?"

"Yes. I'll run."

And he was off.

Verlaque rushed to his interview, not at the underfunded hospital where Paulik and Schoelcher now were, but at an elegant former *hôtel particulier* in the Quartier Mazarin. He would have just enough time to speak to the doctor before driving out to Domaine Beauclaire. As soon as he was buzzed in by the secretary, he walked quickly up the stone steps, glancing at the wall frescoes of gardens as he did. The massive wooden door to the doctor's office was open, an elegant woman in her mid-fifties holding it for him. "Come in, Judge," she said, stepping aside. "But I'm afraid Dr. Charnay just left last night for vacation. How may I help you?"

"Dr. Charnay visited a patient last Thursday in the hospital. . . ."

The secretary looked at him as if he were a dimwit. "Dr. Charnay regularly visits his patients in the hospital, Judge."

"Yes, I would assume so, Mme . . ."

"Blanc."

"Mme Blanc," he continued. "We're interviewing all hospital staff who paid this woman a visit, because she died while in the hospital. Dr. Charnay wasn't this woman's general practitioner, so I'd like to know why he visited the young woman."

The secretary flinched for the briefest of moments. "Dr. Charnay is an otolaryngologist."

"Excuse me?"

"An ear-nose-and-throat specialist. It's very likely she was one of his patients."

Verlaque nodded. "Could I see his patient list, Mme Blanc?"

"You may."

"Thank you," Verlaque said. He felt as if he were walking on eggshells.

"Next week," she added, "when the doctor returns from his vacation."

"Where is he?"

"The doctor?" the secretary answered. "I believe he's in . . . the Ardèche."

Verlaque stared at the woman. "I'm an examining magistrate, madame," he said. "And I can look . . ."

"*Cher monsieur,*" she answered, "I don't care what kind of judge you are. Please have some respect for my position as the keeper of the doctor's records while he is away. You may look at them with Dr. Charnay's permission, next week."

Verlaque opened his mouth to speak, but the sound that was heard in the office was his cell phone ringing. He excused himself and took the call, seeing it was Bruno Paulik on the other end. "*Oui,* Bruno?"

"Sorry to disturb, sir. But I have bad news."

"Go on, Bruno."

"We found Mme d'Arras's body; she's been dead for a few days."

"I see," he answered, glancing in the direction of the secretary, who was watering a small plant on her desk and seemed to be speaking to it. "I'll be right there. Tell me where to find you."

He hung up and said to Mme Blanc, "I have to go, but I'll be back, with or without Dr. Charnay's permission to look at his patient list. Thank you for your . . . your . . ."

"Goodbye, Judge," she answered quickly, walking across the room to hold the door open for him. "I will tell the doctor you called."

Chapter Sixteen

౿

A Love Story

*T*he Bonnards sat at their twelve-foot-long wooden kitchen table with Antoine Verlaque and Bruno and Hélène Paulik. "If you want to cry, son, go ahead," Olivier Bonnard said to Victor, reaching over to put a hand on his shoulder.

"Bugger off, Dad!" Victor said. He got up and left the table so quickly he almost upset his chair.

"What did I say?" Olivier asked.

Élise Bonnard rolled her eyes and tilted her head in the direction of Hélène Paulik.

"Oh . . ." Olivier and Élise had talked about Victor's crush on Hélène. Olivier felt stupid and realized that he would once again have to apologize to his son. Or perhaps he should just let it go? Pretend that he and Élise hadn't noticed the crush?

"Olivier?" Élise said. "Bruno asked you a question."

"I know harvest is around the corner," Paulik repeated, "but we'll have to rope off part of that vineyard as a crime scene. Will that be a problem?"

Olivier Bonnard shrugged. "Cinsault is a bulk grape, so it's not a catastrophe. It's never good to lose grapes, but we'll just have to deal with it."

"We'll try to disturb as little as possible," said Paulik. "Unfortunately, last night's rain will have removed any foot or tire prints."

"What happened to her?" Olivier asked.

Verlaque leaned forward. "Someone hit her on the head with a rock. We don't know if it happened in the vineyard or if her body was dragged there; we'll be able to establish that after the autopsy."

"Oh, my word," Élise said. "*Chez nous!*"

"And that purse?" Hélène Paulik asked.

Bruno Paulik turned to his wife and rubbed her shoulders. "Her wallet was gone, so there's a chance it was a robbery."

"Imagine that," Élise said. "Killing an old woman for money."

Paulik and Verlaque exchanged looks; they were both thinking of the same person: Didier Ruère, who three years ago attacked an elderly woman in Aix in order to steal her purse. The old woman lived, and Ruère was thrown in jail, but he would soon be released, if he hadn't been already.

The kitchen door opened and an elderly man walked in, wearing a plaid wool beret. "Dad!" Olivier Bonnard said.

The old man looked at the people gathered around the table. "What's going on? A meeting of some kind?"

"Sort of," Olivier answered. "We're meeting with Hélène and her husband . . . you know him . . . Bruno . . . we're just discussing the . . ."

"The new proposal to build an *hypermarché* in Rognes," Élise said. "Commissioner Paulik and his colleague are giving us ideas on how to stop the megastore from being built."

"Very good, very good," Albert Bonnard said. "Well, I'm going up into the vines to check on them."

Olivier shot up out of his seat. "I'll go with you, Dad."

Élise Bonnard mouthed the word "Alzheimer's" to Verlaque, and he nodded slightly in acknowledgment. He thought of Mme d'Arras, found dead in the vines, her body now at the morgue in Aix, and how she too had probably had the disease.

"As you wish," replied Albert Bonnard.

When Olivier and the old man had left, Élise said, "Albert takes long naps in the afternoon, thank goodness. He slept through everything; I was worried he would hear the ambulance come into the courtyard, but he didn't. They didn't have their sirens on, since she was . . ."

"He must be upset about the wine thefts," Bruno Paulik said.

Élise shrugged. "Oddly enough, he's taking it better than we thought he would. He even told us the other day that he preferred a French thief over a German."

"German?" Hélène asked.

"He's talking about the war again," Élise replied. "He does that now and again. He was a small boy when his uncle Bertrand was killed because he was *un résistant*. With the dementia, all that stuff is coming back to him."

On his way back into Aix, Verlaque telephoned Marine and proposed that they have dinner at a restaurant in the perched village of Ventabren, a fifteen-minute drive west of Aix. It was a clear, warm night, and they'd be able to eat out on the restaurant's terrace, which had a view south almost to the sea. The chef had just been given his first Michelin star, and Verlaque was relieved that they were open and that he was able to reserve the last remaining table.

"It's odd, these stories," Verlaque said, once they had been seated and were sipping Champagne, "how they're all beginning to overlap. Mme d'Arras's body found not far from Rognes, in the Bonnards' vineyard. Coincidence?"

Marine crossed her arms and stared at Verlaque. "No, I don't think so."

"Really?" Verlaque bit into a petit four and waited for Marine to answer.

"It's *too* coincidental," she said. "What was Pauline d'Arras doing in Rognes, and why did she meet her death there, so close to where she grew up and where there have been recent wine thefts?" Marine picked up one of the petits fours and tasted it. "Oh my," she said, wiping her mouth with a large white linen napkin, "what's in these things?"

"Sun-dried tomatoes?" Verlaque asked. "Mme d'Arras's Filo-fax was still in her purse. "We'll go over it tomorrow morning; her lists of phone numbers and appointments may be useful."

"People still use Filofaxes?"

"You do if you don't have a cell phone," Verlaque answered. "And I may go visit Mme d'Arras's sister Clothilde, who's a nun in the southwest. Care to join me?"

Marine shook her head. "Tempting, but I have too much work, and way too many useless meetings to prepare for the new semes-ter. I was supposed to hand in my syllabus two weeks ago. This happens every year—I think I have all summer to prepare and then, all of a sudden, *c'est la rentrée.*" *I'm still not telling him about the lump: the little pea.*

"It's not like you weren't doing anything." Verlaque leaned back so that the waitress could bring their first course, a sea bream delicately spiced with chervil and tarragon, surrounded by thinly sliced potato rounds. "How's your writing going, anyway?"

"I'm very excited about it," Marine answered, cutting into her fish. "You gave me the strength to move on and try another disci-pline. I've picked my subject for the biography and started research-ing. It's not law-related, which somehow feels very liberating."

"But you seemed sad the other day," Verlaque said.

Marine set her fork down. *Perhaps it is time.* "Yes, I was. But going to church helped, and today I had a long talk with . . . my doctor."

Verlaque leaned forward across the table. "Doctor? Marine, what's going on? Are you ill?"

"I found a small lump in my breast last week," she replied. "And . . ."

"Why didn't you tell me?"

"Because it may be benign—we don't know yet. I'm having a bit of it taken out tomorrow morning, at the hospital."

"You should have told me!" Verlaque said. "I'll go with you." Just then his cell phone, which was sitting on the table, beeped.

"Shit!" Verlaque cried in English. "I'm sorry, Marine, it's Bruno. I'll have to take this." He grabbed his telephone and left the restaurant's terrace to cross the tiny village street so that he was out of earshot of the restaurant's patrons.

Marine watched him, admiring his thick black-and-gray hair and broad shoulders, which were hunched over as he spoke. She was glad she had been honest with him; it had been her father's advice, and her doctor's. But something about Antoine's reaction bothered her. She couldn't put her finger on it.

Her doctor had felt the lump that morning and was confident. "Most of these are benign, Marine," she had said. "Noncancerous breast lesions are very common, and they are never life-threatening. We'll take a sample of it, but don't worry. I'll set up an appointment for you. It's a fast procedure: you'll be in and out in a jiffy. Are you afraid of needles?"

Marine shook her head. "No. Worms, yes; deep seawater, yes. Needles, no."

Her gynecologist smiled and explained the procedure that a radiologist at the clinic would perform with a thin, hollow needle.

"He or she will take some fluid from the cyst with the needle and perhaps use an ultrasound to guide positioning the needle. The fluid will then be sent off to the lab."

Marine had walked home, not happy exactly, but calmer than she had been in days. She spent the afternoon reading a dull but thorough biography of her subject that had been written in the 1960s. She hadn't seen the time go by and was still reading when Verlaque called her, suggesting dinner out. It was a fantastic idea, and she treated herself by running across the street to agnès b. and buying a blouse that she had been eyeing. She had been waiting for the blouse to go on sale, but agnès b. rarely did sales, and when they did it was for clothes that no one wanted. It was frivolous to do this the night before a biopsy, but she wanted to think of other things. That very night she wore the blouse, which was covered in pink roses, with white jeans and flat Tropézienne leather sandals.

She sipped on some white wine but put her glass down the moment she saw Verlaque's face as he crossed the restaurant's terrace, his phone call ended.

"You don't look so good," Marine said. "What's up?"

"Your intuition may be right," he replied, sitting down. "A young woman's body has been found in Rognes."

"Another one?" Marine asked. She felt sick to her stomach.

"Yes. She was raped and strangled, like Mlle Montmory, that girl from Éguilles." He leaned back. "I'm not hungry anymore." He realized that he would not be able to go to the doctor's with Marine in the morning, would have to go straight to the Palais de Justice.

"Nor am I," Marine answered. "We can cancel the rest of the meal, can't we?"

Verlaque nodded and went into the restaurant. "It's not a problem, we can go," he said when he returned. "They hadn't started cooking our main dish yet."

He left a stack of one-euro coins on the table as a tip, and they walked to his car, arm in arm. "Why didn't you tell me?" he asked.

"I'm not sure," Marine answered truthfully.

Verlaque sighed. "I'll try to go with you tomorrow morning."

"That's really not necessary," Marine answered. "With this new murder, you'll be needed elsewhere." She could hear Sylvie's voice: "Martyr!" She changed the subject. "This really is a picturesque village. . . ."

Verlaque looked at Marine and wondered what she was *really* thinking. "Yes," he replied. "And so close to Aix."

"The chef wasn't upset that we had to leave?" she asked.

"I promised him we'd come back, with friends. How about Jean-Marc and Pierre?"

Marine stopped at Verlaque's antique Porsche. "Perfect. And maybe we can invite José and his wife, Carmé."

"Good idea. You spoke with her a lot at the party," Verlaque said. He knew that they both wanted to talk of other, lighter things, if only for a few minutes.

"Yes, she's funny and bright. And not as unctuous as that Philippe Léridon. Yuck."

"He's Mme d'Arras's neighbor," Verlaque said, frowning. "I'm going to go and speak with him."

"When did this woman from Rognes die?" Marine asked as they got into the car.

"Dr. Bouvet is performing an autopsy tomorrow morning," Verlaque answered. "He said that the body had been there, in the woman's house, at least two, maybe three days."

"Who found her?"

"Her ex-boyfriend, who came by the house because she wasn't

returning his phone calls. In the meantime, we've got a killer who has raped twice, and definitely murdered once, if it's the same guy." Verlaque stayed silent as he drove the car down the twisty road from Ventabren's old town to the flat *route nationale* that led back through the valley to Aix. "I'd like you to sleep at my place until we find this guy," he finally said.

"Okay," Marine answered. "If you just double-park in front of my apartment, I'll run up and get my stuff."

"Is Sylvie back yet from Mégève? Can she take you to the clinic tomorrow, if I can't?"

"Yes, but Charlotte starts school tomorrow."

Verlaque said, "Imagine coming from a place as mythical as Mégève."

"That's why she's such a great skier," Marine replied.

"That's for sure. She can ski backward—I've seen her do it. She's a much better skier than I am. But, then again, Charlotte can ski better than I can," Verlaque said, smiling.

Marine looked over at him and squeezed his knee. A year ago, Antoine Verlaque would never had made such a joke. She would only see glimpses of his warmth; then he would quickly clam up, as if he were stopping himself from revealing too much. Something had changed, for the better. He was now more honest and natural, but she noted that the subject of her breast lump had been dropped.

They quickly got back to Aix, and Verlaque waited in his car, double-parked in front of agnès b., while Marine gathered her things. She was back in the car in five minutes, balancing a load of books on her knee. Verlaque pulled away from the curb and tilted his head to look at the spines. "Jean-Paul Sartre," he said. "I should have known you'd pick him. You're writing his biography, right?"

Marine smiled. "Not only his."

Verlaque turned right and drove up the Rue Frédéric Mistral. "You're writing two books?" He looked again at the stack of books on her lap. "Simone de Beauvoir! That's a heavy project. They both lived, and worked, a long time. Two books is perhaps overdoing it, don't you think?"

"One book," Marine answered. "I'm not writing about their philosophies or their works. I'm writing about their relationship. It's a love story."

Chapter Seventeen

❧

Malibu Boy

*B*runo Paulik leaned his thick forearms across Verlaque's desk. "'Gisèle Durand,'" he read aloud from a file. "'Age forty-two. Born and raised in Rognes. Both parents deceased; an older brother who emigrated to the U.S. more than twenty years ago. She worked for thirteen years at a small clothing store in the village, but it recently closed. She's been unemployed for six months. Body found by ex-boyfriend, André Prodos, age thirty-seven. Apparently, he had been trying to call her but kept getting the answering machine, and so yesterday evening, after work, he went by her apartment.'"

"Where does he work?" Verlaque asked.

Paulik looked at the file. "He's a mechanic in Pertuis."

"Let's find out everything we can about him. And the clothing-store owner? If they worked together for thirteen years, he or she would be a good source."

"Right," Paulik said. He turned the page of the file and read. "The clothing-store owner is Laure Matour. It gives an address in

Rognes here for her, and a cell-phone number. No cell-phone number for the ex-boyfriend, but a landline, and I think I know where the garage is." He turned to Jules Schoelcher. "Got your little book with you?"

Jules Schoelcher patted his right breast pocket. "I'll start right away?"

"Yes," Paulik answered. "Flamant will be working with you."

"Look for any connections between the two women," Verlaque said. "Dr. Bouvet told Commissioner Paulik last night that Mlle Durand was attacked in the same way that Mlle Montmory was, and that the marks on her neck were similar. Strangulation, this one successful, at the throat, with bare hands. The two women have very different profiles: one a good fifteen years older than the other; the younger one from a good family with a good steady job, the other unemployed with no family in the area. So we need to find out what they had in common—where they did their shopping, if they went to church, if they ever lived in the same building, anything. Go to their apartments and go through their desks: look at their bills, letters, receipts from purchases, phone calls in and out, everything." Verlaque's telephone rang; he glanced down at the caller's number. "It's Bouvet.

"*Oui?*" Verlaque said into the phone. "You're already finished? It's only nine-fifteen a.m."

"I started at six this morning, I was so pissed off at this attack," the coroner said. "Besides, when you get to be my age, you sleep less and less. You'll see."

"Thanks for the warning."

"Mlle Durand was raped and strangled on Friday evening—as best I can determine, between six and eight p.m. There's some skin under her fingernails that I'm going to send to the lab; she may have scratched her attacker. And I've started examining Mme

Pauline d'Arras. She died around the same time, between six and eight p.m. on Friday, and she was killed right there, in the vineyard. Tell your guys to look for a bloodstained rock about the size of a baseball. I'll be in touch." He hung up.

Verlaque had just repeated the gist of the conversation to Paulik and Schoelcher when there was a knock on the door. "Come in," he said.

Alain Flamant came in, holding a red Filofax. "Lots of good stuff here," he said.

"Thank goodness for pen and paper," Verlaque said. "Sit down."

"Mme d'Arras made a visit to her lawyer ten days ago," Flamant said. "And her husband didn't know about it."

"How do you know?" asked Paulik.

"Because she wrote beside the appointment time, 'Don't tell Gilles.'"

Verlaque laughed, despite the heaviness of the morning's news and the stuffiness of his office. He got up and opened the window. "Who's the lawyer?"

"It just says Maître Bley."

"Éric Bley," Verlaque said. "I'll go and see him." He was about to speak when another knock sounded.

"Your office is like Charles de Gaulle airport on a long weekend," Paulik said.

"Hello, gentlemen," Yves Roussel said as he entered the room.

Flamant leaned over toward Jules Schoelcher. "Prosecutor Roussel."

"We're in quite a fix," Roussel said, pacing the room. Bruno Paulik bent down, put his elbows on his knees, and turned his head sideways to look at Roussel's feet.

"You're not wearing your turquoise cowboy boots," Paulik said.

"They're getting resoled," Roussel said, glancing down at his feet. "While you guys were in here chatting and drinking coffee, I just had to make my way through a crowd of reporters who are standing outside the front doors. Even the national stations are out there; TF1 and M6! The attacker of the girl in Éguilles, and now this woman in Rognes, are one and the same, I take it?"

"Yes," Verlaque replied. "Bouvet just confirmed that likelihood."

"And the old lady?"

"Mme d'Arras," Verlaque said curtly. "I think it was a coincidence that she was attacked in Rognes, but her murder and Mlle Durand's were both committed between six and eight p.m. on Friday night. Her killing was very different, and her wallet was gone, although the wallet could have been taken to throw us off."

"Well, get me someone to arrest, and quickly!" Roussel said.

Verlaque ate a sandwich at his desk and called Marine's cell phone. "Marine, how are you?" he asked when she answered on the second ring.

"Fine," she answered.

"And your father was able to take you to the appointment?"

"Yes. He wanted to come into the room, where they did the puncture, but I wouldn't let him."

"And how are you feeling now?"

"I feel good; I'm trying to read, but I'm having trouble concentrating. Send me on an errand if you can."

Verlaque pushed his half-eaten sandwich aside. "Do you really want something to do?"

"Yes, I said so."

"Two things, then, if you really want to," Verlaque said. "Your friend Philomène. Could you pay her a visit and ask her if this address—6 Rue de la Conception, in Rognes—means anything to her?"

"Fine," Marine said, writing the address down on the back of an envelope. "Is that where the Durand woman lived, and was murdered on Friday night?"

"Yes. And I was hoping to ask Éric Bley some questions, but we have an appointment any minute with an ex-thief who attacked an old woman a few years ago, and then I'd like to go to Rognes. Would you be able to go over to Bley's office as you've known him for ages?"

"Yes," Marine answered slowly. "Why?"

"Bley is the d'Arras family lawyer, and Mme d'Arras had an appointment with him last week that she was keeping from her husband. His office is on the Rue Thiers."

"I know it," Marine said. "I'll go." She sat back in her chair and rested the phone on her chest for a second. Éric Bley had asked her out twice in the past year, and both times she had turned him down. "I'll call you as soon as I have any answers," she said.

"Thanks."

"You guys work quickly," Didier Ruère said, twisting in his seat and crossing his legs. "My parole officer called me and here I am, right on time, at twelve-thirty p.m."

"Then I'll get to the point quickly, so you can go to lunch," Verlaque said. "Where were you on Friday evening between six and eight o'clock?"

"Wait a minute!" Ruère replied. "I saw the news this morning! I wasn't anywhere near Rognes!"

"Good. Where were you?"

Ruère paused. "I was . . . Let's see, Friday evening . . . Oh yeah! I remember! I was here in Aix, at the Bar de Zinc, on the Rue Espariat. You can ask anyone."

"We will," Paulik replied. "Who else was there?"

"My buddy Louis," Ruère said. "We watched the Marseille

soccer game on the bar's television. The waiter and barman know us and will be able to vouch for us. We left around nine p.m., 'cause we were hungry and all the bar has to eat are peanuts."

Verlaque watched beads of perspiration form on Ruère's forehead. "You'll leave us Louis's phone number, please," he said.

"Of course."

Verlaque slipped Ruère a piece of paper, and the thief wrote down a cell-phone number, his hand shaking.

"Saved by the beautiful game," Paulik said.

Ruère smiled weakly. "I just wish Marseille would win once in a while."

Marine walked to the top of her street and down the Rue d'Italie a block, then turned right on Rue Cardinale. She walked down the right side of the street and rang the doorbell at number 18, at the buzzer marked "Joubert." There was no answer; she waited and rang again. She looked up the street and heard the organ playing in Saint-Jean de Malte, so she walked up toward the church. Perhaps Philomène was at choir practice. A crowd of locals and tourists were on the cobbled square in front of the church, coming and going from the Musée Granet, which was showing a colossal Cézanne exhibit. She and Verlaque had been invited to a special showing before the exhibit had officially opened and had come away with admiration for Cézanne that bordered on fanaticism on Verlaque's part. She walked into the church and stood for a few minutes at the back, listening to the music. She saw Frère Benoît, a monk, coming down the aisle and approached him, introducing herself as the daughter of the Drs. Bonnet.

"Pleased to meet you," Frère Benoît said. "Are you looking for Père Jean-Luc? He's over at the Cézanne exhibit, for the third time."

Marine laughed. "It is a great show," she said. "I'm actually looking for Philomène Joubert. I'm her neighbor."

"Ah, Mme Joubert isn't here, as you can see. She's with some of the other parishioners on a pilgrimage to Santiago de Compostela. They should be somewhere around Conques by now."

Marine's heart sank. "They're doing the whole thing? That would take months!"

"Oh no," Frère Benoît replied. "Only two weeks at a time; they're doing another stretch in the winter. She even convinced M. Joubert to go along."

"And can she be contacted?" Marine asked.

"With much difficulty," the brother replied. "They have no cell phones and are sleeping in hospices that I would describe as extremely rustic. Is it an emergency?"

"No," Marine replied. "Thank you."

She walked away and out into the bright sunshine. Was it an emergency? She wasn't sure. What if Philomène did know the address? What if there was a connection? She turned around and ran back into the church, hurrying up the aisle to catch Frère Benoît before he entered the sacristy. "I think it might be an emergency," she said.

Frère Benoît turned around and nodded. "Very well."

"It concerns the . . . violent death . . . of Pauline d'Arras. She and Mme Joubert grew up together."

"I see. Why don't you call me this evening, after Vespers, around eight-thirty p.m.? I'll try to find a phone number for one of the hospices along the route."

"*Merci, mon frère*," Marine said. She walked up the Rue Cardinale and then north along the Rue d'Italie, which at the top of the street would turn into the Rue Thiers. Once on the Rue Thiers, she stopped and looked in the windows of Cinderella, a shoe store that had been there since she was a little girl, and where her mother had bought shoes when she herself was small, in the 1950s. Most of the shoes were old-fashioned and sensible, with low heels and good-quality leather, although they did have some multicolored Repetto ballerina flats. The shop was still closed for lunch, and Marine walked on, knowing that she was procrastinating. She wondered if Éric Bley would also still be out, but it was almost 2:30 p.m. When she rang at his office, she was buzzed in, and walked up the elegant stone staircase to the Bley brothers' law offices on the second floor.

"Hello," Marine said to the well-dressed secretary, "I'm an old friend of Maître Bley's, and was wondering if he is in."

"I'll ring his office," the woman said. "What is your name?"

"Marine Bonnet. Dr. Bonnet." She rarely used her doctoral title, except on occasions when she thought it might help her get more efficient service.

The secretary called Éric Bley, spoke for a few seconds, and then told Marine that she could go on in, the second door on the left.

As Marine gently opened the door, Éric Bley was already halfway across the room to meet her. They stood awkwardly facing each other, not sure if they should shake hands or exchange *la bise*. Marine broke the silence by laughing. "*Quand même*," she said, "we should do the *bise*. We've known each other long enough."

Bley laughed. "You're right. I joined the choir just because you were in it." He put a hand gently on her waist and they kissed each other's cheeks.

Marine's face flushed, and she stepped back. "You really joined the choir for me?"

"No, my mother forced us to join. But you were an added bonus for us Bley brothers."

Marine laughed.

"How are you?" Bley asked, stepping back to look at her.

"Fine," she answered. "Thanks for letting me visit." She quickly took in Bley's delicate features: his long aquiline nose, thin lips, and pale-blue eyes. His hair was receding, which only showed off his fine tanned forehead, his eyes, and his high cheekbones. As teenagers, Marine and her girlfriends had nicknamed him "Malibu Boy."

"You're welcome," he said. "But this isn't a social call, is it?"

"No," Marine said. "Do you have a few minutes?"

Bley nodded and motioned to a chair, then walked around to the far side of his oversized wooden desk, the same desk his grandfather had used, in the same office. Marine sat down and set her purse on the floor; as she did so, her silk top slipped off her left shoulder. She quickly readjusted the blouse and looked up to see Bley staring at her. He had seen the small bandage on her upper chest, where the puncture for the biopsy had been performed.

"Are you all right?" Bley asked.

Marine sat up straight. "Yes, I'm fine."

"I'm sorry. I shouldn't have asked."

"It's all right," Marine answered. "I went in for a biopsy this morning; that's why the bandage's there. It didn't hurt, but it was extremely uncomfortable. It's hard to describe."

"I'm sorry," Bley said. "When will they know something?"

"Possibly by the end of the day," she answered. "My dad put a phone call through to the lab to hurry things up." Marine's father was Aix's most sought-after general practitioner; he had been the Bley family doctor for years.

Bley reached across the desk and squeezed Marine's hand. "I'll keep my fingers crossed."

Marine smiled. "Thank you, Éric."

"So . . . what's going on?" he asked.

"It's Mme d'Arras's death," Marine said. "And you're the family lawyer. . . ."

"That's right."

"We know that Mme d'Arras had an appointment with you that she wanted to keep from her husband."

Bley nodded. "That's confidential, Marine."

"But she was murdered," Marine said. "On Friday night."

"What?" Bley asked, his face ashen. "I heard this morning that she died, but not how. I was in Paris all weekend and just came back on the morning train. I'm speechless. How did it happen?"

"We don't know yet. Her body was found in a vineyard; she had been hit on the side of the head with a rock, and her wallet was missing."

Bley sat back and ran his fingers through his hair. "What do you want to know? And why are you here, and not the police? Or are law professors branching out these days?"

"I'm helping Antoine Verlaque."

Bley stayed silent for a few seconds and then said, "Still seeing him, are you?"

Marine nodded. "We need to know why Mme d'Arras had to keep the appointment with you a secret," she said. "It seemed an odd secret to keep: I'm told that she and her husband did everything together."

"Poor Gilles," said Bley. "Yes, they were inseparable. But Mme d'Arras came to see me about her money, the Aubanel family fortune."

"Ah, I see."

"She had a separate section of the will, independent of what she and Gilles had written up. I can show it to you if you have a warrant—which, since you're not a police officer, I assume you don't."

"No, I don't. But Judge Verlaque doesn't need one."

"Then send him over," Bley said, his voice curt. "I might even ask why you're here instead of him."

Marine knew that she was now being punished for dating Antoine and for turning down Bley's advances. It was also, as Bley had pointed out, unusual that Verlaque had sent her on this mission. She thanked him and got up, shaking his hand this time, and quickly left the office. Out on the stairs, she called Verlaque's cell phone.

"Hey, it's me," she said. "How soon can you walk over to Éric Bley's office?"

"In about two minutes," Verlaque said. "I can practically see it from my office."

"He won't tell me what Mme d'Arras came for, but it has to do with her will."

"I'll be right there."

"And as an examining magistrate, you don't need a warrant, right?"

"Correct. Just my badge."

She hung up and sat on the stairs, which were surprisingly cold given the warm September day. She pulled out a slim volume of Simone de Beauvoir's memoirs and began reading, but after a few lines her mind started wandering, and she put the book away. She realized that she had just told Éric Bley more about her state of health than she had told her boyfriend, at least until their dinner last night. Was it because she wanted to be strong and healthy for Antoine Verlaque? Was she afraid that he wouldn't be supportive if she fell ill? Or was it because she had known Éric Bley since they were children, and as all of Aix knew—at least her set of friends and acquaintances—Bley had recently nursed his elderly father through a long and painful cancer?

Verlaque arrived in two minutes, as he had predicted, and bounded up the stairs. "Lead me to him," he said, kissing Marine.

They walked into the office, interrupting the secretary and Bley, who were deep in conversation.

"*Bonjour*, Maître Bley," Verlaque said, and strode across the reception room to shake the lawyer's hand. "I'm Antoine Verlaque, examining magistrate of Aix-en-Provence. Do you have a minute?"

Bley motioned with a wave of his hand for Verlaque and Marine to enter his office, and closed the door once they were settled. Verlaque removed his badge from his jacket and showed it to Bley. As required, the lawyer laid it on his desk. "You'd like to see the changes Mme d'Arras made to her will?"

"Please," Verlaque said.

"Mme d'Arras made the changes to her *private* will," Marine explained. "She had her own fortune, from the Aubanel family."

Bley removed a file from a turn-of-the-century wooden filing cabinet that had obviously been purchased along with the desk decades earlier, and set it on the desk, beside Verlaque's badge. He opened the file folder and turned to a typewritten page on his office's letterhead.

Verlaque leaned over and put his reading glasses on. "What exactly did she change?" he asked as he read. "It seems that she is giving her fortune, eight hundred ninety thousand euros, to the"— he bent down closer to look—"Société pour la Prévention de la Cruauté Envers les Animaux," he said. He took off his reading glasses and looked at Bley. "The SPCA?"

Bley nodded.

"Who was the recipient before she changed it?" Marine asked.

"Her nephew," Bley replied. "Christophe Chazeau."

Chapter Eighteen

❧

Verlaque Suspects a Friend

Y ou're an ass!" Fabrice yelled into the phone. "I never thought I'd say that about you, Antoine, but you're a total ass! Christophe just called me; he said that the prosecutor was raking him over the coals."

"I'm sorry, Fabrice," Verlaque said, "but Christophe's aunt was murdered on Friday night, and he was disinherited a few days prior to that."

"He was with us Friday night, or don't you remember?"

"He would have had time to go to Rognes," Verlaque answered. "Before the party."

"And how did he know he was disinherited?" Fabrice asked. "Huh? Huh? Answer me that!"

"Mme d'Arras called Christophe's mother, her sister Natalie, and told her. M. d'Arras confirmed that today."

Fabrice stayed silent for a few seconds. "It's all very circumstantial. And you arrest him for that?"

"I didn't arrest him, Fabrice," Verlaque replied. "I only called him in for questioning. He's at home now."

"He must feel like shit. Way to go."

Verlaque didn't tell Fabrice that, while he was questioning Christophe, Officers Flamant and Schoelcher were out in the parking lot, taking samples of mud from the tires of Chazeau's new Porsche SUV. "What's most unfortunate is that he doesn't have an alibi for Friday night from the time he left work at five-thirty p.m. until he came to the cigar-club dinner at eight p.m.," Verlaque said.

"I'm not sure I have an alibi for those hours!" Fabrice yelled into the phone. "So am I a murderer?"

"Don't be ridiculous," Verlaque said.

"You're upsetting *la fraternité*! We're a club!"

"'We few, we happy few, we band of brothers . . .'"

"*What* are you going on about? *No one* is happy at the moment, especially poor Christophe. I'm going to hang up now, Antoine, and I want you to think very hard about what you've just done. Goodbye."

Verlaque hung up and put his head on his desk, resting it on his forearms. Someone knocked at the door. "*Entrez*," he said without looking up.

"Oh, sorry, sir," Jules Schoelcher said. "Should I come back?"

"No, no. What is it?" Verlaque lifted his head.

"Since it rained the other night, M. Chazeau's car was pretty clean. . . ."

"*Merde.*"

"But there was some dried mud clinging to the inside of the wheel well that we managed to scrape off. It's already in the lab."

"Excellent," Verlaque said. "Let's hope it's not from a vineyard."

"Sorry, sir?"

"Christophe Chazeau is a friend."

"Oh, I see. That must be very awkward."

"To say the least. Have you seen the commissioner around?" Verlaque asked.

"Yes, he's at his desk."

"Could you send him in, with Flamant, please? You come back too."

"Certainly, sir."

Within minutes, the three men were in Verlaque's office. "Please tell me that there's something linking Mlles Durand and Montmory," Verlaque said.

"*Nada*," Paulik answered. "We've checked all we can think of, from hairdressers to dentists."

Verlaque said, "Keep going over everything. I'm going to meet with Gisèle Durand's old boss from the clothing shop. She works in Aix now, and we're to meet at a café in"—he looked at his watch—"five minutes. Keep me posted if you find anything, and I'll see you all here tomorrow morning, in my office, at nine."

Verlaque had suggested a café on the Rue Gaston Saporta that he rarely went to, where he knew he wouldn't run into people he knew, especially cigar-club members; they tended to frequent the cafés on the Cours Mirabeau, their favorite being the Mazarin. He wanted Mlle Matour—or Mme? he wasn't sure if she was married—to feel as comfortable as possible. He was relieved that she now worked in Aix and he didn't have to drive to Rognes to meet her. When he got to the café, a few minutes late, he scanned the terrace for women who looked as if they might work in the garment industry in Provence. Since most of the patrons looked either like preppy-type Sciences Po students who had come to Aix before the term started, in a mad rush to find an overpriced studio apartment, or like old men drinking pastis, the choice was easy.

"Excuse me," he said, leaning down over the only woman who was alone. "Mlle Matour?"

"*Oui*," she said, holding her hand out for Verlaque to shake it. "Sit down . . . please."

Verlaque sat down and ordered a coffee from the waiter, who then disappeared.

"Thanks for agreeing to meet on such short notice," Verlaque said.

"You'll have to excuse me if I'm not good company," Mlle Matour said, taking a drag on her cigarette and then placing it in the ashtray. "I'm in shock over Gisèle's . . . murder. There, I said that word. I never thought I'd have to say 'murder' along with the name of someone I knew."

"I'm very sorry," Verlaque said. "You worked with Mlle Durand a long time, didn't you?"

"Twelve years. She was a good employee, and I hope a good friend."

"You hope?" Verlaque asked.

Mlle Matour nodded, taking another drag on her cigarette. "I worked alongside her for twelve years, but when I look back on it, I'm not sure we were ever friends. Colleagues, yes, but friends?"

"Was she hard to get to know?"

"Yeah. Easy to like, but hard to get to know. I think she had a bad childhood, and then seemed to pick rough guys as boyfriends. It never worked out. They flocked to her, though."

"*Ah bon?*"

"Yeah, she was a beauty. Still, even into her forties, she got mistaken for a woman in her late twenties or early thirties. Petite, healthy hair, clear olive skin. The poor thing." Mlle Matour lowered her head and rubbed her eyes, crying softly.

Verlaque looked across the street at the Cathedral's Gothic statues, guarding its front doors, and waited for Mlle Matour to collect herself.

"Who needs a drink?" she finally said, wiping her eyes on a paper napkin.

"Pastis?" Verlaque asked. He looked at her streaked, dyed hair and tattooed shoulder and guessed that she might like the anise-flavored drink.

"I will if you will," she replied, a smile forming at the edges of her mouth.

"*Allez,*" Verlaque said, waving to the waiter. "*Deux pastis, s'il vous plaît!*"

Mlle Matour took a deep breath and said, "You don't know who did it, do you?"

"No, not yet." He paused and then said, "Do you?"

Mlle Matour shrugged. "Any one of her useless past boy-friends, except the last one, André. One of them . . . Georges . . . I had to chase out of the shop with a broom."

Verlaque smiled. He liked her spunk. "Can you give me a list of names?"

"Delighted."

The waiter brought two tall, thin glasses with an inch of yellow liquid in the bottom of each, a carafe of water, a bowl of ice cubes, and two swizzle sticks.

"*Merci,*" Verlaque said. "May I?" he asked Mlle Matour, holding the carafe of water over her glass of pastis.

She nodded. "Go ahead. I'll tell you when to stop."

He poured the water in, watching the pastis turn cloudy. Mlle Matour signaled with her hand and he stopped, then poured water into his own glass and stirred in two ice cubes.

"Chin-chin," Mlle Matour said, holding her glass up to his.

"Salut," he answered. He took a sip of pastis, surprised at how refreshing it tasted. He loved licorice, and yet this was a drink he rarely ordered. Was it out of snobbishness? he wondered.

"You either love it or hate it," Mlle Matour said.

"Pastis?"

"Or licorice in general."

"You're right. Like coriander," he said, thinking of his love of the herb, and Marine's dislike.

"Or . . . oysters."

"Love them," he answered, smiling.

"I hate them."

The waiter brought a small bowl of peanuts and one of popcorn, setting them down on the table.

"Why did you close your shop?" Verlaque asked, taking some popcorn.

"Too hard to compete with the big clothing stores in Aix, especially since they've built that new shopping complex at the bottom of the *cours.*"

"I'm sorry about that," Verlaque replied. "I can't imagine who wanted it, except for the real-estate promoters, big clothing-store chains, and the mayor. And Mlle Durand left when you closed the shop?"

"Yes. I found a job in Aix straightaway, and I encouraged her to do the same. I even offered to drive her into Aix, since she didn't drive. But she sort of got depressed, I think, and then rarely went out."

"Was she dating André Prodos at the time?"

Mlle Matour drank some pastis and nodded. "Yes, but they broke up about a month or two after I closed the shop. He's an okay guy, if you want to know. I ran into him shortly after they broke up, and he seemed pretty sad. He said that he just couldn't get her out of her blues, so they stopped seeing each other. But he still called her now and again. I think he really loved her."

"He found her," Verlaque said. "Last night."

"Oh my God. I didn't know that." Mlle Matour lit another cigarette. "Poor André. I've seen enough television shows to know that you'll have to question him," she said, taking a drag of her cigarette and blowing out the smoke. "But André's not your man."

Philippe Léridon was relieved that his wife was on a shopping spree in Paris, picking out furniture and drapes for their new house. How could someone take so long looking at fabrics? he wondered. His wife couldn't stand Pauline d'Arras, and now, with the old woman dead . . . murdered . . . any moment now the police would come ringing his doorbell. He knew he must be a suspect; Mme d'Arras had harassed him over and over again, and he had finally blown up at her—in the post office, of all places. And the judge's girlfriend had been there; he had recognized her at the cigar club's party. Who wouldn't recognize her? A tall, thin, elegant woman with hazel eyes and curly auburn hair, and those charming freckles . . .

He walked across his small back lawn; actually, it was big for a downtown garden, narrow but fifty meters deep. The garden had been neglected, and the only plants that remained were two tall palm trees at either edge, near the back, and a couple of oleander plants. He felt his loafers sink down into the grass, surprisingly green and lush for Provence, thanks to the recent unexpected rain, and stopped at the edge of the garden, under a lean-to that his mason had built quickly to protect the digging site. He got down on his hands and knees, removed the tarp, and shone a flashlight below, where his state-of-the-art wine cellar would one day be. He had purposely stopped the construction of his wine cellar and redirected the workers into another big project, the Italian kitchen. Each day, he couldn't wait for his workers—the ones who showed up—to leave, at 6:00 p.m., so that he could go and inspect his prize. He almost shooed them out the front door.

He needed time to decide what to do, and how to do it without anyone's knowing. Mme d'Arras was now no longer around, but her husband could be watching him. Perhaps she had told her husband about Léridon's secret? He looked up at the Hôtel de Barlet's windows, but since the sun was still shining he couldn't see anyone at the windows. It was a risk to come out and look at it during the daylight hours, but he got too impatient thinking about it sitting there, waiting for him. No one knew about this, except him and his mason, who was sworn to secrecy. The mason had been paid in cash for keeping his mouth closed. Philippe Léridon had never seen anything like it; it brought tears to his eyes to imagine that it was his.

Verlaque stopped in the middle of the Place d'Archevêché on his way home. With his hands on his hips, he looked around at the tall plane trees that lined the square, and then tilted his head and looked up at the sky to watch the swifts flying overhead.

"Salut, Antoine," someone said, reaching out to shake Verlaque's hand.

"Oh, salut, Omar," Verlaque said, and shook the hand of the owner of the café on the northwest corner of the square.

"Doing some thinking?" Omar said.

"Yes."

"Well, I'll leave you to it." Omar smiled and walked on.

Verlaque stayed in the square, pivoting around once to get a 360-degree view of it. Then he stopped turning and looked at the ground again, kicking aside a leaf. What could Mlles Montmory and Durand have in common? Neither lived in the same village, and Gisèle Durand apparently hardly ever left the house. But the murderer was someone who knew both women, and who knew where they lived and when they'd be alone. Was it someone in

Aix? Laure Matour had told him that Gisèle didn't drive, so she probably rarely came into Aix. He supposed that she could take the bus, though. He often saw them on the ring road, usually full of high-school students from the country who came into Aix to school. Mme d'Arras had taken a bus too, so they must run frequently. . . .

Chapter Nineteen

ꝛ

Southern Charm

*V*erlaque ran up the four flights of stairs to his apartment and, out of breath, fumbled with his keys to open his door. "Salut, Marine!" he called when he was inside.

"Hello! I'm in the bedroom," she answered, "working."

"Okay, I'll be there in a minute!" He grabbed his cell phone and called Paulik. "Hello, Bruno. Sorry to bother you. Can you text me Mlle Montmory's boss's phone number? What's his name again?"

"Kamel Iachella," Paulik replied. "I'll send it to you right away."

"Thanks. I'll call you after I talk to him. *Ciao*."

As soon as the bank manager's cell-phone number beeped on Verlaque's telephone, he hit dial and waited for Iachella to answer. "Come on . . . come on . . ." Verlaque mumbled.

On the fourth ring, Iachella answered. "*Oui, hallo?*"

"Hello, M. Iachella," Verlaque said. "It's Judge Verlaque. I have a quick question."

"Go ahead."

"Did Mlle Montmory drive a car?"

"Yes."

Verlaque sighed. "Oh, I see."

"But not recently," Iachella replied. "Her car conked out about six months ago, and she was saving to buy a new one."

Verlaque straightened his back and looked up at the ceiling. "So how did she get into town?"

"She caught a ride with a colleague or took the bus."

"Thanks a million," Verlaque said. "Sorry to disturb you."

"No problem. I hope it helped. We're completely saddened by her death." He sniffed and choked a little, and then added, "Perhaps we'll see you at the funeral? It's tomorrow, at eleven a.m., at La Madeleine."

Verlaque closed his eyes. "I'll try to be there. Goodbye."

Marine came out of the bedroom carrying a book. "Hello there," she said, crossing the kitchen to kiss Verlaque. "Mmm, pastis," she said.

"Suzanne, Pauline, and Gisèle all took the bus," he replied quickly.

Marine stepped back. "You're kidding?" she said. "That's more than a coincidence, wouldn't you say? A bus driver?"

"Possibly, but how would he know where they lived?"

"And why go after Mme d'Arras?" Marine asked. "That's the bit that doesn't fit. By the way, have you spoken to Philippe Léridon yet?"

"You really don't like him, do you?" Verlaque asked. "Tomorrow I'll go. Gilles d'Arras told Bruno about the argument you overheard in the post office; Mme d'Arras had complained to her husband about it."

"And Mme d'Arras didn't hear what Léridon said after she

left," Marine said. "That the world would be better off without women like her, or something to that effect."

Verlaque nodded and walked over to the fridge, taking out a bottle of Mâcon white. "I would have said the same thing about her, from what I've been told." He looked at the bottle and saw that it had been opened already. "Hey! How is it?"

"Delicious," Marine answered. "Helps with the reading."

"I'm sure it does."

"I went to try to speak with Mme Joubert . . . Philomène . . . today," Marine said.

Verlaque poured himself a glass of white wine. "Thanks. What did she say?"

"She's away on a pilgrimage," Marine said.

"*Merde!* Is there any way we can contact her?"

"Frère Benoît tried to find me a phone number; I just got off the phone with him. Their hiking group was held back because of rain, and now they're off schedule. He's trying to figure out where they are right now. He also wants to tell Mme Joubert about Mme d'Arras's death, since they were once good friends. How was the rest of your day?"

Verlaque took his wine up the five steps that led from the open kitchen and dining room to his living room, and sat down in his club chair. "Shit," he answered. "Fabrice bawled me out for calling in Christophe for questioning. I felt like I was a teenager."

"He'll get over it," Marine said, sitting down on the top step, one of her favorite spots. "Do you remember that mud you saw on the tires of Christophe's fancy car, the night of the party?" she asked, looking over at Verlaque.

"Well done, remembering that detail," he answered, smiling. "I did remember, but probably after you. Some of the guys managed to scrape off some of the mud and send it to the lab."

"Poor Christophe," she said. "I hope it's not mud from a vineyard."

"That's what I told one of my officers today. Christophe doesn't have an alibi for early Friday evening, before he came to the cigar club."

"What did he say he was doing?"

"Bruno thought he was being cagey," Verlaque said. "Christophe claims that he was at home, alone."

"Did you ask him about the mud?" Marine asked.

"No. I wanted to have it tested first. I'm not sure if that was a good decision." Verlaque leaned back, enjoying the Chardonnay from the southern tip of Burgundy, a quarter of the price of its fancier cousins north of Beaune. "What's for dinner?"

"Chickpea salad and cold ham," Marine called from the kitchen. "With fresh chèvre and figs for dessert."

"More figs?" Verlaque asked, swirling the golden wine around and watching its legs drip slowly down the sides of the glass.

"My parents had a bumper crop this year, as did everyone else in Provence."

Verlaque laughed. "I sounded spoiled. Sorry." He picked up the volume of Czeslaw Milosz's poetry and chose a poem at random in the middle of the book. He read a bit and then set the book upside down on his knee, open, and then picked the book up again. "Listen to this," he called to Marine. "'And on and on, into winding dells, until suddenly / It appears high, so high, that jewel of wayfarers. . . .' It's about Rocamadour," he said. "That's on the pilgrimage route, isn't it? Have you been there?"

"A couple of times. 'Winding dells' is a perfect description of that countryside; I always used to get carsick from the switchbacks that led up to the village. There's a Madonna and Child in the church that you have to climb to; my parents were nuts over it. I preferred the little round cheeses that came from there. That was our treat for the long car ride."

Verlaque sighed. "And your carsickness," he yelled. "You poor thing. I'm glad I never had to vacation with your parents."

"And your vacations?" Marine asked from the bottom of the stairs, a tea towel thrown over her shoulder. "Michelin three-star restaurants with whichever mistress your dad had along that week?"

"Touché."

Marine stopped on her way back into the kitchen, then came up the stairs and sat on the arm of Verlaque's chair. "It bothered me that when I told you of my lump you took it personally."

"At the restaurant? But how else was I to take it?" Verlaque asked, surprised at the change of topic.

"You should have been concerned for *me,* and not upset just because I took a while telling you. It seemed a selfish response."

"I was in shock, I suppose. And with these murders . . . I'm sorry. I should have asked you how you're feeling."

Marine kissed his forehead. "You did, but after."

Marine showed Verlaque the bandage. He ran his fingers gently over it, leaned over, and kissed her. "When will you know?"

"The lab should have called tonight, but they didn't. So I hope first thing tomorrow." She jumped up. "Dinner awaits, on the dining-room table. I'm just going into the bedroom to change."

Verlaque tried to smile; he loved the fact that Marine changed for dinner, out of what she called her "town clothes" into her "comfy clothes," both equally elegant. He loved Marine's strength of character; she had obviously been bothered by the lump over the weekend but now seemed to be taking it in stride. Something had changed in her mood. Had it been going to church on Sunday? Had she spoken to her parents about it? He certainly hadn't helped, and he felt like an ass—just as Fabrice had called him.

He sighed and read some more of Milosz's poem about the pilgrimage. That was one of the things he loved about poetry: he could select one or two lines at random and he'd have something to take away from it, something to reflect upon. "Nor the maiden in the tower, though she lures us with a smile / And blindfolds us before she leads us to her chamber." It was Monique to a tee; she had lived on the sixth floor in Saint-Germain, without an elevator. And she had died of breast cancer, years later.

He closed the book and went down the steps into the dining room, to watch Marine lean over the table and light two candles.

Jules immediately regretted that he hadn't reserved a table ahead of time. He walked down the Rue Frédéric Mistral with Magali; it was impossible for them not to bump into each other, for the sidewalk was impossibly narrow, and he purposely walked on the street edge of the sidewalk, giving Magali the interior. He had been raised that way and hadn't given it a second thought. Magali had immediately noticed Jules's chivalry and been impressed. Years later, she would tell their two daughters that she fell in love with her young policeman that very night.

Jules would have a different story to tell of their first date. He always began it the same way: how they had bumped into each other in the Place Richelme, Jules on his way home from work and Magali having just closed the café, which wasn't open in the evening. Something about her smile when she saw him gave Jules the courage to ask her out that night. He made it sound like a whim, suggesting that they try Lotus, a trendy new restaurant, but in fact he had been thinking of inviting her there for days. Now, just a few meters away from the restaurant, he regretted his decision. Not in asking Magali out for dinner, but in choosing Lotus. It was packed; they could hear the music, and a crowd spilled out the door and down onto the sidewalk. "*Scheiße . . .*" he mumbled under his breath.

"Pardon?" Magali asked, stopping in front of the restaurant.

"I didn't reserve," Jules said.

Magali shrugged. "That doesn't matter. We can go someplace else."

Jules smiled weakly. "I'll just pop in and try."

"I'll wait out here," she said.

With much effort, he finally made his way through the crowd and managed to get inside to talk to a big burly man who was standing at the door. It seemed to Jules more like a nightclub than a restaurant. When he looked at the kitchen, which was open to the dining room, he suddenly felt very hungry. "Is there any chance of getting a table for two?" he asked.

"What do you think?" the bouncer/host asked.

"I guess your answer is no," Jules said. "Even for later?"

"We're fully booked, even for later." The man handed Jules a business card.

Jules mumbled a thank-you and went back outside, where he found Magali standing against the stone wall across the narrow street.

"No chance," he said, walking beside her. "Should we try Les Deux Garçons?"

Magali frowned. "What did it look like in there?" she asked.

"Cool. Open kitchen. The place was buzzing."

Magali raised an eyebrow. "I might know some of the staff," she said. "Everyone gets coffee sometime or another at our café. Mind if I try?" She would later tell friends and family that she knew she was risking their date, and future ones, right there. Jules had proved himself a gentleman and was probably a little old-fashioned, and here she was taking the situation in hand.

"Go ahead," he said after some thought. "I'll wait here." It was at this point in telling the story that Jules always reminded his listeners of the short life span of Aix's restaurants. Within six months, the lines at Lotus had disappeared. The prices had gone up, the guys in the kitchen had gotten sloppy, and Lotus was no longer the place to be. Two years later, it was closed.

Magali skipped across the street and made her way through the crowd, saying hello to some and giving the *bise* to others. He could hear her loud laughter, and then he watched her go in and speak to the same bouncer/host, who now had a smile on his face. Jules watched the bouncer scan the restaurant and say something to Magali; then he saw Magali motion to him with a wave. He walked across the street, saying *pardon* every few seconds as he edged his way through the crowd.

Magali reached out and put her arm through his. "They're setting up a place at the end of the bar for us, with two stools."

Jules tried to smile. It wasn't normal that the rules had been changed, even for a girl as pretty and charming as Magali. Either you're full or you're not full. Either you have a place available or you don't. That's the way it was in Alsace. He felt guilty about the people waiting outside too. But perhaps they also knew the secret code, as Magali had?

A waitress came and said, "Follow me," and they made their way through the restaurant and sat down. Magali leaned over toward Jules and put her hand on his forearm. "I hope you don't mind what I just did. That's the way it works here."

"You mean Lotus?" Jules asked, almost having to shout over the noise of music, laughter, and clattering cutlery and plates.

"No, in the south," she answered. She squeezed his arm, delighted to feel his muscles.

The bouncer/host appeared and slapped Jules on the back. "Sorry, man," he said. "I didn't know you were with Magali!"

"Next time, I'll make sure to tell you," Jules answered, trying to sound lighthearted.

"I'll bring you guys something nice from Corsica to whet your palates," he said. He snapped his fingers, and a bartender appeared and leaned over the bar.

"Bring my friends two glasses of our sparkling wine of the month," the bouncer/host said. "Domaine Martini!"

The bartender nodded, and in under a minute, two flutes of sparkling wine appeared. Jules and Magali toasted each other, and the bouncer/host, now back beside the front door, waved and winked.

"It's going to be hard to speak tonight," Magali said over the noise.

"I know," Jules answered. "But at least we'll eat well, from all I've heard about this place. The commissioner raves about it."

Magali laughed. "That's the first time I've ever had a restaurant recommendation from a commissioner of police!"

Jules laughed and sipped his wine. He looked up, surprised. He was loyal to Alsatian wines, and at family gatherings they always drank an Alsatian Crémant as an apéritif. "This is good. Really good."

Magali took what he thought was a rather large gulp, hiccupped, and laughed. "It is!" She set her glass down. "So where do you get these?" She squeezed his forearm again, and then reached up and squeezed his biceps.

"What do you mean? My arms?"

Magali let out a howl of laughter. "No! Your muscles! Do you work out at a gym?"

Jules laughed at his own naïveté. "No, I row."

"Really?" Magali asked. "Where?"

"Well, when I was in Alsace it was on rivers," he answered. "But I've just joined the Rowing Club de Marseille."

"I've seen it! Well, I've walked by it. By the Pharo, right?"

Jules nodded. "What do *you* do, when you're not working at the café?"

"I paint."

"Pictures?"

"Yeah."

"What kind?" Jules yelled. It seemed to him that the restaurant was getting noisier. A waitress appeared with a plate of thinly sliced figatelli sausage from Corsica, took their orders, and then disappeared.

"Promise you won't laugh," Magali said.

Jules made the sign of the cross, immediately regretting it.

Magali leaned over. "Still lifes."

"Really?" Jules asked. "With fruit and stuff?"

"Yeah. It's been my obsession for a while. I love going to the market and buying fruit and veggies, and then bringing them back to my apartment and painting them. I have a collection of old jugs and vintage tablecloths that I use. It's really fun."

Jules beamed. This was by far the most interesting date he had had in a long time. "Could I see them sometime?" he asked.

Magali winked at her tall blond Alsatian. "Of course!"

Chapter Twenty

༃

A New Bus Pass

*I*nstead of thinking of what they did in common," Paulik said as they stood in Verlaque's office Wednesday morning, "you thought of what they didn't do . . . drive."

Verlaque nodded as he snipped the end off a Partagás double corona. "Neither Gisèle Durand nor Mme d'Arras drove," he said. "When Durand's ex-boss told me that Gisèle didn't drive, I remembered M. d'Arras saying the same thing about his wife."

"Do you think it's the same bus route?" Paulik asked. "Éguilles to Rognes, and then to Aix?"

Verlaque shrugged. "No idea. We need to send someone to the bus depot and do some interviews. But I have an appointment after lunch with a nun, Pauline d'Arras's sister. I need to hit the road soon if I want to be on time." He checked his watch. "When is Gisèle Durand's boyfriend coming?"

"I'm meeting him early this evening," Paulik said. "He lives and works in Pertuis, pretty close to our house. I know his garage;

they specialize in old Citroëns. And I'm meeting the other sister, Christophe Chazeau's mother, after lunch."

"Could you go to Mlle Montmory's funeral at eleven a.m.?" Verlaque asked. He was beginning to feel like a shit again—or an ass, as Fabrice had called him. He hadn't taken Marine to the clinic, and he wasn't going to the funeral.

"I was planning on it," Paulik replied. Verlaque nodded and thought to himself, *God bless you, Bruno Paulik.*

"By the way, Didier Ruère's alibi sticks," Paulik said. "Both his drinking buddy and the barman confirmed his claim that he was in the Bar de Zinc on Friday night."

Verlaque's phone rang, and he ran to his desk to answer it. "*Oui.*" He nodded and whispered to Paulik, "It's the lab guys who tested the mud." Verlaque listened and nodded a few times, thanked the technician, and set down the phone. He ran his fingers through his hair and sat down behind his desk.

Paulik took his cue and sat down opposite his boss. "What is it?"

"There are traces of vineyard on the mud," he said. "Grapes, even. Syrah, apparently."

"Domaine Beauclaire's bestseller. I'm sorry."

Verlaque sighed and leaned back. "*Merde, merde, merde.*"

"I'm afraid we'll have to hold him here for questioning."

"You're right," Verlaque said, looking out of the window. "When it rains it pours. How are the Bonnards?"

"Morale is at an all-time low, Hélène reports."

Verlaque tapped his desk. "Well, regardless of what it looks like for Christophe, we need to get someone down to the bus depot, as quickly as possible."

Paulik got up. "I agree. It's the best angle we've got, and it's one that makes total sense."

"What we should do is send one of our officers down there, in plain clothes, and ask around. Pretend he's buying a bus pass. He can even take the bus to Éguilles and Rognes if he has to."

"You're right," Paulik said. "Let's not let this guy know we're on to him. After we get the information we need, our guys here can tap into their computer system."

"I love technology."

Someone knocked on the door, and Paulik got up to answer it. Jules Schoelcher entered, reporting for his morning shift.

"Ever taken the buses in Aix, Schoelcher?" Paulik asked.

Marine watched her mother, Dr. Florence Bonnet, retired professor of theology, as she stopped, staring at the shop and its glossy window displays. After a few seconds, Dr. Bonnet seemed to remember that she was on her way to have a coffee with Marine. She mumbled something to herself and walked toward the Café Le Verdun. "Where did the bookshop go?" Dr. Bonnet asked when she saw her daughter.

"Hello, Maman," Marine said, standing up to give her mother the *bise*.

"Hermès?" Dr. Bonnet asked no one in particular. "Who shops there?"

Marine grinned despite herself; Antoine Verlaque shopped there.

"I saw an ashtray in the window for two hundred and fifty euros," Florence Bonnet went on. "Are you having a coffee?"

"I've just ordered one," Marine said. "The Hermès shop has been there for over two years, Maman." Marine loved the way that their conversations, this one in particular, were split into two parts.

"I didn't see it happen," Dr. Bonnet replied. "I must be blind. I loved that bookstore."

A waiter appeared with Marine's coffee, and her mother ordered a tea. "Terrible about Pauline d'Arras," her mother said as she fastened up the buttons on her cardigan. "It's cold out all of a sudden, isn't it?"

"You knew her?" Marine asked.

Dr. Bonnet shrugged. "We weren't best friends, but I certainly knew her, yes. She didn't attend Mass at Saint-Jean de Malte. The Aubanel girls went to the Cathedral. Always."

"The Aubanel girls? They were well known?"

"Of course! They were beauties—well, except for Natalie. . . ."

Marine hadn't realized that her mother was almost the same age as Mme d'Arras. For Marine, Florence Bonnet always stayed in her mid-fifties; she went most places on bicycle, was never sick, and, although retired, she still went to the university most days for meetings, to advise young students, and to continue her own research. "Do you know the story of Natalie Chazeau's birth?" Marine asked, leaning in.

Mme Bonnet laughed. "Of course! Nazi father."

Marine set her coffee cup down. "Boy, there really are no secrets in Aix."

"It used to be like that," her mother answered. "But now no one knows anyone here. The town has changed. . . ."

"What do you know about Natalie, and her son, Christophe?" Marine asked.

"Only that Natalie has a grudge against Pauline," Dr. Bonnet said. "She always did. It was obvious to us all that they hated each other. It reminded me of an old Bette Davis and Joan Crawford movie they used to play late at night on television."

"I know the movie you're talking about. Joan Crawford was an invalid—"

"And that Christophe," her mother cut in. "If it wasn't for his mother's real-estate agency, he wouldn't have any money or a job. He's just bling. Bling bling."

Marine tried to hide her smile at her mother's attempt to use current slang. "Do you know him?"

"Of course not! How could I know him?"

But you know him well enough to say that he couldn't find a job without his mother's help. "Well, the same way you knew the Aubanel girls, I guess. Which is how, anyway?"

"High school, naturally," her mother said, finishing her tea. "There wasn't a high school in Rognes back then. They came on the bus to Sacré Coeur. Pauline and Natalie I didn't care for, but Clothilde was nice. I always knew that she would become a nun. She was always following the Sisters around."

Marine sat back, thinking that she would phone Antoine and tell him of the supposed antagonism between Pauline and Natalie Aubanel.

"Is that the time?" her mother said, jumping up from the table. "I'm late for a meeting at the church." She fumbled with her purse; Marine had remembered her mother buying it at the insistence of her father, in Tuscany, when Marine was twelve years old.

"It's okay, Maman," Marine said. "My treat."

"You're an angel," her mother said, leaning down to kiss her forehead but missing, and instead kissing the side of Marine's head. "Père Jean-Luc said how lovely it was to see you at Mass. . . . I'm off! *À bientôt!*"

Marine waved and watched her mother as she quickly removed her bike lock, which was wrapped around a plane tree, jumped on her bike, and rode down the Rue Thiers. Her mother hadn't asked why Marine had gone to the church, nor why Marine had suggested they have coffee together. Did her parents really communicate so little? Marine stood up, placed some coins on the table, and left the café.

. . .

Verlaque had been driving for two hours when he finally pulled over at a gas station rest stop to buy lunch. After zigzagging his way around stands full of videos and CDs he would hate to watch or listen to, then past a shelf full of the usual Provençal trinkets—ceramic cicadas of garishly bright colors, lavender sachets, soaps made from olive oil, and chewy nougat candy—he finally made it to the food area. He spent too long looking over the selection of sandwiches, and finally settled on ham and cheese, picking out a shrimp salad to go along with it. He ate his lunch standing up, trying to avoid the spilled coffee on the bar. He resisted the temptation to buy a Mars bar; however good they tasted at the moment when you ate them, he knew that afterward he would feel slightly sick to his stomach. He walked across the parking lot to his car, thankful that the summer vacation rush was over and the Parisians were all back at home.

Back on the *autoroute,* he listened to a jazz CD and strained his neck to get a glimpse, off to his right, of the medieval city of Carcassonne. He remembered that there was a hillside rest stop with a lookout that gave over the walled city, and he hoped that he would have time to pause there on the way back. He drove on until Narbonne and looked at his watch. He had promised Marine that he'd try to stop off at Narbonne's city hall and see a photography exhibition of France's best photographers that included Sylvie. He had just enough time, if he found the city hall soon. Within minutes, he had not only found the city hall but also parked his car in the shade almost in front of the building's front doors. *It was meant to be,* he mused. He opened the door and ran down the marble-floored hallway, following the posters advertising the exhibition. Once inside the exhibition room, he spotted a group of immense photographs of bathers—one of Sylvie's favorite themes—and crossed the room to look at them. They were portraits; people of all ages were bathing in a green-blue river, each one staring directly at the camera. The water was perfectly still, and so rich in color that it looked like a sheet of glass. He put his reading glasses on and got as close as he could to inspect one of the photographs. He stood back, slipped off his glasses, and moved on to the next one. When he had looked at six or seven, he stopped. A boy of twelve or thirteen stood in chest-high water, his back to the camera but his head turned to it, as if his name had just been called. *Antoine,* she had called. *Come here and help me towel off.* He turned around and left the room quickly; the docent's "Good afternoon, sir," followed him as he walked down the hallway.

He got into his car and sat back with his eyes closed. After a minute or two, he started the car and saw that his appointment with the nun was in under an hour. He left Narbonne and headed south on small departmental roads, marked in yellow on his Michelin map. Every so often he pulled over, next to vineyards heavy with fruit, and checked his map. He drove onto even smaller roads, and then signs began appearing for the abbey, open every morning for guided tours. It was rugged countryside, more rugged than Aix: sparsely inhabited, its hills smaller and older, and the plants that covered them even drier and more meager than in Provence. He rolled his car windows down and let the smells waft in. It was a landscape for cloistered nuns and monks, medieval hermits, and fanatical winemakers; it couldn't be any more different from his green Normandy, and he loved it.

The abbey's parking lot was bigger than he expected, but it was almost empty now that summer, and the morning tours had ended. He parked under a small tree, hoping this would give his car a little shade, and walked up to the abbey's reception area. To get to the front desk, visitors were forced to go through a gift shop, and Verlaque smiled at the nuns' business sense. Since he was ten minutes early, he strolled around the shop, looking at their hand-made soaps, honey, and liqueurs, the packaging in better taste than at the gas station. He flipped through their extensive collection of ecclesiastical-architecture books and selected one for Marine, with stunning photographs and what looked like detailed maps. It could be for weekends away—a present to her after the murderer was caught.

"That's the best one we have," a soft female voice said.

Verlaque turned around and saw a small, elderly nun with wire-rimmed glasses smiling at him. "I'm glad," he answered, smiling back. "Soeur Clothilde?"

"Yes," she replied. She extended her thin, age-spotted hand and gave him a firm handshake. "You looked like a judge; I'm glad I wasn't mistaken."

Verlaque laughed. "Oh dear, I'm not sure if that's bad or good."

"Good. It's good," she replied. "Follow me; we'll go someplace where we can talk."

Verlaque paid for his book and followed the nun back outside and through a cobbled courtyard lined with potted plants. "This is beautiful," he said, looking around him at the golden stone buildings built in various centuries.

Soeur Clothilde nodded. "I'll show you the rose garden after-ward, if you wish. It's one of my duties here, to select varieties for planting and then tend the roses."

"My grandmother was a great one for roses," Verlaque said as they entered what looked more like an elegant manor house than a convent.

"It's our bit of paradise," the nun said. "Roses don't belong here, in this wild countryside, but I think God will forgive us." They moved down a hall, lit with what looked like expensive Italian wall sconces. Wooden doors lined both sides of the hall; she opened one toward the end and gestured for Verlaque to enter. He walked in and stepped aside, letting the nun pass, then looked around the small whitewashed room and stood still, speechless. Finally, he said, "This is your cell."

"Yes," she answered. "Please, sit down." She motioned to a cane-seated chair; Soeur Clothilde sat opposite him, on the edge of her small bed, her feet dangling.

"I'm very sorry about the death of your sister," he began.

"Thank you."

"I don't know if you heard, but two other women were attacked the same week, one also in Rognes, and the other in Éguilles."

Soeur Clothilde closed her eyes and then opened them. "No, I hadn't heard. Are they . . . ?"

"They're dead, yes."

"And you're here because there may be a relationship between their deaths and my sister's murder?"

Verlaque said, "Yes." He let the nun think while he glanced behind her head, where a small bookshelf was hung over her bed. Not wanting to be nosy, he looked back at the nun, who again had her eyes closed.

"As Pauline got older, she got more and more angry," Soeur Clothilde finally said, her hands on her knees. "I rarely spoke to Pauline, but on Saturdays—our day off—my sister Natalie would call me. Complaining."

"Pauline, Mme d'Arras, had been harassing her sister, *non*?"

"Yes, and it wasn't right. All Natalie's life she had to deal with . . . with . . . her parentage, and now Pauline was reminding her of it. Do you know our story?"

Verlaque nodded. "That Natalie's father was an SS officer? Yes, I know."

Soeur Clothilde retold the story, very much as Philomène Joubert had told Marine; it took her ten minutes. "Family secrets," she said. "They have to be dealt with, don't they?"

Verlaque hesitated. "Yes."

"And since you already knew the Aubanel story, I can't think of why you drove three hours from Aix to here, unless it was because you have your own story you'd like to talk about."

"That's preposterous."

"Is it?" she asked, smiling. "Why did *you* come here, instead of sending one of your officers?"

"I was available." Verlaque shifted in his chair and crossed his legs. He looked around the room and asked, "What do *you* do all day, if you don't mind me asking?"

"I think, pray, read," she said. "And tend to the garden. I saw you trying to read the spines of my books. I love historical novels— big thick ones that sweep generations, and even centuries."

"Leon Uris–type stuff?" Verlaque asked. "My grandmother liked his books."

"Ah, your grandmother again. The rose gardener."

Verlaque smiled. "Coincidence."

"What do *you* read?" she asked.

"Poetry," he answered. "Twentieth-century."

"Oooh," she said, teasing, "very dark."

"More like . . . lonely," he said.

"Do you want to be lonely?"

"No, I'm tired of it."

"What's your next step, then?" she asked. "To rid yourself of this loneliness and get back into the world? The world of love and roses and . . . unloneliness."

"I don't know," Verlaque said. "This afternoon I saw a photograph that a friend had taken—actually, a series of photographs— and one triggered some memories. The memories weren't all bad, but they were ones I'd been hiding, or ignoring. I'm tired of it, that's all."

"You could tell me, and then you'd be rid of them," she said. "We could throw them out the window." She leaned over and looked at her barred window, about a foot in width. "There's not room for many, though," she said, winking.

Verlaque tried to smile. "Could we go outside and talk in the garden?" he asked.

"Of course. Your grandmother will be by your side there, won't she?"

"*Oui.*"

L'Agence de la Ville was Aix's biggest and most luxurious real-estate agency, in a town that could almost boast more Realtors than doctors. It had a prime location on the Cours Mirabeau—on the north café side, not the south bank side—so that one could stroll after a coffee and gaze at the framed, backlit color advertisements of bastides, stone *mas, hôtels particuliers,* lavish apartments, and even the converted barn or two. The houses were located in the most desirable areas of Provence: Aix and its environs, the southern Lubéron, and the Marseille coast. Most of the properties had prices in seven digits; for others, no price was given, only the words "Inquire with us. . . ."

Paulik had never been inside—he and Hélène abhorred Realtors and had bought their house in Pertuis from a cousin. His shoes squeaked on the marble floor as he walked in; marble also shone on one of the walls and on the receptionist's desktop. A young Aixoise greeted him with a huge smile and a perfect set of teeth. "Welcome to L'Agence de la Ville," she said. "How may I help you?"

"I have an appointment with Mme Chazeau," Paulik replied. "Commissioner Paulik."

The girl jumped up, still young enough to be nervous around policemen. "I'll tell her you're here," she said. As she left the reception area, she remembered what she was supposed to do, turned around, and asked Paulik if he would like a coffee or a glass of water. He declined.

Within seconds, Mme Chazeau walked out of a double-doored office and came to shake the commissioner's hand firmly. "Commissioner," she said, "please, come into my office."

Paulik followed the Realtor into her spacious, high-ceilinged office. Framed oil paintings hung on the wall, showing off Provence's bounty: fields of red poppies, the rugged red cliffs of Cap Canaille in Cassis, and of course, Mont Sainte-Victoire against a deep-blue sky. Mme Chazeau was almost as tall as Paulik, and much slimmer. She had the wide shoulders of an athlete—a swimmer, possibly—and a head of thick, wavy black hair that she kept short, tucked behind her small, delicate ears. Her only jewelry was a pair of large diamond stud earrings. She wore no wedding band, so Paulik assumed she was divorced, or widowed. He knew that Natalie was the oldest of the Aubanel sisters, although she didn't look as if she could be in her late sixties or early seventies.

"My secretary offered you a coffee?" she asked.

"Yes, thank you, but I declined."

"So . . . we'll start, then. I assume you're here to ask questions about my sister Pauline, but I must begin this . . . interview . . . by telling you how very angry I am that my son was called in for police questioning."

"I understand," Paulik answered. "But we have to ask everyone who knew Mme d'Arras the same questions. . . ."

"You know very well you are not answering my question," she said. "Why was he called in to the police station?"

"He was to inherit. . . ."

"And that makes him a murder suspect?"

Paulik didn't reply. "Was he angry that he was cut out of your sister's will?" he asked.

"No," she answered quickly and, it seemed to Paulik, honestly. "Christophe wasn't expecting any money from her, so he thought it was a lark that he was even mentioned."

"When was the last time you saw Mme d'Arras?"

Mme Chazeau paused, resting her large hands on the desk. "Months ago," she finally said. "Before the summer. May."

Paulik deliberately showed his surprise. "May? That's four months ago."

"Precisely. I'm sure it was May, because that's Christophe's birthday, and I had Gilles and Pauline over for dinner. With Christophe, naturally. May 12."

"And your husband?" Paulik asked.

"My husband died over twenty years ago, of a heart attack."

"I'm sorry," Paulik said. "So you haven't seen your sister, who lives in the same town, in four months?"

Mme Chazeau nodded. Paulik could see that she wasn't going to offer any information for free. "Is that normal?" he asked. "To get together with your sister . . ."

". . . who lives in the same town, only every four months," Mme Chazeau cut in. "Yes."

"Why?" *If she can answer in one-word sentences, I'll start asking in one-word sentences,* Paulik mused to himself.

"We didn't get along."

That was obvious. "Why not?"

Mme Chazeau sighed and glanced at her gold watch. "Oh, it's a long story. . . ."

Paulik didn't say anything, just sat back in his chair and crossed his legs. *I have the time.*

"We've never been close," she answered, "since we were very young. Do you have siblings, Commissioner?"

Paulik nodded. "Five."

"And do you get on with all of your siblings?"

"Yes." *Liar.*

"Well, that's great for you. Pauline and I didn't get on." Mme Chazeau looked at the field of poppies on the wall and then turned to Paulik. "But I didn't hate her. I used to, but not anymore."

"Why did you hate her?" he asked, sitting forward again.

"We competed for everything," she answered. "Don't ask me why. It was always like that. And I've stopped competing." She then added, "I'd stopped competing *before* Pauline was killed." She looked at a newspaper sitting open to her right and quickly closed it in half.

"Do you know who may have killed your sister?"

"No. I have no idea."

"Was she an easy person to get along with?"

"No, as I've been telling you."

"I meant with strangers, with shop owners, neighbors. . . ." Paulik said.

"She was . . . difficult. . . ."

Paulik sat back again. "And last Friday evening . . . where were you?"

"I was here, working. With another sales agent and the secretary," she said, pointing toward the door. "She stayed late to help us conclude a sale."

Finally, Paulik stood up and shook her hand; he realized that he could get nothing more from her now. Natalie Chazeau walked him to the door. "Goodbye, Commissioner," she said.

He nodded, thanked her, and left, saying goodbye to the secretary on the way out. Outside the agency, he looked at a framed notice for one of the houses for sale. "Six bedrooms, two salons, swimming pool and pool house, one acre of landscaped grounds, views of Mont Sainte-Victoire. 6,150,000 euros." He could remember when no house in Provence cost more than a million euros—francs back then—except for certain seaside estates on the Côte d'Azur. It didn't seem so long ago.

Mme Chazeau went back into her office and opened the newspaper that had been sitting on her desk. Had the commissioner seen it? she wondered. She picked up her new cell phone, put on her reading glasses, and texted her son: "Have you seen the front page of *Le Monde* today? I think it may interest you."

Aix's bus station wasn't a bus station as such, just a street where the buses came and went, with a temporary portable that served as an office. Jules Schoelcher walked up the ramp and into the stuffy room, where he saw two long queues, each with about eight or nine people waiting. On a whim, he selected the second queue, because it had a female employee. He hoped to work some charm, as Magali had done at Lotus. If that was how the south worked . . .

Amazed by how long some people took to buy bus passes or get directions, he tried to hide his frustration when he finally got to the front of the line. "Hello," he said, working on sounding as cheery as possible.

The middle-aged employee didn't look up but continued typing something into the computer. After a few seconds, she replied with a weary "Yes?"

"I'd like to buy a bus pass, for the Aix region, please."

"You'll need to show a student card."

Annoyed, Schoelcher coughed. "I'm not a student anymore."

"Lost your license, then?" she asked, her voice starting to show the tiniest bit of enthusiasm. Schoelcher noticed it right away and decided to run with it.

"How did you guess?" he asked, laughing. "Lost the last two of my twelve points this week, talking on my cell phone while driving. Not handy if you're a gardener."

The bus-station employee looked at Schoelcher's tanned, muscled forearms and smiled.

"So . . . I need a pass that will get me to my clients out in Éguilles . . . and Rognes." He paused and took a gamble. "My pickiest clients too, with the fanciest houses."

"Ah oui," she replied. "Big houses out that way. Show-offs. There's a pass you can buy that will get you from Aix to all the villages north. But how will you get your equipment around?"

He stood still, stunned, and then said, "They're letting me use theirs, until I do my driving lessons over. Generous of them, eh?"

She laughed.

"Is there a bus that goes directly from Éguilles to Rognes?" he asked.

She looked at him as if he had asked the stupidest question in the world. "No, of course not."

"Oh, that's a drag," he replied, getting out his wallet. "Do the drivers share the routes? You know, mix it up?"

"What's it to you?" she asked, her gaze narrowing.

"Oh, it's nothing. It's just that the guy I had yesterday was in a foul mood. I didn't have the bus pass yet, and I took a long time finding the right change."

"Hey, it's a tough job. Yeah, they switch routes. So don't worry."

"Great. I'll buy the pass."

"Thirty-six euros. I'll take down your information." She asked Schoelcher for his address, phone number, even an e-mail address, which he declined. Easy for any bus employee to find the street address of a young woman living alone, he noted silently. But how would the bus employee know that both Mlles Montmory and Durand had lived alone?

When he had paid her in cash, she said, "Smile into the camera poised at my left."

"You're taking my picture?" he asked.

"Yeah! It's for your bus pass. Smile!"

They'd have the women's photographs too, he noted.

"The bus to Rognes," he asked as she was waiting to print out his card, "is it busy?"

"Of course!" she answered, opening a box of candy and putting one in her mouth. "Especially before and after school."

"Oh, kids coming into Aix in the morning?"

"Yeah, to their high schools. And at night, going home." She glanced at his downtown address. "But you'll be coming back into Aix at night, against the flow."

"Right! Thank goodness. A whole busload of teenagers," he said, raising his eyes and trying to laugh.

"They're total brats," she replied, handing him his pass. "No respect anymore. But you'll be fine; the night buses back to Aix should be pretty empty. Probably just you and the driver."

Schoelcher nodded and put the shiny new pass in his wallet. "You have no idea how much help you've just been."

She yawned. "My pleasure."

Chapter Twenty-one

ﻬ

La Politesse

Jules Schoelcher arrived back at the Palais de Justice to find Paulik and Flamant in Paulik's office, hunched over Paulik's computer. "How did it go at the bus station?" Paulik asked, looking up.

"Brilliant," Schoelcher replied, tossing his bus pass on the commissioner's desk. "They have records of your address and phone number and your photograph. There's no direct route from Rognes to Éguilles, but the drivers share routes. And a bus-station employee could easily look up the information on the computer. But on my way back here, I kept thinking: how would they know that the women lived alone?"

"They couldn't," Paulik replied.

"Right," said Schoelcher. "But a driver could."

"How so?" Flamant asked.

"By talking to the women."

Flamant sat back. "Yeah, you're right. By chatting them up."

Schoelcher nodded. "If you're a single woman, and you go

into Aix sometimes at night, the bus is often empty. So where do you sit?"

"Behind the driver," Paulik answered. That's where he would sit too—not for protection or out of politeness, but because of his motion sickness. "Did you say the bus is often empty on the way back to Aix?"

"Yes," replied Schoelcher. "I thought right away of Mme d'Arras. Her body was found not far from the road."

Paulik turned to Flamant. "Alain, can you break into the bus-station employee Web site?"

Flamant pretended to roll up his sleeves. "*La magie commence,*" he said, waving his fingers in the air. "Just give me two seconds."

"How was the funeral?" Jules Schoelcher asked Paulik, whispering.

"Terribly, terribly sad," the commissioner replied. "I introduced myself afterward and got accused by Mlle Montmory's oldest brother of not doing enough to find this guy."

"I'm sorry, but I understand his anger."

"So do I," said Paulik. "I have two sisters."

"And the interview with Mme Chazeau?"

"Not very useful," Paulik said. "She seems to have hated her sister, but she has an alibi . . . at the office with two colleagues. She confirmed that Pauline d'Arras was difficult to get along with, but that we already knew. And she's furious that we called her son in for questioning. I didn't tell her that he's coming back here at the end of the day."

"Bingo," Flamant said, looking up.

"Already?" Paulik asked.

"Yeah. I was just waiting for you two to finish talking. What are we looking for?"

"Well," Paulik said, sitting down, "male bus drivers . . ."

"Gisèle Durand preferred younger men," Schoelcher said. "Her former boss wrote that in her statement."

"So under the age of forty," Paulik continued, impressed with Schoelcher.

"With a police record would be useful," Paulik said.

"*Nada*," Flamant answered, staring at the screen. "They're all clean. They probably have to be to get a bus driver's license."

"Ones who *weren't* working the nights that the women were attacked," Paulik said. "With the possible exception of Mme d'Arras."

Flamant took out a pencil and began taking notes. "They're having an employee picnic next Sunday," he mumbled.

Paulik rolled his eyes and smiled. "Keep looking. . . ."

"Okay, here's last Friday's schedule," Flamant said. "Doing the Rognes–Aix route in the afternoon was Guy Mézery. That's the guy that recognized Pauline d'Arras, right? Who said she seemed confused?"

"Yes," replied Paulik. "And the evening shift?"

"Jean-Pierre Bondeau," replied Flamant.

"What time did he get off?" Paulik asked.

"Eight p.m."

"He could have driven back to Rognes after his shift," Schoelcher said. "Dr. Bouvet could have been an hour off on the estimate for the time of death."

Paulik nodded. "Did Bondeau work last Wednesday?"

"I'm looking, I'm looking," Flamant replied, squinting at the screen. "Yes, the day shift, it looks like—from seven a.m. to three p.m."

Paulik clapped his hands. "Suzanne Montmory was attacked after work, in the early evening. Give me his address, please, Alain."

Flamant read off the address of an apartment complex on the west side of Aix. He looked at his watch and added, "Bondeau just finished his shift."

Roger Caromb knocked at the door and stuck his head in the office. "Christophe Chazeau is here, boss," he said. "I've put him in interview room number two and given him a coffee. But he looks like he could use something stiffer than that."

"Thanks, Caromb," Paulik replied. He looked at his watch. "I'll go and interview Chazeau, and then go to the bus driver's house on my way home. Flamant, if you could come with me, and, Schoelcher and Caromb, if you guys could pore over the files one more time, trying to link these three women together, in case we're wrong about the bus employees. What kind of man would be able to see where they live, and that they lived alone?"

"Plumbers, electricians," Schoelcher suggested.

"Great; go through their bills again, phone Mlle Montmory's colleagues, and ask if she had any work done to her apartment recently," Paulik said. "Who else?"

"Deliverymen," Caromb said. "Those big grocery stores deliver now."

"Excellent, Roger," Paulik said. "You find out which grocery stores deliver to Rognes and Éguilles and see if the women were on the client list. They'll have records of recent deliveries."

Caromb saluted the commissioner. "Consider it done!"

Flamant thought of his fiancée, looking at the La Redoute catalog until late in the evening, obsessing over drapes for their new apartment. He hoped that, once they were married, she'd calm down a bit on the interior-decorating thing. "The big catalogs deliver too," he said.

"You're right," Paulik said. "My wife loves the home furnishings in La Redoute. That's yours, then, Alain."

"Yes, sir," Flamant replied. So it didn't end at marriage, apparently.

Paulik and Flamant walked downstairs and into the room where Christophe Chazeau was waiting, his head in his hands. He looked up at the policemen and asked, "Where's Antoine?"

"Not here," Paulik said, sliding a chair out and sitting down. Flamant stayed in the back of the room, leaning against the wall.

"I have some bad news for you," Paulik said.

"What now?"

"Your car had mud from a vineyard in its wheel wells. And traces of grapes."

"Oh no," Chazeau said.

"Care to explain?"

"I was at a vineyard on Friday night, before our cigar-club party," Chazeau answered, sighing.

"Why didn't you tell us?"

"I freaked out when I found out that Aunt Pauline was killed in a vineyard, and then, when you called me in about the will . . . I knew it would look so bad!" Chazeau said. "Like it does now! I didn't think you'd be low enough to take a mud sample off my car!"

"I'm afraid that's part of our job," answered Paulik. "Which winery were you at, then?"

"Not at Domaine Beauclaire," Chazeau answered. "I was on the other side of Aix, at Domaine Frérot et Fils. I wanted to buy a few bottles to take to the party, and a friend had recommended their reds."

"Why didn't you tell us?" Paulik said. "I still don't get it. That's your alibi."

Chazeau shook his head. "They weren't around; there was a

note on the door that they were all in the vineyards. I didn't want to be late, so I turned around and left."

"The vineyard mud?" Paulik asked.

"I have a new Porsche Cayenne," Chazeau answered. "Their parking lot, and the dirt road into the domaine, were muddy, but I didn't mind because of the new SUV. I was having a bit of fun, driving through the mud."

Paulik leaned back and sighed.

"Doesn't look good, does it?" Chazeau asked.

Paulik paused. "So you went straight to the cigar party?"

"Yes. Well, no, I first bought some wine, then went home and changed for the party." Both men looked at each other, and Chazeau slapped his forehead. "The wine! I stopped at a little wine shop by the Pont de Trois Sautets!"

"I know that place," Paulik said. The owner, a tiny, bustling woman, had limited stock, but what she did sell she had selected herself, including Domaine Beauclaire. "Will she remember you?"

"I think so," Chazeau said. "We talked about the wines for a bit, and I told her I was on my way to a cigar club. She might remember that."

"What time was it?"

"It was just before seven, because I caught her just before closing."

"I'll send someone over to her shop with your photograph," Paulik said. "You're free to go, but stick around Aix, okay?"

"I'm not going anywhere," Chazeau said. "My aunt's funeral is on Saturday, and I'm going, even if she did give all her money away to puppies."

Paulik was about to leave the Palais de Justice, the bus driver's address in his hand, when he almost ran into M. d'Arras, coming into the building.

"Sir," Paulik said, holding the door open for him, "can I help you?"

"Yes," M. d'Arras said, his voice trembling. "I want to talk to you about our neighbor, the annoying Philippe Léridon."

Bruno Paulik tried not to sigh. While Antoine Verlaque was driving across southern France to visit a nun—which would amount to nothing, Paulik was sure—he was being run off his feet: delegating work; interviewing Christophe Chazeau, André Prodos, and Natalie Chazeau; and attending one of the saddest funerals he had ever been to. And his wife's employer was having wines stolen from right under his nose, and Paulik hadn't done anything about it. He had sent a team to dust for fingerprints, but only family and winery employees' hands had touched the cellar door.

"Let's find somewhere to talk, shall we?" he said. They walked down the hall and went into inquiry room number two, the same one that Christophe Chazeau had been in fifteen minutes before. "What is it?" Paulik asked, closing the door behind him.

"He's out in his garden all the time," M. d'Arras said. "My dear wife thought he was up to no good there, and now I'm convinced of it too. He's hiding something. I know it. I tried talking to him about it, and he told me to mind my own business!"

"I would have said the same thing," Paulik said. "People do garden, M. d'Arras."

M. d'Arras looked up in shock. "At night?" he asked. His eyes started watering, and he took out a yellowed handkerchief from his pocket to dab his eyes.

Paulik leaned toward Gilles d'Arras. "I'm sorry, M. d'Arras."

The old man blew his nose and whispered, "It's all right. . . . I just don't know what to do."

"It's up to *us* to find out what happened to your wife," Paulik said. "You go home and get some rest. I'll send someone around to your neighbor's." He looked at the old man, whose eyes were red, his skin pale. In two days' time, he would bury his wife. "I promise," Paulik added.

It took Bruno Paulik ten minutes to find a parking spot and the right building at Jean-Pierre Bondeau's sprawling apartment complex on the west, and poorer, side of Aix. He was taking a chance that Bondeau would be there, but it was almost dinnertime, an hour when most people were at home. He phoned André Prodos and told him he'd be late. Prodos said that was fine; he was behind schedule, and so would stay at the garage and work until Paulik got there.

Paulik parked his beat-up Range Rover and walked along a sidewalk, looking up at the buildings until he found Bâtiment D; he rang the bell marked "Bondeau."

"*Oui?*" a male voice answered.

"M. Bondeau?" Paulik asked, trying not to speak too loudly.

"*Oui?*" came the answer. "Are you selling something?"

"No, I'm the police. May I come up?"

"*Oh mon dieu,*" Bondeau mumbled. "Third floor." The door clicked open.

Jean-Pierre Bondeau was standing in his open door when Paulik got to the top of the landing. He looked older than the thirty-seven years that the bus-station Intranet site claimed he was and, by the looks of it, didn't seem to be Gisèle Durand's type. Bondeau was short—under five five, Paulik thought—and overweight. He kept his gray hair in a brush cut and wore glasses. "Come in," he said, stepping aside. "What's going on?"

Paulik showed him his badge and thanked him. "I'm sorry to come at dinnertime." He looked over and saw what he assumed was the Bondeau family—mother and three children—sitting still at the dining-room table, watching him.

"Good evening," Paulik said to them.

Mme Bondeau nodded; the children continued to stare, mouths open.

Jean-Pierre Bondeau motioned for Paulik to sit down on the sofa, and he sat across from him in a rocking chair. "Does this have to do with that old lady who took the bus to Rognes?" Bondeau asked.

"Yes," Paulik answered. "Your colleague took her to Rognes on Friday afternoon, and remembered her."

"Yes, Guy. He was really shaken up when he heard the news."

Paulik nodded. "You drove the evening shift back to Aix, right?"

"Yes, sir, I did."

"Was Mme d'Arras on the bus?" Paulik asked, watching Bondeau closely.

"No," he answered immediately. "Of course not. I would have said so, wouldn't I?"

"Yes . . ."

"Hey! You don't suspect me, do you? What's going on here?"

One of the children dropped a fork or spoon on the floor, and Paulik heard Mme Bondeau whisper, "Just leave it."

"Was there anyone on the bus that night?" Paulik asked.

"Let me think a minute, would ya?" Bondeau replied, leaning forward with his forearms on his knees. "Friday, Friday . . . Wait, yes, there were. The bus is often empty on the way back into Aix, but there were three teens, three boys, who were going into town to see a movie. A three-D movie or something like that." He sat up straight and smiled. "I remember them because they were polite. Not like some of the other kids I have to drive around." He looked over at his own children and repeated, "*Polite!*" He turned to Paulik and added, "They were getting picked up by their parents after the film. I heard them say that because it wrecked their chances of going to some club."

Paulik nodded. Bondeau had confirmed that the bus was often empty going back; that seemed honest. And Paulik had seen the posters advertising a 3-D movie, but perhaps Bondeau had as well. "And you didn't see anything unusual on the road back into Aix?" Paulik asked.

"No," Bondeau replied. "I would have said something if I had."

"Is there any way you could help us identify those boys on the bus?"

Bondeau leaned forward. "Yeah," he said, straightening up. "One of them was named Victor, if that helps. That's my oldest son's name." He looked over at his son, who was about eleven years old, Paulik estimated, and also wore glasses. "Stand up, Victor, and say good evening. *Politesse!*" his father said.

Victor Bondeau stood up, bumping the dining-room table as he did. "Good evening, sir," he said to Paulik, and quickly sat down again, bumping the table once more.

Paulik smiled. "Good evening," he answered. He turned back to M. Bondeau and asked, "Victor? What did he look like?"

Bondeau looked up at the ceiling. "Taller than my Victor, lanky, with those skinny low-hung jeans that *some* boys wear," he replied. "Messy curly hair, but a nice face, and polite. Well brought up."

Paulik paused and then continued writing. "And the other boys? Names? Faces?"

"Um . . . not much. One was perhaps younger than the other two, or at least shorter. Oh! And one was named Jérôme. . . ."

"Like Uncle Jérôme in Toulouse!" cried one of the children excitedly.

Bondeau gave the children an impatient look. "Yes, like my brother."

"Anything else?" Paulik asked.

"No," Bondeau replied. "It's a miracle I could remember that much." He sat up straighter and put his hands on his thighs.

"Very well then, thank you," Paulik said. He stood up and shook Bondeau's hand. "Mme Bondeau, I'm very sorry to have interrupted your dinner. I'll see myself out."

On the way out to his car, Paulik walked quickly and dialed the phone number for Domaine Beauclaire.

"*Oui*," Élise Bonnard answered.

"Élise, it's Bruno Paulik here. I'm sorry to call at dinnertime."

"That's all right," she said. "We haven't started yet, but Hélène left about an hour ago, if you wanted to talk to her."

"No, I'd like to ask Victor something, if I may."

He heard Élise call Victor and tell him it was Commissioner Paulik on the phone.

Victor Bonnard came slowly to the phone, his palms sweating. Olivier Bonnard looked at his son with a worried look, and thirteen-year-old Clara, setting her book down, whispered, "Way to go."

"Shut up, Clara," Victor said, gently cuffing her on the head as he walked by her.

"Um, yeah?" Victor said, standing in the kitchen with his whole family around him.

"Hey, Victor," Paulik said. "I just have a quick question. Did you take the bus into Aix last Friday evening?"

Victor looked around at his family, perplexed. "Yeah, I did."

Paulik smiled. "You might have just proved someone's innocence."

"Really? Cool."

"What were you going into Aix for?"

"A movie, with my friends Jérôme and Thomas."

Paulik smiled again. "Which movie?"

Victor laughed. "I wouldn't recommend it. Some three-D crap. None of us liked it."

"Thanks a million, buddy," Paulik said.

"Hey, anytime."

Paulik hung up and tried Verlaque again; the judge's phone was still on his *messagerie,* so Paulik left him a message, bringing him up-to-date, and telling him of M. d'Arras's most recent visit. It was unusual for Antoine Verlaque not to answer his phone, and Paulik thought it was perhaps because he was driving back to Aix. Paulik got into his Range Rover and turned out of the parking lot, happy for the half-hour commute to Rognes, to his stone *maison de village,* and his wife and daughter, who would be waiting for him, and then he realized that he still had one more appointment.

Chapter Twenty-two

☙

The Car That Saved a President

*P*aulik set his cell phone on the passenger seat and turned it off. Hélène had left two messages, which he hadn't had time to listen to, and his daughter, Léa, one. He thought of ten-year-old Léa as he drove north out of Aix; he couldn't remember the last time he had sat down with her and really been with her, reading or talking or even watching a film. He stopped at a traffic light and listened to Léa's message: "Hello, Daddy. I know I'm not allowed to phone you at work except if it's an emergency, but I just wanted to tell you that I got nineteen out of twenty on my math test. Mommy's in a bad mood. See you soon!" He would love to go straight home; it was almost 8:00 p.m., and Léa usually went to bed at 9:30 p.m. But he had to interview André Prodos. As he drove on, he thought of the three deaths that remained, after a week, unsolved. Murders of women. "I'm sorry, Léa," he said aloud, and turned up the opera CD.

Prodos's garage was almost in walking distance of the Pauliks' house. As he pulled up in front of the garage, he could see lights on through the streaked window glass.

Prodos heard Paulik pull up, and knew by the sound that he was driving an older Range Rover that needed work on the fan belt. That squealing sound it made as it turned was unmistakable. He came out of the garage to meet the commissioner, wiping his oily hands on a small blue towel.

"*Bon soir,*" Prodos said, extending his elbow. "I've wiped my hands, but they're still pretty oily. My elbow will have to do."

Paulik shook the mechanic's elbow. "No problem. I'm Commissioner Bruno Paulik."

"Come inside, Commissioner."

Paulik followed Prodos through what looked to him like any office in a working garage: an old metal desk was piled high with old invoices and dirty coffee mugs. Posters and framed photographs covered every wall surface, along with a collection of trophies. There were no girlie posters or photos of Ferraris or Maseratis. The cars proudly featured were Citroëns, mostly from the 1960s and '70s, and only two models, the DS and the ID.

"Have a seat," Prodos said, gesturing to a chair across from the desk.

From where he sat, Paulik could see into the garage; a two-toned black-and-white DS 21 was on a hoist about six feet high, and a burgundy-colored ID was next to it, parked on the garage's concrete floor. Paulik said, "I'm sorry about Gisèle's death."

Prodos nodded. "Thank you," he said quietly.

Paulik tried to study the mechanic without making it obvious. Prodos didn't look like a mechanic, or at least like other mechanics that Paulik had dealt with. He was tall and thin and wore small wire-rimmed glasses. His hair was brown, and receding, and he spoke and carried himself with . . . grace, Paulik thought. Grace.

"I imagine you're here to ask me about where I was this weekend," Prodos said, looking straight at Paulik. "Gisèle looked like . . . looked like she had been dead for a while. . . ."

"Yes," Paulik answered. "She was murdered on Friday evening, between six and eight p.m."

Prodos bit his lip and thought for a few seconds, and then said, "I was here, in the garage. No alibi, I'm afraid."

Paulik nodded. "Did anyone call the garage, by any chance?"

Prodos shook his head. "No, I don't think so. It was just me and the cars."

"When did you and Mlle Durand split up?" Paulik asked.

"We stopped seeing each other about a month after she stopped working at the clothing store in Rognes," Prodos said. "It was more my decision than hers, and it was very hard on both of us."

"But you still kept in touch, and went to see her on Monday."

"Yes," Prodos replied. "Neither of us have cell phones; Gisèle felt she couldn't afford one, and I'm too old-school for such advanced technology, so the only way I could get hold of her was on her landline. But she didn't answer all weekend. I was worried about her. And so I closed the garage early on Monday evening and drove over to Rognes to see her."

"I'm sorry," Paulik said. "Did she have any other friends?"

"No, not many," Prodos replied. "We're both loners."

"How was her mood recently?"

"Gisèle was in a real funk—a depression, really—but I just couldn't reach her anymore. I needed to protect myself—my mother was a depressive, before she killed herself when I was thirteen—and Gisèle's mood reminded me too much of . . ."

Paulik watched the mechanic closely. André Prodos looked down at his crossed arms and took a deep breath. "I'm sorry," he said. "And to think I've had years of therapy," he said, trying to smile.

Paulik smiled and said, "Take your time. Anything you can

tell me about Mlle Durand's habits, and moods, will help." Paulik thought to himself: a garage mechanic who not only has seen a therapist, but admits to it.

"Anyway," Prodos went on, "Gisèle and I had stopped dating, but that didn't stop me from loving her. So I checked up on her, tried to boost her morale."

"Was she seeing anyone?"

"No, I really don't think she was. She would have told me."

"I was told that some of her previous boyfriends were not so nice," Paulik said.

"She went for the tough guys," Prodos answered. "Until me. At least I like to think of myself as a gentle soul."

Paulik looked at Prodos; he spoke like a poet, not a mechanic. "Any of those guys on your suspect list?"

"I thought of one of them, Georges Hoquet, right away," Prodos replied. "I even phoned him up, ready to accuse him, or at least ask him to a duel. But his brother answered the phone: Hoquet is in Paris."

"Paris isn't that far away. . . ."

"In jail," Prodos went on. "For armed robbery. Has been for over a year."

"I see," Paulik said. "What did Mlle Durand do all day?" he asked, changing the subject. "What were her habits?"

"I think the only time she went out was to do a bit of grocery shopping," Prodos said.

Paulik wrote, "Double-check shops in Rognes," in his notebook. "Did she go into Aix often?"

"Nah," Prodos replied. "Even when we were dating and I could drive her in, she didn't like it. She found it too snooty. I go about once a week to the Cinéma Mazarin, but she wouldn't come, so I ended up going to films alone."

Paulik nodded. The Cinéma Mazarin showed foreign movies—in their original languages—and art films.

"That was the big problem for me," Prodos went on. "Gisèle was a great woman, but was too easily intimidated. She lacked so much self-confidence. I tried to help her. . . ." Prodos again looked down at his folded arms and then took off his glasses and wiped his eyes.

As Paulik waited for Prodos to collect himself, he saw, across the office, toward the door that led to the garage, a bust of Charles de Gaulle.

Prodos put his glasses back on and looked up. "President de Gaulle was a huge Citroën DS 19 fan," he said, noticing the commissioner's puzzled expression. "It saved his life."

"Really?" Paulik asked. "I didn't know."

"In 1962. The president's car was ambushed, and shots were fired. The would-be assassins fired at de Gaulle but hit the tires instead. The DS kept rolling along, with two flat tires. Got the president out of harm's way."

"My grandparents had one," Paulik said. "Sort of like that one you have up on the hoist, but it wasn't as fancy. Definitely not two-toned. It was light blue. Eggshell blue, my mother used to say. I thought it was the sleekest car in the world." Paulik sat back and laughed. "The way those headlights moved with the steering wheel! Talk about avant-garde!"

Prodos smiled. "Wanna come into the garage and look at them?"

Paulik got up and stretched his legs. "I'd love to."

Prodos held the garage door open for Paulik. "That one on the hoist is a DS 21, 1970."

"I remember when I figured out for the first time the puns Citroën was using for its car names," Paulik said, staring up at the strange lemon-shaped car. "'DS' sounds like *déesse*. I ran and told my father."

"Yes, 'goddess,'" Prodos replied. "And that's what these cars are: goddesses. I hate long trips when I'm not in one of these."

"I'm with you. That hydraulic suspension—the way the car would float along, hardly even slowing down at potholes or speed bumps. The suspension had its bad side too—I used to get carsick."

"Ah yes," Prodos said, resting a slender hand on the car's rear. "That soupy-floaty motion did have its negative side effects, but I've never felt that way in one. It's just ice-smooth to me."

"I remember my grandfather using the hydraulic suspension to change a flat tire," Paulik said. "We used to beg him to drive the car with the suspension all the way up. He did once, but he only drove about twenty kilometers an hour. The car was sitting up about one meter off the ground. We hung our heads out the window and yelled like warriors."

Prodos laughed. "There were warriors in West Africa who actually did that for big-game hunting, with the suspension hiked all the way up, just like you say—except they weren't going twenty kilometers an hour, but sixty."

"Really? Can the car handle that kind of speed while sitting one meter off the ground?"

"No way," Prodos replied. "They busted the suspensions. Citroën couldn't figure out what was going on with all of these broken cars until it realized they were driving them with the suspension hiked up in order to chase antelopes. But ten or twenty kilometers an hour, over rough terrain, is no problem. Just the other day, before the rains . . ."

"Do you sell these?" Paulik cut in as he walked around the burgundy ID.

"All the time," Prodos said. "There's a waiting list. There are fan clubs all over the world."

"Makes you proud to be French, eh?" Paulik asked.

"I've always been proud to be French," Prodos said. "Except when Pompidou chose a Citroën SM for the presidential car."

Paulik groaned. "I agree! That was an eyesore compared with earlier Citroëns, even if it did have a Maserati engine."

"I'm thinking of selling the Range Rover," Paulik said as he came into their kitchen. Hélène Paulik looked up at her husband, pushing aside her glass of red wine.

"You're so late tonight, Bruno," she said.

"I'm sorry," he replied. "I must have conducted a record number of interviews today. And everyone has an alibi, or no motive."

"Did you listen to my messages?" she asked. "Léa even left you a message. She's in bed, sleeping, by the way."

Paulik looked up at the kitchen clock; it was after 10:00 p.m. "I heard Léa's message. I'll write her a note and put it by her bed."

"A *note*?"

Paulik set the bottle down; he had been about to pour himself a glass of red wine. "Hélène, I'm sorry. I know that Léa misses me, and that you're under stress at work. . . ."

"Stress? That's what you call it, Bruno?"

Paulik shrugged. "Yes, stress. Hélène, I'm doing everything I can. . . ."

"It's more than stress! Olivier is now accusing his employees of stealing wine! He's gone through all the family members, and he's so desperate he's started in on us. . . . Cyril quit today!"

"He quit? Well, I'm sorry about Cyril quitting, but the Bonnards' little wine loss is nothing compared with these women being attacked and killed!"

"I'm not saying it is!" Hélène said. "Do you think I'm thick? I'm not comparing wine theft to rape and murder, and I know that Beauclaire's wines aren't worth as much as famous Bordeaux and California wines, but the sentimental loss . . ."

"Sentimental loss? I went to a funeral today for a twenty-eight-year-old girl!"

Hélène put her head in her hands and then looked up at her husband. "I'm so sorry. I had no idea."

Paulik sat down across from his wife. "And there'll be two more funerals this week: one for Mme d'Arras, with the church full of people who didn't like her but pretended they did; and the other in Rognes, with maybe ten people, one of whom cared very much for the dead woman."

"That's terrible, honey."

"And so your Cyril is quitting," Paulik said. "You'll be overworked."

Hélène nodded. "He's the best assistant I've ever had. A real natural." She took a sip of wine and ate a handful of salted cashews. "I can't stop eating these things."

Paulik grabbed a handful. "Yum. Dinner." He got up and pointed to the bottle. "Do you mind if I have a glass?"

Hélène laughed. "Go ahead. I could see that you needed one, but I kept interrupting."

"I was thinking today that I haven't been doing enough on the Bonnards' wine caper," he said, pouring one of Hélène's special-reserve Syrahs in a glass.

"Caper? You make it sound like a board game."

"Sorry," Paulik replied. "God, you don't know how many times I've said 'sorry' today."

"Sorry," Hélène said, and they burst out laughing. "I think we're both exhausted," she said.

"I'm sure you're right. I'm stumped on these attacks, and stumped on the Bonnards' wine theft." He sat back and had a sip of wine, swirling it in his glass and then sniffing it. "Wild raspberries. You make great wine, honey."

"Thanks."

"Do you really think Cyril's leaving?" Paulik asked. "He could be bluffing."

"Oh yeah," Hélène answered. "He's already found another job, in Burgundy, for some Chinese who have just bought Château Baron Dubreuil. At double the salary."

"Are foreigners buying up all our wine estates?"

"Almost! Soon we'll have to buy our own wines back from them!" Both Pauliks laughed. "Luckily, Victor is very sharp in the cellar, and he loves it out in the field too. The two don't always go hand in hand."

"Good for him, since he'll inherit," Paulik said, looking at his wife.

Hélène sighed. "Pity me, not being born into a wine family."

Chapter Twenty-three

ℳ

A Secret in the Garden

*V*erlaque parked his car in his garage and listened to his messages while walking into downtown Aix. He had turned his phone off while speaking to Soeur Clothilde and forgotten to turn it back on. He realized that he had been so mesmerized by their conversation that not only had he not switched his phone back on—something he never forgot to do—but he had also forgotten to pull off at the rest stop to look at Carcassonne. He had a text message from Marine that read "Still no word from the lab. Sylvie and Charlotte are back, so I'm at their place celebrating their return. Don't wait up. . . . S. had a very exciting summer; we have much to talk about."

He listened to Paulik's message about Philippe Léridon and decided to walk straight there. It sounded as if Paulik had had a busy day, while he himself had been walking in a rose garden, getting psychoanalyzed by a nun. He laughed for the first time that day, and it felt good.

He zigzagged his way through Aix's medieval streets until he got to the Palais de Justice. Verlaque looked up at the justice hall's upper stories and noticed for the first time that instead of shutters on the windows there were flimsy blinds, many of them broken, flapping in the wind. "How embarrassing," Verlaque muttered, and he turned up Rue Émeric David. He knew that wooden Provençal shutters would look out of place on a neoclassical building, but there must be a better solution than using metal blinds that were meant for interiors.

On Émeric David he noticed how many storefronts had recently changed, and he was thankful that the antique dealer on the northwest corner was still in business. From across the street he looked at its interior, dimly lit, its walls painted a dark burgundy, and he remembered his grandmother Emmeline saying that antique shops were both welcoming and intimidating at the same time. He walked on, noticing that across the street from the d'Arras apartment was a tattoo-and-piercing salon. Verlaque didn't have to guess twice about what Mme d'Arras had thought of it.

He rang at number 16, Hôtel de Panisse-Passis, admiring its elaborate door carving as he waited. A crown was carved in huge relief in the center, and branching out from it were a variety of weapons: swords, an ax, bows and arrows, knives. Delicately carved ribbons and foliage offset the manly weapons. Scaffolding covered most of the façade, and a piece of tarp blew in the breeze, making a flapping sound against the metal poles of the scaffold. Verlaque stretched his neck and looked up between the wall and the blue tarp; much of the stonework was heavily carved into busts or foliage, and the second-story balcony was a riot of twisted wrought iron. It was all very wedding-cake-like. Someone in the seventeenth century had certainly been showing off.

Verlaque was about to ring again when a male voice answered, "*Oui?*" A camera and speakerphone had already been installed at the front doors, even though the building was still being renovated.

"Philippe? It's Antoine Verlaque. We met at Jacob Lévy's house last Friday night."

"*Ah oui!* Come in." The door clicked, and Verlaque pushed it open and stepped inside—not into a hallway, as he had expected, but into a paved inner courtyard, open to the sky. Léridon walked across the courtyard and shook Verlaque's hand. "*Bon soir,*" he said, smiling.

"*Bon soir,*" Verlaque said. "I'm afraid this isn't a social call."

Léridon's smile faded. "In that case, let's go inside to talk." He gestured with his hand to the far side of the courtyard. They were walking across the cobblestones when Léridon stopped and said, "Is it about Mme d'Arras? Her husband's on my case now too."

Verlaque nodded.

"Follow me," Léridon said, and they walked through a second set of doors—not wood, as they once would have been, but clear glass edged in matte-black aluminum frames. The contrast was striking between the old and the new. Inside the hall, the floors were laid in worn black-and-white-checkered marble, common in Aix's *hôtels*. They turned left and walked into a living room whose central focus was a huge flat-screen TV. Verlaque winced. "This room's finished," Léridon said, his hands on his hips. "Can I get you anything? Coffee? Whiskey?"

Verlaque chose a seat with his back to the television and wanted to say, "I'd love a whiskey. I've had a hell of a day." Instead, he answered, "A coffee, if it's no trouble."

"I have an espresso machine; it'll take two seconds," Léridon said. "I'll be right back; the machine is in the temporary kitchen. Sugar?"

"One lump. Thanks." While Léridon was gone, Verlaque mused on his day; he had wanted to describe it as "hellish," but it hadn't been hellish at all. Reliving his past had been hellish, yes, but it had been eased by the company of the nun, especially in that environment. He sat back and looked around Léridon's living room. The abstract paintings on the walls were probably expensive, but not to his taste: the colors were too garish. The white leather sofas were probably Italian, and expensive as well, but cold both to the touch and on the eyes. The color scheme seemed to be white, with highlights of red in the light fixtures, vases, and carpets, a color Verlaque didn't like in decoration. The dark, almost brown red of Burgundy wine, perhaps, but not this bright red.

Léridon came back balancing two espresso cups on a small tray and held the tray in front of Verlaque. "The blue cup is the one with sugar," he said. "I always take it black."

"Thanks," Verlaque said, stirring his coffee with a tiny silver spoon.

Léridon sat down and drank his coffee. "So what's d'Arras complaining about now?" he asked. "The noise? I told my workmen to knock off early, around six p.m., because I know how much it's been bothering the d'Arrases."

"Him now, not them," Verlaque answered. He brought his demitasse to his mouth, but the smell of the coffee turned his stomach. He forced himself to have a tiny sip, to be polite.

Léridon finished his coffee in two sips and set the cup on a glass coffee table. "She wasn't my favorite person in the world, but I'm sorry she died."

"She was murdered," Verlaque said, leaning forward. "And, unfortunately, you were overheard threatening her. Multiple times."

Léridon laughed uneasily. "I have a hot temper," he said. "Ask anyone who's ever worked for me."

"I will." Verlaque forced himself to finish his coffee and set his cup beside Léridon's. "I'll have to ask you if you have an alibi for Friday evening—"

Léridon cut in. "I was at that cigar party."

"Between six and eight p.m.," Verlaque said, "before the party."

"I was here."

"Were there any workmen still around? Or family members?" Verlaque watched as Léridon lowered his eyes and then rubbed them.

"My wife's in Paris. . . ." he mumbled. "But the electrician was still here. I'll get you his phone number." Léridon went into another room and came back with a business card. "I don't recommend him," he said. "Every time I put the microwave on, the power downstairs cuts off. But here's his phone number. I made him stay late Friday night to fix his mess."

"Thank you," Verlaque said. "I'm sorry to have bothered you." He went to get up and fell back down on the white sofa.

"Are you all right?" Léridon asked, hovering over him.

Verlaque looked at Philippe Léridon and saw two men standing before him. He rubbed his eyes and said, "Could I have a tall glass of water?"

"Done," Léridon said, quickly leaving the living room. Verlaque closed his eyes; when he opened them, Léridon was standing over him, holding a glass of water.

"Thanks," Verlaque said. "My mouth is incredibly dry." He drank half of it and rested the glass on his knee. "M. and Mme d'Arras complained that you have something in your garden that you're hiding. My commissioner reminded me of it earlier this evening." Verlaque realized he had almost left Léridon's without asking about it. Something was not right with him this evening, and he tried to ignore the churning noises his stomach was making.

Léridon laughed uneasily. "Are they worried I'm building a swimming pool without a permit?"

"No, they seem to think that it's something more sinister," Verlaque replied.

Léridon sneered. "It's none of their business, as I told both of them."

Verlaque finished his water and set the glass down. "It's my business now, since Mme d'Arras was murdered. What's out there, Philippe?"

Léridon said nothing. He crossed the living room and looked at the front courtyard through the tall living-room windows.

"You can show me tonight," Verlaque said, rubbing his stomach, "or I can have four guys and a van in your courtyard tomorrow at eight a.m."

Still Léridon said nothing and continued looking out the window.

"I can also tap your phones, have you followed, and go over your business and private bank accounts with a team of accountants from Paris who get their kicks finding holes in accounts. . . ."

Léridon turned toward Verlaque and held up his hand, the palm facing the judge. "All right, all right," he said, "I get the point! But you'll see; I haven't done anything wrong."

"So let's go and see it," Verlaque asked.

Léridon sighed. "I knew I couldn't keep it a secret forever." He looked at Verlaque, who was half slumped over on his sofa. "Let's go outside, then." Léridon went to the door, and Verlaque got up, trying not to groan. They walked through what Léridon referred to as a temporary kitchen, which looked to Verlaque like an already decent one, and exited through a set of French doors into a garden that was in total darkness. Léridon led, with a flashlight in his hand, toward a lean-to set against the rear stone wall. Once there, he motioned for Verlaque to squat down at the edge of the lean-to. Verlaque almost fell down onto the lush lawn.

"You have to stick the upper half of your body over the hole to see it," Léridon said, pointing his flashlight to where a blue tarp was laid. "Way over."

Verlaque did as he was told, awkwardly poising his body over the tarp, which made the same eerie flapping noise as the one by the front door. Verlaque's forearms shivered, and he could feel sweat dripping down his back. Léridon stood behind him, shining the light on the blue tarp. "Are you ready?" he said. "Lean out a little more."

Verlaque set his aching stomach on the grass and craned his neck. He felt woozy; it must have been the long drive . . . or had Léridon put something in the coffee? His dry mouth . . . If Léridon had murdered Mme d'Arras, would he be stupid enough to kill an examining magistrate? But, buried in this hole, Verlaque's body might never be discovered. The voice of Soeur Clothilde rang in his head, and her words: "It's not your fault; you did nothing wrong."

He was struggling to get on his knees when he felt a hand on his shoulder. He imagined that it was Soeur Clothilde's, forgiving him. Léridon said, "Lean over more or you won't see it," and Verlaque groggily obeyed. Léridon reached over and lifted the blue tarp off with a fast, practiced gesture; he shone his flashlight twelve feet below. "Do you see it?"

Verlaque blinked and waited until his eyes had adjusted to the light. He gasped. Léridon was now lying on the grass beside him, looking down, his chin resting on the end of the flashlight. "Isn't it amazing?" he asked.

Below was a large mosaic floor, laid in small black and white stone. "It's Roman, isn't it?" Verlaque asked, not able to take his eyes off it. He blinked and looked down again, scanning the squares, diamonds, and circles that created a vivid geometric pattern. He couldn't see any missing tiles—it was in perfect condition.

"Of course," Léridon replied. "Aix was a Roman spa town."

Verlaque sighed. "Thanks, Philippe. I didn't know that."

"Oh, sorry if I sounded uppity. I've just never been excited by any . . . art . . . like this before. I did some research at the library, and did some asking around. I think this dates from the first or second century A.D."

"Who else knows about this?"

"One of my workmen, the guy who discovered it while digging to install a wine cellar," Léridon answered. "I've had to pay them off to keep them quiet, but who knows how long that will last. Plus, the head research librarian at the municipal library probably suspects something."

Verlaque laughed. "You were asking a lot of questions?"

"Yeah. I kept pestering her for articles on the history of Roman Aix."

Verlaque looked over at Léridon, noting his expensive moccasins, open shirt, and tanned forearms. Léridon was right: he probably hadn't been mistaken for a historian. "And you didn't want to report the mosaic," he said.

Léridon laughed. "Of course not. The librarian showed me articles about people finding Greek and Roman remnants while renovating their houses. Work can be stalled for up to ten years. And *I've* found a whole floor, not just some pieces of jars or a few coins. Who knows what else is down there?" He shone his light around the floor, tracing its zigzag pattern with the light. "It looks like it could have been designed in the 1960s, eh? It's almost psychedelic."

Verlaque laughed. "You're right." A tiny bit of bile came up from his throat into his mouth. "Philippe, you need to show me to a toilet, fast."

Léridon jumped up and pulled Verlaque to his feet. They ran back across the garden and into the house. Ten minutes later, Verlaque found himself lying on the tiled bathroom floor, his head on a towel. Léridon was sitting next to him, his back against the wall, arms resting on his pulled-up knees. "Feel better?" he asked. "You passed out."

Verlaque sat up and wiped his mouth. "I do. Did I throw up?"

"About a million times," Léridon said. "No, just twice. What did you have to eat today, my friend?"

"Only a sandwich, and a shrimp salad."

"From a place in Aix?"

Verlaque wiped his brow with his linen handkerchief. "No, from a highway gas station."

"*Putain!*" Léridon cried, hitting his forehead. "You should never eat anything from those places!"

"I thought you'd drugged me," Verlaque said before he could stop himself.

Léridon let out a loud laugh. "That's the funniest thing I've heard in a long time!"

Verlaque laughed and said, "Can we go and sit in the living room?"

Léridon helped Verlaque up for a second time and led him to the living room. Verlaque fell back onto the sofa. "I'll bring you a blanket," Léridon said, laughing. "And another glass of water."

"Bring some of that whiskey you suggested earlier too," Verlaque said, taking off his shoes.

"Sounds like a great idea. I was wishing you'd taken me up on the offer earlier. I've had a hell of a day."

"*Your* day?" Verlaque said, leaning back. "Couldn't have been worse than mine!"

Léridon returned with two cut-glass tumblers, each with a generous serving of golden whiskey. Verlaque thanked him and sniffed. "Islay?"

Léridon nodded. "Ardbeg . . . with a touch of arsenic." He laughed and toasted Verlaque. "So why was your day hellish?"

Verlaque looked up. "I got cross-examined by an old nun."

Léridon laughed. "Excellent! Did she get a confession out of you?"

"You could say that. And your day?"

"My wife finally told me she's leaving me."

Verlaque set his glass down on the coffee table, unsure whether whiskey was a wise choice. "*Merde.* I'm so sorry."

Léridon sighed. "I've been waiting for her to do this; it's not like I didn't see it coming. The worst part is, she sent me the news via a text message."

"Oh God." Verlaque reached for his glass and took another sip. It tasted good and, oddly enough, settled his stomach. "A text message. Really?"

"Yep." Both men remained silent. "Tonight," Léridon went on. "While watching you toss your cookies . . ."

Verlaque laughed. "Thanks."

"I decided what to do. I'm going to sell this place. I'll have to report the mosaic, and then I'll put the place on the market. Perhaps the city will buy it."

"They might," Verlaque said, although he secretly knew that

the city of Aix preferred real-estate transactions that made them a huge profit.

"And then I'll go back to Morocco." Léridon took a gulp of whiskey. "I liked it there. Workmen actually show up on the job site, for one thing."

"But they don't have this," Verlaque said, lifting up his whiskey glass.

"No," Léridon said, "you just have to bring it with you."

Chapter Twenty-four

❧

Honey and Buttered Toast

*C*offee in bed?" Paulik asked as he fluffed the pillows behind his head and sat up.

"We need to take it easy this morning," Hélène said. "Léa got a ride to school with the Villards; they owed me. And I called Olivier and told him I'd be late."

Paulik rubbed his eyes. "I need to phone Judge Verlaque, then." He reached over and grabbed his cell phone. After a short call, Paulik hung up. "He slept in too," he told Hélène. "Ate something bad yesterday. We've agreed to meet at Domaine Beauclaire after lunch. Sound good?"

Hélène sat on the edge of the bed and sipped her coffee. "That's great! You mean you're interested in trying to solve the 'caper'?"

Paulik grimaced. "I've been wanting to, believe me—as has Judge Verlaque. We also agreed that it may be a good idea to return to the scene of one of the murders and work our way over it again."

"When you've finished your coffee, come downstairs and we can have breakfast," Hélène said.

"Actually, when I finish this coffee, I'm going to roll over and go back to sleep," Paulik replied. "Wake me up for lunch."

Verlaque's Porsche was parked in the Bonnards' courtyard when Bruno and Hélène Paulik pulled up. "Coffee?" Élise asked as they came into the kitchen.

"Please," Bruno Paulik answered. He looked at Hélène, who said, "I'm actually going to pass. I don't think I can drink any more espresso. I've been living on it since these wine . . . thefts."

Olivier Bonnard jumped up. "I agree," he said. "Let's say no to more coffee and try your new white, Hélène." He looked at Victor and quickly added, "Yours and Victor's."

The boy beamed and then bent toward Hélène. "I bow to the master," he said.

Élise Bonnard looked anxiously at Antoine Verlaque. "I'm up for a wine tasting," Verlaque said. "I always think better with a little wine."

"That's what Dad always says," Victor said. "I'll go and siphon some wine from the barrel."

"What kind of white is it?" Verlaque asked.

"Rolle," Hélène answered. "It's our premium white-wine grape in Provence, but it's so underrated, and undervalued. The Italians and Corsicans have been working at elevating its status, and that's what Victor and I have been trying to do."

"By putting it in barrels for a few months?" Paulik asked his wife. "I don't like that too-oaky taste that was a fad a few years ago."

"Don't worry," she said. "We used *old* barrels we bought from a Burgundian estate, not new ones, so the oak won't overpower the fruit."

"Do they do Rolle in Italy?" Verlaque asked. "I've never had it there."

Hélène nodded. "You've had it, but they call it Vermentino."

Victor came back carrying two decanters balanced on a tray. "*Et voilà!*" he said.

Élise tried not to sigh too loudly as she got up and gathered wineglasses from the china cabinet. She didn't approve of drinking in the middle of the afternoon.

Victor poured everyone an inch of golden wine, and Olivier, unable to hide his excitement, passed the glasses around. "The moment of truth! And may this golden nectar help solve our wine heist!" Olivier said, holding his glass in the air.

"Hear, hear!" the others bellowed as they all, even Élise, swirled the wine in their glasses, sniffed, and then swirled some more.

Verlaque put his crooked nose in the glass and inhaled. "It does smell like honey," he said.

"And buttered toast," Bruno Paulik offered.

Verlaque swirled the wine in his glass and then drank. "If you hadn't told me," he said, "I would have guessed that this was a noble Chardonnay, from the Beaune region."

Victor did a high five with Hélène.

"Our Rolle has never tasted like this," Olivier Bonnard said, closing his eyes and taking another sip. "Don't tell your grandfather I just said that," he added, looking at Victor.

"Where *is* Grandpa?" Victor asked.

"He's getting ready for his *boules* game," Élise replied. "Rémy should be here to pick him up any minute."

As if on cue, a car swung into the courtyard, stopping with a jerk just a few feet away from the kitchen window.

"He's in a rush today," Élise said, opening the door. "Come in, Rémy!"

"Rémy's been our mailman for years," Olivier Bonnard explained to Verlaque.

"He's been the *only* one I've ever known," Victor said. "He's one of Grandpa's best friends too."

The group turned to the open kitchen door as a tall, blond man walked in, wearing a lime-green merino-wool suit and carrying a straw hat, as if he had just been on the set of a turn-of-the-century film. "Excuse me, ladies and gentlemen," he said, bowing.

"M. Thébaud," Olivier said, getting up to shake the wine expert's hand. "Do come in." Hippolyte Thébaud shook hands with the people gathered around the table; Verlaque was quite sure that he had winked at him.

"My fair judge," Thébaud said with a slight bow.

Élise Bonnard gestured for the wine expert to sit down, but he refused a seat with a motion of his hand. "I just love your suit," she said. Victor snorted.

"We weren't expecting you back," Olivier Bonnard said, throwing Victor a stare.

"I hadn't meant to come back," Thébaud said, "but I found myself fascinated with the games of *boules*."

Olivier looked at Thébaud in wonderment. The wine expert was the last person he expected to play bocce ball. "*Boules?*" He asked, looking around the table to see if his guests were just as bewildered as he was.

"Is that your new white?" Thébaud asked, changing the subject.

Olivier Bonnard quickly poured Thébaud a glass and handed it to him. Thébaud held the glass up toward the ceiling, then swirled it and put it to his mouth quicker than Olivier expected him to. He tossed the wine around in his mouth with a loud slurp, walked over to the kitchen door, and spat the contents outside.

The group looked on until Verlaque asked, "So . . . what did you think?"

"One of the finest Rolles I ever tasted," Thébaud replied. Victor let out a cheer, and Élise gave her son a look as if to say, "You see, don't judge a book by its cover." "It has great strength of character," Thébaud went on, sipping more of the wine, and swallowing this time. "And it reminds me of a Vermentino I had years ago on the Ligurian coast, at the summer home of a dear friend, the Contessa de . . ."

A second vehicle broke Thébaud's reverie, coming to a roaring stop beside Thébaud's rental car. "*That* would be Rémy," Victor said. "Here for the *boules* game."

"*Boules,*" Verlaque said, looking at Thébaud with a twinkle in his eye. "You were going to tell us about *boules*. . . ."

Élise Bonnard introduced Rémy, who had rushed into the room and then froze when he saw the guests sitting around the kitchen table. He put himself shyly against the kitchen wall, twirling a cap in his hands.

"Come in, Rémy!" Olivier motioned. "It's your day off today?"

"Yes, s-s-sir," Rémy replied nervously. "I've come to pick up Albert for our game. And I've also come to . . ."

"That can wait," Thébaud said, stepping out of the shadows. "Taste the wine first."

"M. Thébaud!" Rémy said. "I thought you had gone back to Paris."

"What's going on here?" Olivier Bonnard asked. "Do you two know each other?"

Thébaud smiled. "We met in the village, playing *boules*."

"You're good," Rémy said, rocking back and forth on his tiptoes. "A real natural."

"Sit down, Rémy," Olivier said. "And try this white wine we've just created."

Rémy quickly sat down, bumping into the table. "Um, yes. A little wine will go down well right now."

Victor poured the mailman a glass, and Rémy sniffed and then tasted, swirling the wine around loudly in his mouth, like an expert. Hélène hid her smile and winked at Victor.

"Magnificent," Rémy replied. "That's the way Rolle should taste."

As the others stared in silence, Élise came back into the kitchen and said, "Albert will be down in a minute, Rémy. He didn't notice the time go by and is getting ready."

"And we should go out and look at the scene of the crime once more," Paulik said, getting up. Verlaque nodded and gulped the rest of his wine.

Rémy jumped up. "Eh? The scene of the crime?" he asked. "The wine theft?"

Hippolyte Thébaud grinned.

"No, Rémy," Olivier said. "It has to do with that woman, you know, whose body was found in our vineyard."

"Perhaps you should come outside before your father comes down," Thébaud said to Olivier.

"We have to show you something!" Rémy added, his head bopping up and down.

"Rémy, what's wrong?" Olivier asked, setting down his wineglass and getting up.

"Are you all right?" Élise asked. "Would you like a glass of water?" She glared at her husband.

"Um, no, no water. But you need to come out to my van, M. Bonnard, quickly. I have to show you something."

"All right, all right," Olivier said. He and the rest of the group followed Rémy out to his van, a former yellow post-office van that had been painted white. They crowded around its back doors while Rémy fumbled for his keys, dropping them on the gravel.

Victor bent down and picked up the keys. "Rémy, would you like me to open the doors for you?" he asked.

Rémy quickly nodded, glancing at the kitchen door. Victor put the key in the lock and opened the van's doors wide; then he stood back and looked from his father to Rémy. "Rémy," Victor said, "it's full of wine."

"Y-y-yes."

Olivier Bonnard reached in and pulled out a bottle at random. He looked at the label and sighed, handing it to Élise. "Rémy," she said, passing the bottle on to Victor, "it's ours."

"Did you figure this out?" Olivier asked Hippolyte Thébaud.

Thébaud replied with a bow.

"I don't believe it," Victor said, looking at the postman. "How could you have done this?"

"It was, er, tricky," Rémy replied. "It took us days to gather what was left."

"What was left?" Hélène asked.

"How did you get into our *cave*?" Olivier asked. "Did you make a copy of the key that hangs in the kitchen?"

Rémy looked at Olivier Bonnard in shock, his mouth open. "Eh? What's this? I've known you all my life," he said. "I can't believe you would accuse me of stealing your wines! *Ça alors!*"

"But, Rémy," Élise said softly, "what are we to think? Where did you get these?"

"The Old Vines 1964," Victor said, passing a dusty bottle to his father.

"From everyone around," Rémy replied, looking anxiously toward the kitchen door once more. "Nobody wanted to admit that they had some of your wine. He figured it out!" the postman said, pointing at Thébaud. "He played *boules* with us and asked us if we had some of your bottles. Then Roger said that Albert had given him a magnum of 1978, and Jean-Philippe said that he had some 1970s from Albert, and we realized what was going on."

"Dad's giving away our wine?" Olivier asked.

Thébaud nodded. "That day I came to see your cellars," he said, "I saw your father leave for his *boules* game, carrying his leather satchel as if his life's worth was inside of it, not his *boules*. I left quickly and followed him into the village, where I saw him stop by the butcher shop and hand the butcher a bottle of wine, and then cross the street to the pharmacy and do the same thing. Disappointingly easy case to break."

"Even your maid got some, and Patrice, who cuts Albert's hair," Rémy excitedly added.

"I wanted to make sure that your father wasn't being forced to give the wine away, so I played *boules* with the . . . lads," Thébaud said. The crowd exchanged looks, each one silently thinking, *What would he wear to play* boules?

"As if we would ever force Albert to do that!" Rémy cried. "It was all his own doing!"

"That's right," Albert Bonnard said. The elder Bonnard had just emerged from the house, cradling his bag of *boules*. "Better our friends than the enemy."

"Dad?" Olivier asked, heading for his father. "The enemy?"

"*Les boches.*"

"Dad, the war has been over for more than sixty years," Olivier said. "We have German friends, and clients."

Albert Bonnard hugged his duffel bag.

"Grandpa," Victor said, "can I take the bag from you? It looks heavy." He walked slowly to his grandfather and gently lifted the bag from his arms, raising his eyebrows at his father at the same time.

"Don't give them to anyone but our friends," Albert said. "Now Rémy and I have to go, before we are late for our match."

Rémy looked at Olivier Bonnard and shrugged.

"Come on, Rémy!" Albert said, walking around the van to the passenger side.

Victor had laid the duffel bag on the ground and removed two bottles of wine. "Here, Grandpa," he called. "Your *boules*!"

Rémy got into the driver's seat and rolled down the window. "We got what we could," he whispered to Olivier, his head leaning out of the window. "But some of the guys had drunk the wine already. I didn't, though. Don't worry. You'll get all mine back."

Olivier put his hand on Rémy's arm. "Thank you so much, Rémy. You should keep a few bottles for yourself."

"Eh? No, no. I wouldn't dream of it. Happy to be of service."

Olivier glanced toward the back of the van and saw that Verlaque, Hélène, Bruno, and Victor had quickly unloaded the wine while Thébaud looked on, his arms crossed. Olivier tapped the van's door and said, "Have a great game." As Rémy waved his cap in the air, Olivier could hear his father loudly complaining about Jean-Philippe, who he thought had cheated during their last game.

"I'll have him back in time for dinner!" Rémy called as they drove through Domaine Beauclaire's gates.

"M. Thébaud," Olivier Bonnard said, shaking the wine expert's hand, "I don't know how to thank you."

"It was nothing."

"Will you stay for dinner?" Élise asked excitedly.

"Thank you, but no, I have to catch the TGV back to Paris." Thébaud smiled and added, "I'm having a late dinner with my editor."

"Are you writing a wine book?" Olivier asked.

"I'm publishing my memoirs."

Verlaque looked at Thébaud and smiled.

"Wow! We'll be sure to buy the book when it comes out," Élise said. "What's the title?"

The wine expert straightened his bow tie. "*Confessions of a Wine Thief.*"

"Ha!" Verlaque laughed out loud.

Thébaud ignored him. "The TV rights have already been sold," he said, smiling. "It will be a series on Canal Plus."

Élise clapped her hands together. "That's wonderful! Who will play you? Oh, I can just see Romain Duris, or perhaps Guillaume Canet. . . ."

Chapter Twenty-five

❧

Big Spender

*I*t's strange," Verlaque said as they walked through the vineyard back toward the house. "We have two separate cases here, but both involve elderly people who are experiencing dementia."

"And both remember the war," Paulik added. "It's like my uncle. The worse it got, the more he kept reliving the past."

"And what dementia and World War II have to do with the deaths of Mlles Montmory and Durand, I just don't know," Verlaque said.

"Maybe they're not connected, and that's all there is to it."

The grapes hung heavy on their branches, many of the clusters hidden by fat green leaves. Paulik looked down at them, remembering harvesting for his father, and the fear that he'd snip off a finger while cutting the grapes off their branches.

The sky was bright blue, and it was suddenly hot again. Verlaque kicked at the dusty red earth; it was as if it had never rained. "They'll be harvesting soon," he said.

"Any day now," Paulik replied. "I was surprised that Olivier was so calm back there. He's usually uptight just before the harvest."

Verlaque asked, "Does it bother Hélène that she has to make someone else's wine?"

Paulik nodded. "It does now. I mean, recently. It never used to, but I think it's now dawned on Hélène that she'll never have her own vineyard. Victor will be the enthusiastic natural winemaker at Beauclaire. When Hélène first started out, she thought that perhaps she could buy some small place in the Languedoc, but even those vineyards are now out of any mortal's price range."

Verlaque stopped to look at the rows of vines. "I don't think I know of any other métier where so many exterior elements have to be dealt with while you produce a product that must be good to, well, taste. Winemakers have to deal with so much: geography, geology, soil science, history, tradition. . . ."

"And trends," Paulik added.

"Yes, you're right, trends and fashions. Not to mention the complicated science involved: chemistry, biology, the science of taste. . . . I'm always very moved when I hear winemakers speak about their work."

"And the wine often reflects the winemaker," Paulik said. "Hélène's wines remind me of her: soft, and yet sometimes surprising and tough in character."

Verlaque nodded. "I once saw a documentary about winemaking, and they were interviewing a father and daughter who both made their own wines in Burgundy. There was a really tearful moment when they had this heart-to-heart, and the daughter accused her father of being cold and impersonal, but she said it through his wines: that his wines were cold and hard to get to know. She was crying her eyes out." They walked on in silence. Antoine Verlaque was thinking about how and when he would confront his family, much as that Burgundian winemaker had confronted her father in the family's damp cellars. Bruno Paulik was thinking about Hélène, and her wines, and the day when he fell in love with her.

"One mystery solved, three to go," Verlaque said as they passed through the gate that led from the vineyard to the Bonnards' courtyard. He brought Paulik up-to-date on Léridon's hidden mosaic floor.

"A Roman floor?" Paulik asked. "No wonder he didn't want to tell anyone. There goes his renovation down the drain."

"Exactly," Verlaque said. "It's like you've found this incredible work of art, and it becomes a hindrance, not a pleasure. I thought of your dad right away. Is he still on his Roman-history kick?"

"Oh yeah," Paulik replied. "He found another Roman coin at a friend's the other day. Do you think . . ."

"That he could have a peek at Léridon's mosaic?"

"Yeah, before the city ropes it off."

"I already asked Léridon and he said yes, bring your dad around anytime, but soon."

"It's a relief that the Bonnards' wine theft was an inside job, and not even theft," Paulik said, laughing. "And now we know that there's no relation between the murder of Mme d'Arras and the wine theft."

"But we still need to determine if Mme d'Arras's death was related to the deaths of Mlles Montmory and Durand," said Verlaque. He suddenly remembered that Marine hadn't heard back from her elderly neighbor, Philomène Joubert. "How did your talk go with Gisèle Durand's ex?"

"Fine," Paulik replied. "He's a Citroën DS buff, and a bit of a poet."

Verlaque smiled. "And his alibi sticks?"

"He doesn't have an alibi," Paulik said, stopping when he got to his car.

Verlaque looked sideways at his commissioner. "Doesn't have an alibi?" he asked. "Shouldn't that concern us?"

"Nah," Paulik said. "He's innocent."

"What's his background?" Verlaque asked. He didn't understand how Paulik could be so certain of the mechanic's innocence.

"Citroën buff, as I told you," Paulik said. "DS in particular."

"That's the long, sleek one with the hydraulic suspension?"

"Yes. My grandfather had one. He drove it for us once with the suspension hiked all the way up. The car was a meter . . ." Paulik stopped talking and started running toward his car.

"Forget something?" Verlaque called after him.

"Prodos drove a car like that last week," Paulik said over his shoulder. He reached his car and jumped in, hanging his head out of the window as he yelled to Verlaque, "I'm going back to the garage. I've been an idiot!"

Verlaque got into his car and cut the end off a Cuban cigar handmade by a young Cuban, purchased on the sly by Fabrice on his last trip to Havana. He smiled, thinking of Fabrice's story about tracking down the mythical young cigar roller and, after several failed attempts because of Fabrice's faulty Spanish, finally locating his apartment. "I'll call him *Miguel*," Fabrice had whispered to Verlaque when he gave the judge the cigar, "but of course that's *not* his real name."

His cell phone rang and he answered it, tilting his car seat back and looking at the plane trees that lined Domaine Beauclaire's drive. "*Oui?*"

"Antoine, it's Marine."

He sat up. "Yes. Have you heard?"

"Positive."

"What?"

"I mean yes, I've heard, and everything's okay!"

He sat back and closed his eyes. "The tests were *negative,* then."

"Yes, sorry to confuse you," she answered. "Everything's a hundred percent fine."

"I'm so happy. We'll have some Champagne tonight."

"Sounds lovely. See you later."

"*Ciao.*"

He put the car into first gear and drove away, listening to Cuban salsa music and blowing cigar smoke out of the open window. Verlaque knew he would have to call Christophe and Fabrice and apologize to them both. However much he liked Christophe Chazeau, his story of getting mud on his tires at another winery had rung as entirely invented. But the wine seller had remembered Christophe's visit on Friday evening, and even the wines he had purchased: a white and a red both from Château Simone. "Big spender," Verlaque mumbled. They were Aix's most expensive wines, and his least favorites.

Paulik parked his car in front of the garage door, about as close as Rémy had parked his van in front of the Bonnards' kitchen. He quickly ran up to the door that led to the office and pulled it; it was locked. "*Merde!*" he said aloud. He banged on the door and called out, "André! I need to speak to you!" and tried the door again, but it was definitely locked. He cupped his hands around his eyes and peeked through the window into the garage's office; the desktop was still covered with invoices and coffee cups. He quickly moved to the front of the garage and looked into the garage's working station; the DS 19 and 21 were gone.

"*Merde, merde, merde!*" he said aloud. "Why was I so stupid?"

A car pulled into the parking lot, and Paulik swung around, hoping to see Prodos, but it was a police cruiser. Paulik walked over to the car as the officers got out.

"Looking for something?" the taller one asked.

"I was," Paulik said, "but he's already flown the coop. I'm Commissioner Paulik from Aix-en-Provence, but I live here." Paulik took out his badge and showed it to the two policemen.

"Do you mean André Prodos?" the taller one asked. "He's had two break-ins within the last six months, so we promised we'd keep a lookout on the garage."

"Yeah, André," Paulik replied. "You know him?"

"Sure," he answered. "Those weird old cars. My brother-in-law knows him; he bought a DS 21 off André a while ago. The thing sucks gas like you wouldn't believe. Is André in trouble?"

Before Paulik could answer, they received another call on their radio and took off, responding to a domestic-violence call in Lourmarin.

Paulik went back to the window and looked into the office again. Bits of the conversation with Prodos came back to him: "We're both loners" . . . "I needed to protect myself" . . . "Just the other day, before the rains." Paulik wiped the dirty glass with the edge of his sleeve and toured the office's interior with his eyes. It seemed to him that the office was emptier than it had been last night; on the walls there were fewer tools—in fact, almost no tools at all. As his eyes scanned the room, he saw the cheap column that had held the bust of Charles de Gaulle, in the corner of the room, beside the coffee machine. But the bust of the illustrious president was gone. "*Merde!*" Paulik yelled, banging the wall with his fist. "*Merde! Merde! Merde!*"

Chapter Twenty-six

❧

Two Glasses of Lagavulin

*Y*ou're home a bit earlier than usual," Marine said, kissing Verlaque. She stood back and looked at the judge; she loved his shaggy black hair streaked with gray, his broken nose, his dark-brown eyes and full lips.

"You can't imagine how happy your phone call made me today," he said, kissing her.

"I was so happy I almost cried," Marine said. "In fact, I think I did."

"Did you tell your folks?"

"Yes, I called my father at his office right away, and he'll tell Maman."

Marine took Verlaque in her arms and ruffled his hair and tightly hugged him. "There was a time I was afraid to hug you," she said, pulling away so that she could look at him. "I mean really hug you, like a best friend does, or a cousin."

"Let's hope we're not related," he said, smiling. "My family is messed up, and cousins marrying are never a good idea."

Marine looked at him in shock, surprised that he would mention marriage, even in an abstract way.

"Let's have another hug," he said, wrapping his arms around her. "I know that for a long time I was distant, and I'm sorry."

"It doesn't matter," she said, rubbing the back of his head. "Hey, how was your day?"

Verlaque laughed. "That's a conversation changer. Actually, I'd like to tell you about my day yesterday."

Marine looked at him; his smile had disappeared. "Okay," she replied. "Does this need wine? Oh! I forgot to buy Champagne!"

"That's okay. I'll take something a tad stronger. Would you join me?"

"All right," she answered. "But put some water in mine."

Verlaque took the whiskey out of the cupboard high above the refrigerator and poured two glasses. He carried them into the living room, where Marine was sitting on the sofa, flipping through an IKEA catalog. "Thank you," she said, putting the catalog down and reaching for her glass. Verlaque smiled when he saw that the catalog was marked with dozens of Post-its.

"I almost called you to have you meet me at those stone picnic tables we like up at Mont Sainte-Victoire," Verlaque said.

Marine shifted, holding her glass and staring at Verlaque. "What is it, Antoine? Those tables we usually reserve for big events—like our birthdays, or when I get a paper published."

"I met with a nun yesterday," he answered. "At the abbey in Jonquières."

"I know of that place," she said. "My mother loves their rose garden. Is the nun Mme d'Arras's sister? Mme Joubert told me about her."

"Yes," Verlaque said. "We talked for over three hours."

"Oh my! She must have given you the whole Aubanel family story."

"Not really. She told me what you had already told me: that Natalie Aubanel's father had been an SS officer. It shed no light on Mme d'Arras's murder, I'm afraid. But it shed a lot of light on me. So did Sylvie's photograph."

"Antoine," Marine said, "I'm sorry, but you're confusing me. Did you have time to go to Sylvie's exhibition?"

"Yes, and I must say that your friend is talented beyond words. You can tell her that for me."

"She'd love to hear it from you."

"She hates me," Verlaque said, pouting and taking a sip of Lagavulin.

"No, she doesn't!" Marine answered. "Well, she didn't like you for a long time. . . ."

They laughed and Marine put her hand on Verlaque's. "What did the photograph tell you?"

"To let go," Verlaque said. "And then the nun told me to forgive."

Marine tilted her head toward his. "Go on," she said. "Forgive whom?"

"Monique, my mother, my father for not doing anything, and even in some weird way my grandmother Emmeline."

"Emmeline?" Marine asked. "But you adored her."

"Exactly," he answered. "But she knew what had happened, so I have to forgive her for *knowing*. That's what the nun said, anyway." He lifted his glass. "Cheers."

"What did Emmeline *know*?" Marine asked, a bit exasperated that Verlaque would try to make a joke of things.

"Well, about me and Monique."

"Antoine, who was Monique?" Marine asked. "You've called out her name in your sleep once or twice."

"I guess you could say she was my girlfriend."

"Why does she haunt you?"

"She was my mother's best friend," Verlaque continued. "My mother introduced us, and knew that we were . . . sleeping together . . . but didn't do anything about it, nor did my father."

"Antoine, how old was Monique? This is sounding very weird."

Verlaque laughed. "It was weird, believe me, but I had no idea at the time, until Emmeline took me away to Normandy with her. Monique was thirty-six."

Marine put her untouched glass down on the coffee table. "You lived with your grandparents in Normandy when you were really young, didn't you? Did you move back there when you were in your twenties? After your affair with Monique?"

"No, I never lived there in my twenties. I went there when I was fifteen."

Marine reached across the coffee table and picked up her glass. "I need a drink," she said, sipping the whiskey.

"You should just hold on to the glass," Verlaque said.

Marine ignored him. "So . . . are you telling me that when you were a boy, *a boy*, of fifteen, you had an affair with a thirty-six-year-old friend of your mother's?"

"It started when I was thirteen," he said. "So Monique must have been thirty-four."

"Oh my God!" Marine whispered, setting down her glass again and putting her head in her hands.

"Hey, it's okay," Verlaque said. "I knew you'd have this kind of reaction." He threw his hands up in mock surprise.

"Antoine!" Marine cried. "Don't make a joke of this!" She got up to pace the room and then sat back down. "This is awful! You were a child! I could wring her neck!"

"She's dead," Verlaque said. "She died of cancer years ago."

"Then I'll go and spit on her grave!"

"I'll join you," he said.

Marine jumped up again. "You're hopping around like a rabbit," Verlaque said, watching her. "But she's not entirely to blame."

"She isn't?" Marine cried. "She knew what she was doing, and you . . ."

"Did too."

"No, Antoine! You were too young!"

"Old enough to know what I was doing—not really understanding it, but conscious of what was going on between us. And I wasn't having a bad time. That's the truth, and the hard thing for me, and probably for you, to understand. I loved her in some weird way."

"Do you think that you knew what love meant at that age?" Marine asked, taking his hand. "You must have been so confused."

Verlaque heard his cell phone ring. He ignored it. "I think that a thirteen-year-old *does* understand love. I know you're upset, but what I want you to know is that I've finally stopped ignoring it. That's what Sylvie's photo nudged me to do, and then Soeur Clothilde."

"What did the nun say?" Marine asked. "Can you tell me?"

"She just had this amazing way of getting me to talk," Verlaque answered. "By the end I was blabbing on and on, and I even cried." He quickly put his hand up. "Don't say anything!"

Marine smiled. "I'm going to have another sip of whiskey," she said. "Cheers back to you." She took a sip. "So . . . did Soeur Clothilde have advice, you know, a course of action you can take, instead of saying the rosary?"

Verlaque laughed. "You know, she didn't once mention God, or praying. She said I'd have to do all the work." He sipped some whiskey and turned his body toward Marine's. "Marine, do you care about my money?"

"No, but I love your car," she said, laughing. "No, Antoine, I don't care about your money. I do like the fact that we take great vacations, I'll admit that, and I love that Venetian painting in your dining room. . . ."

Verlaque smiled. "I do too."

"But I'd be just as happy with framed posters from IKEA, and sleeping in a tent on vacation."

Verlaque frowned. "Let's not get carried away. I hate camping."

Marine laughed despite herself. "Why do you ask, anyway?"

"No reason in particular," he answered. "I'm just thinking of what Soeur Clothilde and I talked about." He reached down and picked up the IKEA catalog. "So let's pick out some prints," he said.

"Stop teasing!"

Chapter Twenty-seven

❧

French, and English, Innovation

I left two messages last night," Paulik said. "Sir."

"I'm sorry," Verlaque answered. "I was . . . still a bit queasy from my food poisoning. Was it important?"

Paulik sighed and nodded, pulling out a chair opposite Verlaque. "I think I was chatting about vintage cars with the killer for over two hours last night."

Verlaque looked at his commissioner in amazement. Paulik recounted his visit to Prodos's Citroën garage, and that the garage was now cleaned out.

"Even the bust of de Gaulle, you say?" Verlaque said.

"Yep. Now, why would he take that if he wasn't planning on skipping town or country? You can just drive across borders in Europe now; he could be in the Italian Alps, or hidden in some remote hamlet in Andalucía."

"But you say that you trusted him, as did Laure Matour, Mlle Durand's boss."

"I can be wrong, and have been before," Paulik said.

Verlaque picked up the phone. "Let's put out a nationwide search on him, then. I assume he drives a DS? That should stick out like a sore thumb. I know he was a loner, but do you have any contacts for him?"

"Yes," Paulik answered. "One of the Pertuis policemen who drove by the garage last night said that his brother-in-law had bought a car off Prodos. I got the brother-in-law's number and left a message late last night." Paulik pulled his cell phone out of his jacket and set it on the desk. "I wish he'd call back." He got up and began to pace around the room. His phone rang, and he ran to the desk. "Bingo!" he said, picking the phone up. "*Oui?*"

"Commissioner? This is Benjamin Talmard. You left a message last night."

"Yes. I met your brother-in-law last night, the policeman, and he told me that you're acquainted with André Prodos."

"Yeah, that's right," Talmard answered. "Is André in some kind of trouble?"

"No," Paulik said, lying, "I just need to speak to him about a case we're working on, but I passed by the garage last night, and it looked cleared out. Do you have any ideas where he might be? He doesn't have a cell phone, I know that."

"Ha, André with a cell phone would be hard to imagine," Talmard answered. "Well, he only closes the garage for one reason, and that's to attend rallies."

"Car rallies?"

"Citroën rallies."

"Is there one on right now?" Paulik asked. He doubted that Prodos was at a car rally; more likely he was hiding somewhere.

"I remember reading about a September rally in a recent DS fan-club newsletter," Talmard answered. "I'll try to put my hands on it."

"Do you remember where it's being held?"

"Not near here," Talmard said. "Otherwise I would have gone. I'm thinking it was somewhere in the middle of France."

"That would be fantastic if you could find out where and when, M. Talmard. A million thanks."

Paulik had just hung up when Jules Schoelcher and Roger Caromb knocked and entered.

"What have you guys come up with?" Verlaque asked. "Anything connecting the three women? Deliverymen? Artisans?"

"Nothing, Judge," Schoelcher answered. "Grocery stores don't deliver that far out of Aix; Mlle Montmory had a La Redoute delivery in July, but Mlle Durand and Mme d'Arras have never ordered from the catalog; Mme d'Arras had a plumber fix a leaky faucet in April, but Mlle Durand has never had a workman in the house. Mlle Montmory had a plumber in, but it wasn't the same guy, and she wasn't even home when he came, she was getting her tonsils out. . . ."

"UPS?" Paulik asked.

"Nothing," Roger Caromb quickly replied. "We checked them, and FedEx."

Verlaque looked at Caromb and wished he didn't chew gum, especially while working; his grandmother Emmeline had taught him that it was a disgusting habit, and he always thought of it that way.

Paulik's cell phone rang, and he lunged across the desk and grabbed it. "*Oui?* M. Talmard?"

"Yes," Talmard answered. "And lucky for you I found the newsletter before my wife recycled it. The rally is this weekend, in the Aubrac." He read to Paulik the rally's location and hours. "It officially opens this evening, but André probably went early to set up his stand."

"Thank you so much," Paulik said, hanging up. He looked at

Verlaque and said, "There's a Citroën rally that begins tonight, in the Aubrac, near Laguiole."

Verlaque nodded and tried to think of Laguiole not as the place where Michel Bras's three-star restaurant was located, but instead where he would probably have to make an arrest. "Well, let's hope he's there."

Officers Schoelcher and Caromb looked at each other with puzzled expressions, and Paulik explained his suspicion of André Prodos. "You guys stay here, and we'll call you from the Aubrac once we know something."

"And if Prodos is at the car rally," Schoelcher said, "are you assuming he's innocent?"

"Stop asking such wise questions," Verlaque said, smiling. "Isn't it obvious we haven't thought that far ahead?"

"Let's go," Paulik said. "It's about a six-hour drive, I'm guessing. *Merde*."

"We're lucky it isn't in Brittany," Verlaque said, grabbing his jacket. "That's a twelve-hour drive."

The drive on the Autoroute du Soleil was a pleasant one; the vacationers had gone home, and both men were able to enjoy the views of olive orchards framed by a bright-blue sky. At Montpellier they exited and got onto a highway heading north, toward Millau, and its famous viaduct that spans the Tarn River. "Have you seen the bridge yet?" Paulik asked his boss, who was driving.

"No, I'm embarrassed to say I haven't," Verlaque replied, turning down the jazz CD so that they could talk. "We keep meaning to go." Verlaque smiled as he realized that he had changed his "I" to "we." He hoped it would be like that from now on—he and Marine. *We*.

"So do we," Paulik said. "Léa would really like to see it too; one of her classmates did a school project about it." He added, "Some

Englishman designed it," rolling his eyes in mock disgust; he knew little of Verlaque's family, but he did know that his grandmother had been English, and that the Verlaque wealth came from the family's flour mills, sold years ago to a multinational food group.

"Norman Foster," Verlaque answered.

"Funny sending an English architect to build a French bridge."

"No more funny than the French sending their math scholars to work in London's banks," Verlaque said. "But if it makes you feel better, I think that the engineer was French. In any case, we're one big planet now."

Paulik sighed. "I was just talking with Hélène about that," he said. "The globalization of vineyards. The wealthy Bordelais vineyard owners buying vineyards in Argentina, pricing out the local vintners, and the Chinese and Americans buying ours."

Verlaque slowed down to pass through the tollbooth, and they stopped talking as the viaduct came into view. "*Oh mon dieu*," Paulik finally said. "God save the queen."

Verlaque pulled over at a lookout point, and they both jumped out of the car. The wind howled around them, and streaks of flat clouds raced by in the blue sky. The white bridge was majestic. "It looks like a series of sailboats," Verlaque said, "floating across the valley." He took photos with his cell phone as Paulik stood, hands on his hips, staring.

Paulik counted the tall, slender piers holding up the bridge. "Seven columns," he said, pointing. "Look at that great detail: there's a narrow opening in the column that splits it in two but then closes up again above the road deck."

"I had no idea it would be this breathtaking," Verlaque said. "It's so elegant—a perfect union of engineering and design."

"And French and English," Paulik added, smiling.

They stood on the viewers' platform for ten minutes, saying nothing. Both were oblivious to cars coming and going out of the parking lot, to the chatter of tourists and the clicking of cameras. Verlaque looked at the bridge, a lightweight masterpiece of construction, floating between two limestone plateaus that were covered in green scrubland. The Tarn River flowed far below, and a smaller, earlier bridge crossed the river just above its banks. Compared with the viaduct, it looked like a toy bridge. "When I see something this beautiful," Verlaque said, "made by man, I feel that all is well with the world."

Paulik nodded. "I know what you mean," he said, watching the clouds race by, not far above the bridge's tallest mast. "Especially given our work."

Verlaque looked sideways at his commissioner and thought of Soeur Clothilde's words: "We must all do something to make the world more beautiful." "I think I could stay here all day," he said. "But we'd better hit the road."

"Yeah, I know," Paulik said. "I'm definitely bringing the girls here."

Verlaque smiled at his expression "the girls." "You're lucky, Bruno."

Paulik pretended he hadn't heard, and used getting back into Verlaque's minuscule Porsche as an excuse not to answer. What could he say?

As Verlaque pulled back onto the road, Paulik looked at the Michelin map. "We get off this road at exit number forty-two," he said, "then head east on the N88 for about twenty-four kilometers, then head north on the D28 toward Laguiole. Talmard told me that the rally should be well marked, and he said if we don't see any signs toward it we should just follow the Citroëns." He set the map on his knees, ready to take in the view from the bridge. "Spectacular," he said, leaning his head against the window and looking at the valley below.

"Look at that," Verlaque said, pointing ahead of him. "Two cars up, there's an old Citroën."

Paulik looked ahead and then over his shoulder. "There's a whole slew behind us, sir."

"We won't need to watch for signs."

The closer they got to Laguiole, the more Citroëns they saw. From the license plates they could tell where the owners of all the cars lived; since they were coming from the south, most were French, but both men were surprised at the number of Italian, Spanish, and even Portuguese fans on their way to the rally. Just before Laguiole, the Citroëns began turning left, onto a small road that led to Montpeyroux, and Verlaque followed suit. "Judging from the number of cars, they must have rented a huge farm field," he said. A teenager wearing a red Citroën jacket waved them into a parking lot, and Verlaque parked the car amid thousands of Citroëns of every color, model, and year imaginable. When they got out of the car, a gray-haired man, also wearing a red Citroën jacket, with a matching baseball cap, got out of his DS 19 convertible and said in English, "Wrong rally, mate."

Verlaque locked his car door and gave the man a forced smile. "Isn't this the antique Porsche rally?" he asked in English. "Oh dear."

"Just joking with you," the man went on. "You'll become a convert, you'll see. Have a good day!"

Verlaque lifted his hand in a vague salute.

"Was he teasing us?" Paulik said.

"Yes," Verlaque said, walking around the long, sleek convertible. "They really are strange-looking cars," he said. "Beautifully sleek."

"I thought they were space-age when I was a kid," Paulik said. He turned around and tried to see beyond the parking lot. "Let's just follow the crowds. There must be a main pavilion here, where we can look up the list of stands."

"And we can get a bite to eat," Verlaque said, looking at his watch. "It's almost three p.m." He could hear his stomach rumbling and smelled a barbecue.

Once out of the parking lot, they walked along a dirt road lined with Citroëns on display. They walked slowly, falling in step with the crowd, mostly male and over fifty, who stopped at almost every car to speak to its owner, take pictures, or peer under the hood or inside. "Let's try not to ogle the cars too much," Verlaque said, craning his neck to see a 1940s Citroën that, judging by the plates, had just been driven down from Belgium.

They moved, stopping and starting again with the flow of the crowd, for almost twenty minutes, and still could not see the main pavilion. "This is like being in a bad dream," Paulik said, "as if we're never going to get there."

"Or eat." Verlaque looked over at the commissioner, who said nothing. "I guess we can eat later," he continued. "We should find André Prodos first."

"If he's here."

Five minutes later, they were at the main pavilion, a long, flat-ceilinged hangar. Inside were older-model Citroëns, and rarer ones: tin-sided vans, racing cars, a camping van, even a red double-decker bus from pre–World War II London. The hall's acoustics weren't made to handle a thousand car fans, or an accordion player, and Verlaque resisted the temptation to cover his ears. A loud-speaker announced events; the grand opening ceremony would begin at 6:00 p.m., with speeches followed by an apéritif. "Let's get out of here before that begins," Verlaque said to Paulik. The commissioner agreed; speeches at this kind of event could go on for hours.

They followed red signs to an information booth, where fortunately there was just one man in line ahead of them. "I can only suggest that you try farther afield for a hotel room," the information host said. "Millau, perhaps. The hotels and bed-and-breakfasts in Laguiole have been booked for months by the rally participants." Verlaque looked at Paulik and raised his eyebrows. "I guess we'll be driving back in the dark," Paulik said.

The hotel-less man walked away in disgust, and Verlaque moved up to the desk. "Do you have a map of the stands?" he asked. "We're looking for André Prodos's stand; he has a garage in Provence."

The host looked at Verlaque bleary-eyed. "Never heard of him," he said, passing a sheet of paper across the desk at Verlaque. "Here's the plan. There are more than one hundred stands. Good luck."

Verlaque looked at the map. "They're not labeled," he said.

"That's correct," the host said. "We didn't get the list of stand renters to the printers in time. *C'est la vie!*"

"*Vive la France*," Verlaque mumbled as he went back to where Paulik was looking at a Citroën ambulance that had been used in World War II. "I have an unlabeled map. We have to do the whole tour of every stand. Some are in here," he said, looking at the map, "and some are outside."

"Let's split up," Paulik suggested. "And call each other by cell phone if we find him. His garage is called Citroën Prodos, and he looks like a schoolteacher—tall and lanky, with little round glasses and a receding hairline."

"I'll start outside," Verlaque said. "See you soon, I hope."

They separated, and Verlaque headed straight for the barbecue stand. There was a crowd in front of him, and he could smell spicy merguez sausages being grilled. When he had advanced to second in line, his cell phone rang. "*Oui, Bruno?*" he asked, just as he got to the head of the line.

"I found him," Paulik replied.

Verlaque looked at the man barbecuing. "Be right back," he said.

"These are the last ones I'm grilling this afternoon," the cook said.

"Oh well," Verlaque said. "My loss."

He walked quickly back into the hangar, and Paulik sent a text message: "Third stand north of the information booth." He saw Paulik standing at the back of a crowd gathered around the Citroën Prodos stand. "We were practically on top of his stand when we were at the information booth," Paulik whispered. "He's putting on a real show." Both men watched and listened as Prodos showed off the two-toned black-and-white DS that had been on hoists in his garage. The shy introvert that Paulik had spoken to was a natural showman before a crowd.

"Let's face it," Prodos told the crowd, "we're all here because Citroën has produced a lot of groundbreaking cars over its almost ninety-year history. And yet, before a model like this one, we're spellbound. At least I am." Prodos approached the crowd. "Sir," he asked an elderly fan, "if you could use just one word to sum up Citroëns, what would it be?"

"Innovative," the man answered.

"And you, sir?" he asked another fan.

"Um . . . fun, I would say."

Prodos pointed to another man, who quickly answered, "Comfort."

A woman offered, "Individual."

Verlaque sighed, rubbing his stomach. "Let's cut this off."

Paulik stepped forward and said, "Hello, M. Prodos."

"Hey, Commissioner!" Prodos said, as if Paulik had come to the rally as a fan. "Remember this one?" he asked, grinning and pointing to the car.

Paulik stepped up and whispered, "We need to talk."

"Well, folks, that's it for now," Prodos announced, glancing at Paulik. "I'll see you all at the ceremony this evening!" He turned off his microphone and set it carefully on a small table. "What's going on?" he asked. "You look angry."

"This is the examining magistrate of Aix," Paulik said, introducing Verlaque.

"I told you everything," Prodos said, his voice rising.

"What's the big idea, skipping town?" Paulik asked.

"Skipping town? I always come to these rallies. It's how I pay the bills; I always sell a car here."

"You didn't think to tell me about the rally?"

"I didn't think I was going to come," Prodos said, "until after your visit. I phoned my friend Laure—she was Gisèle's boss—and she told me it would be good for my head to come this weekend. Gisèle's memorial service is on Monday afternoon, so I'll be back in time. I had to clear out the garage in a jiffy."

Paulik looked over and saw the bust of Charles de Gaulle. "You brought him?" he asked.

Prodos beamed. "He's part of my shtick! I was about to tell the story of the shooting when you showed up."

"And your shop is cleared out of tools," Paulik said.

Prodos nodded. "I bring tools with me to these rallies," he said. "We all do. You have to be ready to help out a fellow DS owner. The cars can be . . . delicate."

Paulik sighed and looked at Verlaque. "Do you have an alibi for Wednesday, September 7?" he asked, thinking of Suzanne Montmory.

"What time?"

"Between four and seven-thirty p.m."

"Wednesday evenings are my therapy sessions," Prodos said. "Between six-thirty and seven-thirty p.m."

"And before that?"

"I would have been in my garage."

"Talking to me," a voice said. Verlaque and Paulik swung around. Before them was François Gros, the examining magistrate of Aix before Verlaque took over. Gros had retired at sixty-two with full benefits to spend on his great love, the Citroën DS 19.

"François!" Verlaque said, shaking the man's hand.

"Sir!" Paulik said, standing straighter.

"I called you that Wednesday afternoon, André," Gros said, "and talked your ear off. I remember it was Wednesday because Wednesdays my wife goes to our daughter's and babysits the grandkids, so I had the afternoon all to myself."

Prodos slapped his head. "I remember now. We talked about—"

"What in heaven's name is going on here, Verlaque?" Gros asked.

"We're investigating three murders, François, in case you haven't been watching the local news."

"You can fill me in later," Gros said. "But, for the record, I would trust this young man with my life. Got it?"

Chapter Twenty-eight

❧

Le Gargouillou

*T*he cars in Michel Bras's parking lot were decidedly different from those they had just seen: no Citroëns, vintage or otherwise. Most of the cars were German made, with the exception of a bright-yellow Ferrari with Parisian plates. Verlaque walked quickly up a flagstone path into the restaurant while Paulik stayed outside, looking at the view of the scrubby Aubrac plains from the restaurant's hilltop. "Would you have a table for two for this evening?" Verlaque asked a well-groomed young man. "And a room or two?"

The young man grimaced. "The restaurant is fully booked, sir."

Verlaque sighed and reached into his jacket for his badge. He showed it to the man, leaning over the desk, and said, "We're here on official business, last-minute."

"I'll see what I can do," the young man said.

"I'd appreciate that."

The man made a phone call and then put the receiver down. "We'll set up a small table for you in the dining room," he said. "And we have one room left, with a double bed."

Verlaque grimaced. "Fantastic. No twin beds, by any chance?"

"No, sir."

"We'll take it. Dinner at seven-thirty?" Verlaque knew it was a horribly unchic early dinner hour, but he wouldn't last any later than that without eating.

"Fine, sir," the receptionist answered. "If you'd like to relax in the lounge before dinner, we'll bring you your menus there."

"Lovely," Verlaque said. "Thank you."

"I'll call someone to show you to your room and take your bags."

"We don't have any bags," Verlaque said. He then whispered, "Remember, official last-minute business." He walked quickly out of the restaurant and found Paulik where he had left him, looking at the view. "We have dinner booked, and a room. Slight problem with the bed, but I think we can work it out."

"That's fantastic," Paulik said. "But, honestly, sir, judging by these cars and this space-age building, I think we're beyond our budget even as commissioner and judge."

"Don't worry about it," Verlaque said, knowing that he wouldn't bill the taxpayers of Aix for their dinner but would pay for it himself. "And if we're going to share a bed tonight, you have to start calling me Antoine."

Paulik laughed uproariously. "I think they'll bring us a folding bed if we're really sweet."

"Do you snore?"

"Yep. Do you?"

"Yes, so I'm told." Verlaque looked out at the sweeping valley before them, at once bright from the fading sunlight and yet dark from racing black clouds overhead. "The Massif Central is a special part of France, isn't it?" Verlaque asked his commissioner.

"Yes," Paulik said. "But there really isn't a corner of France that I don't love, except for certain neighborhoods in Paris."

Verlaque laughed, not sure if Paulik was referring to the snooty sixth and seventh *arrondissements,* or the crowded and dirty nineteenth and twentieth. "My grandmother once told me that this whole region was entirely left out of her English guidebook on France," he said. "My favorite painter is from this area. I have one of his paintings in my bedroom."

"Not Pierre Soulages?"

"Yes," Verlaque answered. "Do you know his art? Very black— I mean the color, not the mood."

"Hélène is a big fan," Paulik replied. "She told me Soulages was from the Massif Central. In fact, I saw a village with his name on the map when we were getting close to Laguiole." He didn't add that Hélène had once taken the TGV to Paris to see a Soulages retrospective at the Centre Pompidou. He could only imagine what one of those paintings cost. Perhaps Verlaque's was tiny.

Verlaque put a hand on Paulik's massive shoulder. "What do you say we go and have showers and pretend to put on clean shirts for dinner?"

"I could get used to three-star restaurants," Paulik said, sitting back in one of the white leather armchairs that were set before floor-to-ceiling plate-glass windows in the lounge, overlooking the plains and valley. "This is my first time."

Verlaque said, "You would probably prefer to have a woman here with you for your first time."

Paulik laughed. "Yes, preferably my wife."

"If Hélène ever bottles her own wines, she'll be wealthy, and perhaps a bit famous," Verlaque said.

"Wealthy, I don't know," Paulik answered. "Famous, perhaps, but only in the wine world, like Lalou Bize-Leroy up in Burgundy, and that Mondavi family in California."

Verlaque crossed his legs and lit a cigar, getting an angry look from a couple next to them.

"France will be the last country left in Europe to pass a no-smoking bylaw, mark my word! And to think it's already 2006!" the man said in English to his wife. "Come on, Margaret." They quickly got up and went into the dining room.

"Was he complaining about your cigar?" Paulik asked. "It's not as if you were going to take it into the dining room."

"Of course not," Verlaque said, lying.

A waiter appeared, bringing two glasses of house Champagne. "Have you gentlemen chosen your menus? Or will you be dining à la carte?"

"I'd like the complete tasting menu," Verlaque said. He winked over at Paulik and said, "You should get that too."

Paulik closed the menu. "Fine, I will."

"Would you like to finish your cigar before you dine, sir?" the waiter asked. "Normally we serve a *tartelette aux cèpes* with the Champagne, but since you're smoking . . ."

Verlaque set his cigar in an ashtray. "Porcini-mushroom tarte? We'll start eating now, thank you. I'll look at the wine menu, please."

Paulik sat back and soaked in the view while Verlaque pored over the wine menu that the waiter had quickly delivered. "Would you like to have a look, Bruno?" Verlaque asked.

"No, you go ahead and choose for us. I'm just happy sitting here watching the clouds race by."

A sommelier appeared, and Verlaque suggested a Riesling to start with.

"Excellent choice, monsieur," the sommelier said in a heavy accent that neither man could place. "Rieslings go so well with M. Bras's vegetables."

"Great," Verlaque said. "And we'll have a red to go with the meat and cheese dishes. I'm having trouble deciding between the Mas Jullien and the Amalaya."

"Ah. As you know, the Mas Jullien is local, so to speak, from the Languedoc," the sommelier answered. "But the Amalaya, that's also a very special wine, from my home country."

Paulik looked over and raised his eyebrows. It hadn't occurred to him that Verlaque would order a non-French wine.

"Argentina?" Verlaque asked.

"Yes, and I'm happy to report that not only will it go well with the second half of your meal, but it's also . . . divine."

Verlaque smiled and handed him back the wine menu. "The Argentinian it will be."

"Look at these," Verlaque said, leaning forward, when the *mise en bouche* arrived. "They look like tiny delicate tartes Tatin." The judge and commissioner tried not to eat too quickly, to savor the thin, buttery pie crust that held slices of plump porcini mushrooms arranged in layers, exactly like the apples on famed tartes Tatin.

Ten minutes later, they were seated in the dining room, facing picture windows that overlooked the setting sun. Their Riesling was uncorked, and Verlaque let Paulik taste it first. Large white plates began arriving in slow succession, mostly vegetables; they ate in silence until a sweet onion—slow-roasted and served with what the waiter called "licorice powder" but what was in fact a sweet and savory mix of olives, sugar, and ground almonds—caused the men to begin chatting again.

"Do you think they'll serve the *gargouillou*, even if it's autumn?" Paulik asked, swirling the golden wine around in his glass.

"I should hope so," Verlaque said. "What does that mean, anyway?"

"It's local slang. It used to be a peasant stew made from potatoes, water, and ham."

"But now it's become the Bras signature dish," Verlaque said as a waiter approached their table. "I've seen versions of it in almost every fine restaurant I've eaten at in the past ten years."

"*Gargouillou*," the waiter announced, gently setting down two white plates covered in a riot of bright colors. Both men tilted their heads, as if to count more easily the number of vegetables, wildflowers, and herbs on their plates. "White rose petals," Verlaque said, thinking of Clothilde, and the abbey's rose garden.

"And poppies," Paulik said, lifting a delicate petal with his fork. "And those dark-purple pansies that are almost black."

"Turnips, and radishes," Verlaque said, taking a forkful of razor-thin vegetables. "Fall veggies."

"Half these things I can't identify," Paulik said. "And I'm from the country."

"I've read that Bras begins his day foraging for edible flowers and wild herbs," Verlaque said.

"This is what I call high dining. Who needs Beluga caviar?"

Somewhere after the sixth course, a bright-white monkfish covered in what the menu called "black olive oil," Michel Bras appeared in the dining room. Happy applause broke out among the diners, who up to that point had been quietly talking with their dining partners.

"I heard that he's going to let his son run the kitchen soon," Paulik said, setting his fork down. "He almost looks like André Prodos, doesn't he?"

"Yes, and my high-school chemistry teacher, right down to the little round glasses. He's coming this way!" Verlaque and Paulik pushed their chairs out and started to get up when the chef came to their table.

"Please," Bras said, "stay seated, Judge Verlaque and Commissioner Paulik. How is your meal?"

"Wonderful . . ."

"Amazing . . ."

"The *gargouillou* was my favorite so far," Paulik said, "and I'm not exactly vegetable-crazy."

"Mine was the monkfish," Verlaque cut in.

Bras looked down, smiling, amused by their enthusiasm.

"It was so . . . black and white," Verlaque went on, feeling foolish that he couldn't describe the dish more accurately.

"That's exactly what I was trying to achieve with that dish," Bras said. "I call it Darkness and Light. It represents the Aubrac plateau: the density of the dark clouds and dark hills, mixed with the brilliance of the bright light that we get up here because of the high altitude."

Verlaque smiled. "Have you been to the Yorkshire moors?" he asked. "They're like the Aubrac."

"I'd love to go," Bras answered. "Perhaps someday."

"And the black olive oil?" Paulik asked. "What makes it black?"

"Black olives that we pit and then roast in the oven overnight," Bras said. "The next day, we blend them with olive oil, and baste the monkfish continually with it as it's gently sautéing."

"Low heat?"

"Yes, or it turns bitter."

"It's pitch black outside now," Verlaque said, wanting to talk more of the landscape and less of recipes, which he knew he'd forget the next day.

"And from November to April it will be bright white," Bras said. "Snow and fog everywhere. Darkness and Light. Good evening, gentlemen."

"Good evening, and thank you," Verlaque and Paulik replied in unison.

"The past week has been like that," Verlaque said. "Darkness and Light."

Paulik nodded as a waiter brought the next course. "I agree," he said. "The unsolved murders, darkness; and Albert Bonnard handing out vintage magnums to barbers and pharmacists, light."

A second bed had been set up in a corner of the large room, the white sheets on both beds pulled down. Paulik sat on the edge of his bed and sent photographs of the meal from his cell phone to Hélène and Léa. "I don't think I've ever seen a dish as beautiful as that *gargouillou* anywhere," he said, pressing the send button on his phone. "It looked like an Impressionist painting—a Monet. And I didn't think I'd ever enjoy Argentinian wine so much, although the Malbec grape does come from Cahors. . . ."

Verlaque smiled to himself as he walked toward the bathroom. He showered for the third time that day, hoping that the hot water would somehow cleanse his body of all of the food he had just eaten. When he had toweled off and gone back into the bedroom, he found that Bruno Paulik was already in bed, snoring. Verlaque tiptoed to his bed, and was turning off the light switch when he saw his cell phone's red light blinking. He had turned it to the silent mode during dinner and then forgotten to check it. Seeing that it was Marine's number, he took the phone into the bathroom and called her.

"Antoine?" Marine answered, her voice sounding sleepy. "Didn't you get my message?"

"Sorry, my phone was turned off."

"How was Michel Bras?"

"Heavenly," he answered. "And inspiring too, the way a good

restaurant should be. I'll tell you about it tomorrow, and bring you here someday."

"Great," Marine said. "Listen, I have some important information for you. I finally spoke to Philomène Joubert."

Verlaque sat down on the edge of the bathtub. "Really? Is she still on her walk?"

"No, she came home early to accompany a friend who twisted her ankle," Marine said. "And the priests at Saint-Jean de Malte told her about Mme d'Arras's death and that I needed to ask her something. That address where the woman was killed in Rognes . . ."

"Six Rue de la Conception?"

"Yes," Marine said. "It's Mme Joubert's address. It's where her childhood house was. It was torn down in the sixties."

"Mme d'Arras was probably there," Verlaque said.

"Yes," Marine replied. "With her dementia, she was probably looking up lost friends, old houses, and neighborhoods that she remembered. My father told me that it's common to do that. So the three murders are related."

"Perhaps," Verlaque said. "But not necessarily the same killer."

"I think it was. Suppose Mme d'Arras saw, or heard, something? She was right there on Friday evening when that woman was . . . Oh God."

"And what if it was someone she knew?" Verlaque asked.

"She would get into the car of someone she knew," Marine said. "It was the end of the day, and she must have been tired."

"Yes," Verlaque agreed. "Well, listen, get a good night's sleep, and I'll see you tomorrow evening." He added, "I love you."

Marine held the phone in her hand, looking at the mouthpiece, and then said, "I love you too."

Chapter Twenty-nine

❧

Bruno Paulik Breaks a Door

Verlaque dropped Paulik off at the Palais de Justice at 4:00 p.m. and called Marine from his car. "Do I have any clean shirts at your place?"

Marine took her phone into her bedroom and opened her closet. "Yes, two white and one light blue."

"Then I'll be right over," he said.

Thirty minutes later, Verlaque had changed, brushed his teeth, and shaved and was sitting in Marine's kitchen, pleased to have five minutes just to look at her face. "I'll have to go back to the Palais de Justice today," he said.

"I know," Marine answered, stirring a sugar cube into her espresso.

"But when we find this guy, I'll take a few days off, and we'll go to Michel Bras."

"Any place would do, Antoine. Eating there last night must have cost you an arm and a leg."

"Stop sounding like your mom," he said. "I don't care about the money." He leaned across the table and kissed her. "I'm so relieved that lump was benign."

Marine took a deep breath. "Me too. My specialist said he wasn't worried, but I was. I consider I got off very lucky."

"Specialist?" Verlaque asked. "I just assumed you went to your family doctor. I'm sorry; I should have been more clued in."

Marine laughed. "I didn't expect you to keep track of my doctors' names," she said. "I have many."

Verlaque got up and put his demitasse in the dishwasher. "Really? Do all women?"

"Of course! You men have it easy. Women have their GP, then their gynecologist, some women see dermatologists, others podiatrists to work on their feet. . . ."

Verlaque suddenly grabbed her and kissed her forehead. "You're amazing!" he yelled. "I have to run!"

"Glad to have been of service," Marine mumbled as Verlaque ran out the front door. She took the rest of her coffee out onto the terrace, where she could look at Saint-Jean de Malte's steeple, its gargoyles poised and watching the city. The church's bells began a slow, mournful ringing, and she wondered if it was for Mme d'Arras's funeral. She looked over at the windows of Philomène Joubert's apartment, their shutters open, and a fresh load of laundry—a set of flowered sheets—flapping in the breeze. The ever-busy Mme Joubert would probably attend her old friend's funeral but would put a quick load of laundry up on the line before leaving. Marine sighed and went back into her apartment. Would she ever be that efficient? She put her cup in the dishwasher, beside Verlaque's. How he had changed. She smiled to think of it. "If you think he's worth it, stick with it," her father had advised. She was so glad she had. And funny the way Verlaque had run out of the apartment like that, at the mention of women's health. Marine leaned against the kitchen counter, her chin resting in her palm, and then it dawned on her.

Antoine Verlaque walked as quickly as he could up the Rue Thiers; he didn't want to draw attention to himself, and he was still full from the previous evening's dinner. He pulled out his cell phone and called Paulik. "Bruno," he said when the commissioner answered, "I'm almost there. Is Officer Schoelcher around?"

"He's sitting across from me," Paulik replied.

"Great. Tell him to get his little notebook, the one that has the list of people who went into Mlle Montmory's hospital room."

Paulik said something to Schoelcher and then came back on. "Done. He has it on him."

"I'll be there in two minutes!"

He was heading across the Place Verdun when he bumped into Vincent, a friend of Marine's who owned a men's clothing store. "Antoine," he said, giving Verlaque the *bise*, "you have to come into the shop and say hello!"

"I will," Verlaque said. "Soon!"

"I have new tweed jackets for the winter!" Vincent continued. "In very nontraditional colors!"

"Pick out your favorite and save it for me," Verlaque replied, walking on toward the Palais de Justice. "You know my size! *Ciao!*"

"*Ça marche!*" Vincent yelled, thrilled to have made a sale while slipping out for a coffee. "Bring Marine in too!"

Verlaque waved behind him, then ran in the door and up the stairs that led to Paulik's office. As he ran past Mme Girard, who was busy typing, he said, "Hello, Mme Girard! You look lovely today!" without losing step; he ran into Paulik's office.

"Mme d'Arras was seeing a doctor about her thyroid," Verlaque said. "And Mlle Montmory had her tonsils out—"

"When the plumber came!" Caromb blurted out.

"Same doctor?" Verlaque asked no one in particular. "Ear, nose, and throat, right?"

"Mme d'Arras was giving her thyroid doctor a hard time," Paulik replied, standing up.

"How so?" Verlaque asked.

"M. d'Arras told me that she thought that surgery was unnecessary. That it was a racket."

"Probably is," Verlaque said. "You guys told me that a specialist visited Mlle Montmory's room. . . . I tried to visit one of the doctors who went into her room, but he's away on vacation. Or so the secretary said. I can't remember his name."

"Did Mlle Durand also see a specialist?" Paulik asked. "I'll call her GP. I have his cell-phone number."

"What day is it?" Verlaque asked. "God, now I'm the one with Alzheimer's."

"Saturday, Judge," Jules Schoelcher answered. Tomorrow was Sunday, Magali's day off, and they were going to Cassis.

"Ask especially if she saw an ear-nose-and-throat guy!" Verlaque said to Paulik as he headed out of the room to make the call, already dialing.

"Officer Schoelcher, get out your little notebook," Verlaque said. "Did M. d'Arras leave you their family doctor's name? We'll have to call him, and not her husband, to get her thyroid specialist's name, because I think today is her funeral. The doctor might even be there. *Merde*."

"I think the GP's number should be here in the file," Schoelcher said. He reached across Paulik's desk and flipped through the drawer until he got to Mme d'Arras's section. "Dr. Hervé Tailly," he said. "There's a cell-phone number. I'll write it down. Should I call him?"

"Please," Verlaque said.

Paulik came back into the room. "Bingo," he said. "Mlle Durand's GP was at home, thank God. Gisèle did see an ear-nose-and-throat specialist, also for a thyroid problem. A guy in Aix. Dr. Franck—"

"Charnay!" Verlaque said.

"Yep!"

Jules Schoelcher put his hand over his telephone's mouthpiece. "That's the doctor who went into Mlle Montmory's room." He tossed his notebook to Caromb. "Show them." He listened to his phone, then set it down. "Answering machine," he said.

"He's probably at the funeral," Verlaque said.

Alain Flamant knocked and came into the room.

"Officer Flamant," Paulik asked, setting down the phone book, "can you get on my computer and look up Dr. Franck Charnay's work history? And his address, since he isn't listed in the phone book."

"No problem," Flamant said, sitting down behind Paulik's computer. After a few taps, Flamant said, "Here's his address." He wrote it down on a piece of paper. "Puyricard."

"Nice and close to both Éguilles and Rognes," Verlaque said. "Have you found his work history yet?"

"Almost there," Flamant said, not looking up. He leaned in closer to the computer and whistled. "He's been in Aix for four years. Before that he was in Lille."

"Probably moved here for the weather," Roger Caromb said, laughing.

"No," Flamant said. "He moved down here because in Lille he was suspended for eighteen months. Sleeping with a patient."

"Let's go to Franck Charnay's house," Verlaque said. "His secretary told me he was away. Charnay is linked with two of the women, and I'm sure he was Mme d'Arras's specialist as well." Verlaque realized he had promised the secretary that he would be back, and because of their last-minute trip into the Massif Central, hadn't.

"I suggest we take three cars," Paulik said. "Judge Verlaque and me in one; we'll drive right up to the house and ring the doorbell. Officers Caromb and Schoelcher in another; you guys should park it somewhere hidden, at the neighbors' if you can, and then try to get around to the rear of Charnay's house to back us up. And, Flamant, get someone to go with you, and the two of you wait out front, but out of sight."

"I'll grab Javallier," Flamant said. "He was downstairs complaining about being bored."

Verlaque watched as his colleagues adjusted their holsters. "Do you want one of these?" Paulik asked.

"No, thanks," Verlaque said. "I trust you to protect me."

In fifteen minutes, they were in front of Franck Charnay's faux bastide, built in the 1990s rather than the 1790s. Two newer-model French cars were in the carport. Verlaque and Paulik got out of their car, walked up to the door, and rang the bell. No one came, but when Paulik rang it a second time they heard a loud thump and a cry coming from inside the house. Verlaque pounded on the door and tried opening it; it was locked.

Paulik said, "Move aside."

"Are you for real?" Verlaque asked.

"I play rugby, remember?" Paulik said. He lunged at the door, and on the second thrust it opened, the wood splintered. "Cheap nineties construction," he said.

"Charnay!" Verlaque called as they ran in, and they heard a moan coming from the living room. Charnay's secretary was on the floor, gasping for air. The sliding doors that led to the patio were open. "I'll go after him," Paulik said.

"Stay still," Verlaque said to her. "I'm calling an ambulance for you."

She swallowed and whispered hoarsely, "He has a gun."

Flamant and Javallier came running in. "We heard the yelling," Flamant said.

"Charnay ran out the back, and he's armed," Verlaque said. "Javallier, stay here with her and call an ambulance. Flamant, go back out to the street in case he makes his way around to the front!"

Verlaque got up and was running out the front door, thinking to check the carport, when he heard a shot. He ran back inside and through the living room, pausing long enough to see the look of fear on the secretary's face and to think, but resist saying, "That's the last time you'll lie for your boss."

He ran across the green lawn and saw Paulik hunched over someone. Verlaque ran up and saw that Paulik was on his cell phone, calling for an ambulance. Jules Schoelcher lay on the ground, breathing heavily. Another shot was fired; it sounded as if it was coming from the front of the house. "*Merde!*" Verlaque yelled as he ran back inside and out the front door. Flamant was at the end of the driveway, his gun pointed at Franck Charnay. The doctor had his back up against a plane tree, and Roger Caromb was handcuffing him.

Verlaque walked down the drive as two ambulances pulled in. He motioned them to the house, and told the driver that an officer on the back lawn had been shot. Alain Flamant didn't move as he continued staring at Charnay, his gun pointed at the doctor. "Officer Caromb caught him from behind," Flamant said. "Charnay's gun went off as it fell."

"Well done," Verlaque said. He went up to Charnay and showed his badge and read the man his rights.

Chapter Thirty

❧

Antoine Verlaque's Gift

Verlaque came into Jules Schoelcher's hospital room as Magali was fluffing his pillows.

"Bet you didn't think you'd end up back here," Verlaque said, handing the officer a wrapped package.

"Luckily, I already knew all the doctors and nurses," Schoelcher said.

"They're spoiling him," Magali said, smiling. "As they should. Hi, I'm Magali." She extended her hand.

"I'm sorry," Schoelcher said, "I should have introduced you."

Verlaque laughed. "No worry." He shook Magali's hand and said, "Antoine Verlaque." He stared at her and then asked, "Where do I know you from?"

"The café on the Place Richelme," Magali said. "By the wild-boar statue."

"That's it! You roast your own beans," Verlaque said. "And how's your leg, Jules?"

"Much better, thanks," Schoelcher replied. "Apparently, the bullet didn't go in very far. Is that woman all right?"

"Yes, she just stayed in overnight for observation," Verlaque said. "She was roughed up and was in shock, but wasn't harmed in any great way."

"Why did she cover up for that guy?" Schoelcher asked.

"Love," Verlaque said. "She loved him, but she didn't know what he did to those women."

"But why kill the old lady?" Schoelcher asked. "I keep going over that part in my head." Magali discreetly pretended to be arranging the vases of flowers and gifts across the room.

"Either Mme d'Arras saw or heard something," Verlaque said, "or he *thought* she did."

"M. d'Arras told us that she accused the doctor of unnecessarily removing thyroid glands. Could she have accused him of that when she saw Dr. Charnay in Rognes, and he thought she was accusing him of murdering Mlle Durand?"

"Or, when she heard about Gisèle's murder and where she was found, Mme d'Arras would have told the police she saw Dr. Charnay at that address," Verlaque said.

"Has he confessed?"

Verlaque nodded. "To all three. He blames all women for his eighteen-month medical suspension in Lille. Are you going to open your present?"

Schoelcher fumbled with the wrapping paper as Magali came back beside him to watch. He tore off the last piece of paper and pulled out five small black-covered books. "Notebooks?" Schoelcher asked.

"For your copious note taking," Verlaque said.

Magali picked one up. "They're Moleskines!"

"Thank you, Judge," Schoelcher said. "I'll make good use of them."

A nurse came into the room, carrying a tray. "Medicine, and rest time, M. Schoelcher," she said. "I'm afraid your friends will have to leave. Your mother will kill me if you're not back on your feet by the end of the month."

Schoelcher grimaced. "I hope she isn't calling your desk too often."

"Only a few times a day," the nurse said, smiling.

It took much less time than Verlaque had expected to sign the papers at the notary's office. Jean-Marc, who had cosigned as a witness, told Verlaque that the fact that he was paying in cash sped up the process. Jean-Marc had tried not to flinch when he saw the amount of money involved.

Verlaque had already made up his mind to put Emmeline's mansion in Normandy on the market, which would help recover some of the costs. His brother, Sébastien, wanted to buy a real-estate company—in addition to the building it was located in, in the expensive Passy neighborhood of Paris—and had immediately agreed to the sale.

Verlaque invited Jean-Marc to have a celebratory glass of Champagne at the Café Mazarin. They chose a table on the terrace, and both sat cross-legged, watching the Aixois stroll up and down the Cours Mirabeau.

"It's none of my business," Jean-Marc said, looking over at his friend, "but does Marine know you're doing this?"

Verlaque sipped some Champagne and nodded. "I told her last night," he said. "She loved the idea."

"She's entirely unselfish, isn't she?"

"Yes, one of her many qualities," Verlaque replied. "But I see this as a winning business deal; it's bound to work and bring in money, and maybe even a little fame. So, you see, I'm not nearly as selfless as Marine is."

"Glad to know you haven't changed," Jean-Marc said, tipping his glass toward Verlaque's. "I was getting worried that you had gone all soft and mushy."

Hélène Paulik drove, with Léa beside her in the front seat. Paulik sat in the back, in the middle, so that he could talk to his girls and see the road. Since the three of them were susceptible to motion sickness, they usually took turns in the back. "Now that I'm ten, I'm always going to sit in the front," Léa said. "The law says I can."

"You can sit in the front the whole way there," Paulik said, trying to concentrate on the white lines on the road. "Do you feel sick?"

"Not at all, Papa," Léa answered. "It's great up here."

"Wonderful," Paulik whispered.

"Can you read me the directions after the traffic circle, Bruno?" Hélène asked.

"'Left at the first traffic circle toward Rousset,'" Paulik read aloud, trying not to look for too long at the printed page. "'Follow the N7 toward Puyloubier and Peynier, making a left on the D12 toward Puyloubier.' As soon as the village's church steeple comes into sight, we'll see a small road on our right with a mailbox marked 'G. Herblin.' We go in there."

Léa sang the rest of the way, and didn't stop until she saw the mailbox. "There it is!" she cried. "Turn here, Maman!"

"Yes, dear, I am."

They drove up a narrow dirt lane bordered by olive trees, their glittering silver leaves dancing in the wind. Through the trees they could see acres of vines, with dried and shriveled grapes on the branches.

"These are old vines," Hélène said, pointing to her left. "No one harvested here; what a shame."

"How old, Maman?" Léa asked. "One hundred?"

"Almost, sweetie," she answered. "Isn't that amazing?"

"I guess. Does someone live here?" Léa asked.

"Not anymore," Paulik said. "This belonged to an old man, but he just died. He had no family." That was all that Paulik had been told.

"G. Herblin," Léa said. "It could be Georges, or Gilles, or Guy. . . ."

"That's right," Paulik replied. He felt his jacket pocket for the letter; it was to be read aloud on the front steps of the house. The house came into view, an old *mas* that had, years ago, been painted an earthy red that matched the soil.

"Pretty!" Léa exclaimed. "Is someone here? There aren't any cars, and the shutters are all closed. I like that they're painted blue. Shutters should always be painted blue. Blue's my favorite color. . . ."

"Léa, please," Paulik said. "I don't know what's going on either. All I know is that we are to get out of the car and read a letter that I have in my pocket."

"Okay!" Hélène said. "Let's go, troops!"

They got out of the car, and Léa raced ahead to stand on the front doorstep. "You can see mountains in front of us!"

"Mont Aurélien," Paulik said.

Léa ran to the back of the house and turned around to look behind her. "Mont Sainte-Victoire!"

The Pauliks followed her and stared up at the mountain. "These vines are all AOC Sainte-Victoire," Hélène said. "The vintners around here were just awarded their status not long ago. They've been trying for years."

"Is it that important?" Paulik asked.

"Sure. It protects their vines, and how the wine is made around here, for one thing," Hélène said. "So somebody can't come in here and make a wine from Merlot grapes."

"Well, they can. . . ."

"Right," Hélène said, "but they can't call it AOC. The AOC status . . ."

"You two!" Léa said. "Let's go back by the front door and read the letter! That's what we're supposed to be doing! Hurry up!"

Hélène and Bruno laughed. "We're coming!"

Dear Bruno, Hélène, and Léa,

By the time you read this, I'll be in Laguiole, having a multicourse dinner with Marine at Michel Bras. You must be wondering why you're here. Léa, I'll bet you especially have lots of questions.

I'll begin by apologizing for the shock. I didn't know how else to go about telling you. It also happened much faster than I had predicted. The idea had been in my head for some time, but when word came about this place, I had to act quickly.

What I would hate to do is insult you. Perhaps that's why I've sneaked away this weekend. But I also wanted to give you time, as a family, to think about my proposition. This land, as you can see, contains ninety-five acres of AOC Sainte-Victoire grapes: Syrah, Cinsault, Mourvèdre, and Rolle. The vines are in a bit of disrepair; even I could see that. M. Herblin was ninety-six when he died at the end of August, and had no offspring save a great-nephew, who is selling the property. My good friend Jean-Marc is a lawyer in Aix and told me about the sale, and I jumped at the chance to buy the estate— beating out two foreign couples, you'll be glad to know, Bruno, and one French company that sells soft drinks and is branching out.

I think that by now I'll be eating my *gargouillou*, and you'll have guessed what I'm about to propose. Hélène, I've admired your wines for a long time, even before I moved to the south. I can still remember my first proper glass of Domaine Beauclaire's Syrah, made by you; it was at L'Arpège in Paris, and I was dining with my grandparents. My grandfather, who was a die-hard Burgundy fan, read your name on the label and said, "This woman is someone to watch." I'd like you to take over the winemaking operations here—I'll leave you to think of a name for the domaine, since "G. Herblin" is somewhat lacking in pizzazz. You'll have complete control, and I've made arrangements that you and Bruno will be part owners of the estate (we'll talk about that on Monday). My only request is that I get as much wine as I want (Marine thinks that this is very unwise), and that your first bottling you call Cuvée Emmeline. The rest will be up to you.

By the way, the house is charming outside, but the interior needs to be gutted.

      Yours affectionately,
      Antoine Verlaque

Epilogue

Natalie Chazeau was sure that another elderly woman, seated one row behind her in first class, had stared at her brooch and nodded and smiled. Mme Chazeau lifted her hand up to her jacket's lapel and felt the silver brooch, embedded with two interlinked flags, one French, the other German. "The woman behind us knows my story," she whispered to her son. "Perhaps she's one of us. Wouldn't that be wonderful?"

Christophe Chazeau smiled and took his mother's hand. "Perhaps, Mother. It's also possible that she just liked the brooch."

Mme Chazeau shook her head back and forth. "Oh no, I don't think so. We're over two hundred thousand. And your generation, there are more than a million of you. Our story has been getting a lot of press, you know. *Le Monde, Figaro*, they're all publishing stories on it. Even *Paris Match*. And there was a television documentary in July. . . ."

"It's about time," Christophe said, stretching his legs.

"It takes *time to heal*."

Christophe looked at his mother in surprise. She had never spoken like that before. He was quite certain she had never in her whole life ever said the words "It takes time to heal."

Mme Chazeau took out of her jacket pocket a newspaper clipping that had been folded and refolded dozens of times, and began to read aloud to her son. "Listen, *chéri*, to what this journalist said of us: 'There were so many cases that I realized I couldn't write an article on these children; it would have to be a book.'"

Christophe looked at his mother and saw the tears forming in the corners of her eyes. He smiled; he had never seen his mother so serene, so at peace.

She read on: "'They really do deserve special treatment after all they have suffered. It would be a last line drawn under the 'century of iron and blood' that was the 20th century.' He's right, isn't he? I was the child of a French woman and a German man who loved each other. But they lived at a time of hatred, didn't they?"

Christophe nodded and asked the stewardess for a Bloody Mary, relieved to be able to have a drink.

"I'll just have sparkling water, dearie," his mother told the stewardess. Christophe tried not to cringe; he hoped that his mother wouldn't become Evangelical, or run off and become a missionary. He preferred his tough-as-nails mother.

"You'll be sure to thank those lawyer friends of yours for their help in finding my half-siblings," she said. "I sent Maître Sauvat a bottle of Champagne, and the judge too."

"Jean-Marc and Antoine will be touched," Christophe said. "They were only too happy to help."

"Do you think we'll recognize each other right away?" Mme Chazeau asked her son.

"I would think so," he answered, realizing she was now talking about her newfound German siblings. "You've seen photographs of them, haven't you?"

"Yes. They both are tall, with black hair, just like me, although Franz's is mostly white now." Natalie Chazeau smiled as she sat back and closed her eyes, trying to imagine what their reunion would be like. "*Chéri*," she said, leaning toward her son.

"*Oui, Maman?*"

"Do you think we'll visit our father's grave?"

"Perhaps," he said. "It's in Bamberg, isn't it?"

"*Oui*. To think that he was shot just days before Germany surrendered, in May 1945."

Christophe said nothing. At any rate, even if he had survived the war, his mother never would have heard from her father during her childhood. Wolfgang Schmidt had led a double life: in peacetime he was an accountant and amateur bass player with a wife and two children, Franz and Ellen, in Bamberg; in wartime, a colonel in the German army with a lover—Francine Lignon, a history student at the Sorbonne.

"My mother wasn't a collaborator," Mme Chazeau went on. "That's what they called them before they shaved their heads and paraded them through town: *les collaboratrices horlizantales*. . . ."

"Maman, please . . ." Christophe whispered, worried that passengers could overhear.

"I'll no longer be quiet!" she hissed, with the force in her voice that Christophe was used to.

"At least Francine . . . Grandma . . . wasn't paraded through the streets of Rognes," Christophe whispered. "When she came back from Paris . . ."

Mme Chazeau made the sign of the cross. "Yes, thank God for that. Her father had it quickly hushed up; he was a powerful man. It was only years later that it got around the village; we never knew how." Christophe silently thanked his grandfather Frédéric Auba-nel, the man who in 1943 quickly married Francine, for he had always loved her, and raised Natalie as his own.

"Do you know, at school, in the playground, they used to call me *sale boche*?" his mother went on. "The funny thing was, I didn't know what it meant. I thought it just meant 'idiot' or some-thing, since I was always at the bottom of the class in math." Christophe smiled, proud of his mother, the bottom of the class in math, she who had single-handedly created Aix's largest and most prosperous real-estate agency. "But I knew I was an out-cast," she continued. "And Pauline made sure to make me feel that way. . . ."

"Maman, put it to rest," Christophe pleaded. Besides, he was hoping to have a glance at a new car-magazine he had just pur-chased. "At least until the plane lands."

The drive from the Munich airport to Bamberg was easy and took only two hours. They drove past Nuremberg, and neither Chazeau said anything until Natalie whispered, "Nuremberg, where the trials were. That's my history now."

Mme Chazeau helped navigate their rental car into Bamberg. She was good at it and prided herself on her navigational skill; since her husband's early death, her son had always done the driv-ing. "There's an upper town and a lower one," she said, looking at the map. "Separated by the River Regnitz." She looked over at Christophe and smiled, secretly wishing that he'd find a wife, soon. "Slow down, here are some hotel signs." She pointed to a brown street sign. "I see it! Turn right for the Hotel Messerschmitt. Lange Strasse." They parked in a small lot reserved for guests and checked in. Before their meeting with Franz and Ellen, they had time to shower. When Christophe came out of his room, he found his mother anxiously standing by the front door, one foot already outside. "Can you see my pin?" she asked.

"Yes, Maman. They'll see it, and you, right away." He held his arm out for his mother to take, and together they walked down the street and across an impossibly charming bridge that led to the upper town. They passed university students, locals of all ages on bicycles, and tourists pausing to read dinner menus.

"It reminds me of Aix," Christophe said.

"Yes," Natalie Chazeau said. "It looks to be a real town, with real services and businesses, not a Disneyfied one. Let's hope Aix stays that way too."

"There's a sign for the Domplatz," Christophe said. "We're meeting them where, exactly? The history museum?"

"Yes," Mme Chazeau replied, quickening her step. "The Ratsstube, it's called. Franz referred to it as a Renaissance gem in his letter. He taught history at the university here in Bamberg."

Christophe patted his mother's hand. "Yes, you told me." *More than once.* "And he speaks French, right?"

"Yes, perfectly, but Ellen only speaks German. What will I do?"

"You'll figure something out."

"And you won't be bored this evening if we go off somewhere, to . . . talk . . . ?"

"No, don't worry about me," Christophe answered. "I'm going to go in search of that smoky beer they brew here. *Rauchbier*, I think it's called."

They arrived at the Domplatz, a big sloping square that was lined with a striking variety of well-preserved buildings. It unfolded before them like a great pop-up book on European Renaissance architecture. The Ratsstube was on the southeast corner, easily spotted by its elegantly tapering gables and ornate bay windows that jutted out over the square. A tall, elderly man and an equally tall woman stood under the museum's sign, their shoulders slightly touching. The man squinted in the late-afternoon sun. Ellen Hoffmann, née Schmidt, pointed to the Chazeau mother and son and said something to her brother. Eighty-year-old Franz Schmidt, still in shape thanks to a daily uphill bicycle ride, took off his hat and began to run across the square.

AVAILABLE FROM PENGUIN

Murder in the Rue Dumas
A Verlaque and Bonnet Provençal Mystery

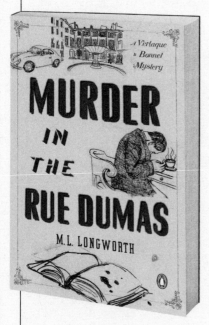

ISBN 978-0-14-312154-1

When the director of the theology department at the Université d'Aix is found dead, Judge Verlaque is stumped. Professor Moutte was about to announce both the recipient of a fellowship and his successor as director—a position that includes a coveted apartment in a seventeenth-century mansion. The prospective recipients and others close to Moutte make up a long list of suspects, but Verlaque isn't convinced any of the eager students or desperate teachers are capable of murder, and he must dig deeper.

PENGUIN
BOOKS

AVAILABLE FROM PENGUIN

Death at the Château Bremont

A Verlaque and Bonnet Mystery

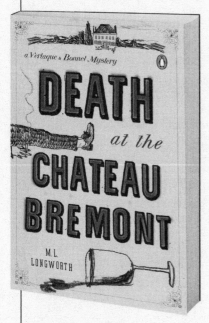

ISBN 978-0-14-311952-4

Set in charming and historic Aix-en-Provence, this lively whodunit introduces readers to Antoine Verlaque, the handsome and seductive chief magistrate of Aix, and his on-again, off-again love interest, law professor Marine Bonnet. When local nobleman Étienne de Bremont falls to his death from the family château, the town is abuzz with rumors. Verlaque suspects foul play and must turn to Marine for help when he discovers that she was a close friend of the Bremonts.

**PENGUIN
BOOKS**